PRAISE FOR WALTER MOSLEY AND
BLOOD GROVE

"Mosley is a master of craft and narrative, and through his incredibly vibrant and diverse body of work, our literary heritage has truly been enriched...From mysteries to literary fiction to nonfiction, Mosley's talent and memorable characters have captivated readers everywhere, and the Foundation is proud to honor such an illustrious voice whose work will be enjoyed for years to come...What sets his work apart is his examination of both complex issues and intimate realities through the lens of characters in his fiction, as well as his accomplished historical narrative works and essays."

—National Book Foundation

"Lest one think Mr. Mosley's middle-age hero—sensitive and contemplative though he may be—is not still up to whatever challenge may confront him, he warns: 'Easy is my name, not my nature.'"

—Tom Nolan, *Wall Street Journal*

"Mosley's authorial superpower remains his razor-sharp perception...This novel is more than a simple mystery meant for entertainment; it and its serial predecessors advocate for the Black hero in literature and in life...A strong entry in a robust series and an even stronger entry into the genre that further solidifies Rawlins as an enduring figure, one who has survived and thrived in a world that sees him as less than the hero he is."

—Aaron Coats, *Chicago Review of Books*

"The ability to simultaneously keep us readers in confusion and in thrall marks Mosley—winner of the National Book Foundation's 2020 Medal for Distinguished Contribution to American Letters—as a mystery master...The central mystery in *Blood Grove*—as in all the Easy Rawlins books—is as much about the brazen contradictions of American society as it is about what happened in that orange grove one night. But that mystery turns out to be pretty gripping too."　　　　—Maureen Corrigan, *Washington Post*

"Rawlins is the greatest contributor to Los Angeles's literary culture and its native son's repute."　　　—Paula L. Woods, *Los Angeles Times*

"In the fifteenth outing for his iconic private detective, Easy Rawlins, Mosley once again chronicles a part of America rendered invisible—and overpowered—by whiteness. The book is set in 1969, with Rawlins on the verge of fifty, still struggling with professional and romantic and familial conflicts in a Los Angeles about to be beset by the berserk."

　　　　　—*New York Times Book Review*, Editors' Choice

"It is a fair bet that if Walter Mosley has a book coming out during any given month, there's an excellent chance it will be the best mystery of that month. Case in point: his latest. Nothing is quite what it seems in this place, in this time, in this book...I read it all in one sitting, as I just could not stop turning the pages."

　　　　　　—Bruce Tierney, *BookPage*

"Walter Mosley's books about Easy Rawlins are crime fiction, not history. But taken together, they're a vivid picture of Black life in Los Angeles in the mid-twentieth century...Easy Rawlins takes a long strange trip in *Blood Grove*, and it's a thrill to take it with him."

　　　　　　—Colette Bancroft, *Tampa Bay Times*

"If Walter Mosely's *Blood Grove* is your first Easy Rawlins book, by the time you finish you'll rejoice that you have fourteen more to catch up on. If you're already an aficionado, Mosley's latest detective creation is the life diversion you know you need now... Easy is smart, self-possessed, and, with Mosley's ear for dialogue, unabashedly funny. *Blood Grove* is ripe to be plucked as one of Mosley's finest and most important novels." —Tom Mayer, *Mountain Times*

"Get *Blood Grove* and you might as well just put that bookmark in a drawer... For fans, Mosley goes the extra step, offering a chance to catch up with the dark characters that Rawlins has called 'friends' in past novels. If you're not a fan, grab this book and you will be quick. Just don't grab it after dark: *Blood Grove* will keep your eyes open all night." —Terri Schlichenmeyer, *Tennessee Tribune*

"Mosley does a fine job highlighting a world of Black survivors who know how difficult their struggle remains, every day of every decade. This marvelous series is as relevant as ever." —*Publishers Weekly*

"Mosley effortlessly moves the series to 1969 in *Blood Grove*, showing just how far Easy has come... A solid mystery, *Blood Grove* will show longtime readers just how much they have missed Easy." —Oline H. Cogdill, *South Florida Sun Sentinel*

"What's perhaps most remarkable about *Blood Grove*—as with all Easy Rawlins novels—is Mosley's undiminished gift for embedding the poignant messaging of the protest novel in hard-boiled crime fiction without ever sacrificing punch or pace... *Blood Grove* does its many antecedents proud—not least among them, Easy Rawlins's formidable first fourteen." —Steve Nathans-Kelly, *New York Journal of Books*

"Both Chandler and Mosley amply reward readers with the beauty of their prose and with the world views of their iconic heroes, men of honor struggling to do right in an unjust world...For Easy Rawlins, it has meant trying to do the same with the added complication of being a Black man in race-torn, post–World War II Los Angeles."

—Bruce DeSilva, Associated Press

"Mosley has his finger on the pulse of racial and cultural issues of the late '60s, and the book is sure to make readers ponder just how much has and hasn't changed today." —Christina Lanzito, *AARP*

"*Blood Grove* may just be one of the best novels in an already iconic detective series...Mosley manages to unfurl a genuinely captivating plot that travels a dark odyssey through the subcultures of 1969 LA, while also adding poignant new depth to the stories of long-running characters. *Blood Grove* is as satisfying as noir gets."

—Dwyer Murphy, *CrimeReads*

"Easy's finely calibrated understanding of and commentary on the social and racial climate around him give the novel its defining texture and power...A new Easy Rawlins novel is always big news in crime-fiction circles, and this fifteenth entry in the series does not disappoint." —*Booklist*

"More than a simple mystery...*Blood Grove* solidifies Easy Rawlins as an enduring figure, one who has survived and thrived in a world that sees him as less than the hero he is." —*Chicago Review of Books*

BLOOD GROVE

BLOOD GROVE

WALTER MOSLEY

MULHOLLAND BOOKS

Little, Brown and Company

New York Boston London

Mulholland Books / Little, Brown and Company
Hachette Book Group
1290 Avenue of the Americas, New York, NY 10104
mulhollandbooks.com

Originally published in hardcover by Mulholland Books, February 2021
First trade paperback edition, February 2022

Mulholland Books is an imprint of Little, Brown and Company, a division of Hachette Book Group, Inc. The Mulholland Books name and logo are trademarks of Hachette Book Group, Inc.

The publisher is not responsible for websites (or their content) that are not owned by the publisher.

The Hachette Speakers Bureau provides a wide range of authors for speaking events. To find out more, go to hachettespeakersbureau.com or call (866) 376-6591.

ISBN 978-0-316-49118-1 (hardcover) / 978-0-316-54179-4 (large print) / 9780316491167 (paperback)
LCCN 2020938668

Printing 1, 2021

LSC-C

Printed in the United States of America

For Diane Houslin and her tireless pursuit of truth

BLOOD GROVE

1

Monday, July 7, 1969

I looked down from the third-floor office window onto the hastily built greenhouse in our back-fence neighbors' yard. The hothouse frame was constructed from pine four-by-fours. This structure was tightly wrapped in semiopaque plastic sheeting that fluttered only slightly in the morning breeze. The structure reminded me of an army barracks at maybe one-third size. Standing around six and a half feet high and wide, it was four times that in length, with a partially flattened triangular roof. These current neighbors, seven long-haired hippies, had moved in five months before. They built the nursery and wired it for perpetual electric light on the first day. Nearly every daylight hour since then they went back and forth armed with bags of soil, watering cans, clay pots, insecticide brews, and various pruning devices.

At night they sometimes had parties. These festivities often spilled out onto the front porch and lawn but never the backyard. The hothouse was off limits to anyone except the Seven.

They were an interesting-looking crew. Three young women and four men; all somewhere in their twenties. All white except for one young black man. Wearing embroidered jeans and threadbare T-shirts, they spent an hour or so almost every afternoon sitting around a redwood picnic table eating food prepared, served, and shared by the women. They poured wine from green-glass gallon jugs of Gallo red and passed hand-rolled cigarettes from one to the other in an endless circle.

I liked the city farmers. They reminded me of life in my child-hood home—New Iberia, Louisiana.

LA was a transient city back then. People moved in and out with predictable regularity. Five months was a long stay for tenants without blood ties or children.

When the back door to the hippie house came open I looked at the round white face of my Gruen *Chronometer mit Kalender*. It was 7:04 a.m. on Monday, July 7, 1969. The hippie I'd dubbed *Stache* came out of the split-level ranch house wearing only jeans. The nickname was because of his generous lip hair. I was standing at that window because Stache came out early every morning toting a long-necked tin watering can, wearing neither shirt nor shoes. This ritual had tweaked my detective instinct.

When Stache bent down to get the garden hose I turned away from the window but remained standing behind the extra-large desk. A case had taken me out to Las Vegas over the past week. This was my first day back at the agency and I was the only one there so far that morning.

For a moment I considered sitting and writing down the specifics of the Zuma case, but the details, especially the payment problem, felt like more than I could handle on my first day. So instead I decided to take a walkabout, reacquainting myself with the offices before my colleagues arrived.

Our bureau occupied the entire upper floor of what once was a large house on Robertson Boulevard, a little way up from Pico. My workspace was the master bedroom at the very back. Walking up the hall from there I first passed Tinsford Natly's office. Tinsford was generally known as Whisper and his room embodied the understated tone of that name. This office was small and window-less, furnished with a battered oak desk barely larger than a writing table you'd expect to find in a junior high classroom. There were two straight-back wooden chairs, one for Tinsford and another to accommodate any visitor or client who found their way to him. He rarely spoke to more than one person at a time because, he said, "Too many minds muddy the water."

The tabletop was bare, which was unusual. As far back as I could remember, Whisper would have a single sheet of paper centered on his desk. It was always a different leaf with writing that seemed to say something pedestrian but most often held deeper meanings. There were no pictures on the walls, no file cabinet or carpet. His office was like a monk's cell where some ageless cleric considered the scriptures—one verse, sometimes just one word, at a time.

A little ways up and across the hall, Saul Lynx's office was three times the size of Whisper's and a quarter that of mine. His desk was mahogany and kidney-shaped. Saul had a blue love seat and a padded leaf-green chair for clients. A burgundy swivel chair sat behind the burnished desk, which was crowded with knickknacks and photographs of his Negro wife and their multiracial children. There were at least two hundred books on the shelves next to the window. He had five maple filing cabinets, a huge standing globe of the world, and a small worktable with an overhead lamp where he mapped out his investigative campaigns.

Saul's office was cluttered but neat. His tabletop and desk were most often disheveled because Saul was usually in a hurry to get out in the street, where detectives like us went up against the jobs we took on. But that Monday morning everything was in its proper place—almost as if he'd left for a vacation.

I wandered from the back offices up to the repurposed foyer, where Niska Redman's desk sat.

Niska was our secretary, receptionist, and office manager. A few years earlier Tinsford got her father out of a jam and she went to work for him. When I had my windfall and decided to start the WRENS-L Detective Agency, she came along with her boss. The caramel-cream biracial young woman was perfect for our needs.

She was a night-school junior at Cal State, friendly, and completely reliable. She knew all our quirks and needs, temperaments and habits. Niska was that rare worker who did the job without direction and was more than capable of thinking on her own.

I sat down at her sleek cherrywood desk facing the front door to our offices. Taking in a deep breath, I noted how it felt good being alone and unhurried. Everything was fine, so I'm not quite sure why the darkness entered my mind . . .

Four years before, I'd been drunk for the first time in many years, driving barefoot down the Pacific Coast Highway at night, far above the rocky undergrowth along the shore. I tried to pass a tractor trailer, met oncoming traffic, and was forced off the pavement onto the soft shoulder, which then gave way to nothingness.

Some hours later Mouse, under the direction of the witch, Mama Jo, found me.

The coma lasted for weeks but I was still aware under that pall, feeling as if I had crossed far beyond the border of expiry. The moments of a wasted life littered the floor around my deathbed.

That same debris surrounded me in Niska's sunlit office space. Breathing became a chore and the memory of a life filled with pain and dying seemed to grasp at me from an incalculable depth. It was as if I had died in the accident and so whenever the specter of that time returned I had to struggle once more against the desire to let go. I could have breathed my last right then and there. Later I'd be found by my friends, having passed away from no apparent cause.

Though assailed by hopelessness I was not afraid. The suffering of my people and my life pressed like tiny embers burning away at the release the numbness of death promised. I took one breath and then another. My chest and shoulders rose and fell slowly. In sunbeams coursing through the windowpane I saw motes of dust illuminated by the light. These floaters were accompanied by unimaginably small insects going about their winged search for sustenance, succor, and sex. Hearing the intermittent sounds of the house creaking in the morning breeze, I somehow slipped back into the rhythm of living.

After all that I was both exhausted and relieved. It was a reminder that the most desperate battles are fought in our hearts and souls, and that death is only one final trick of the mind.

"Hi, Mr. Rawlins."

I glanced at my white-faced watch before looking up at Niska Redman. It was 8:17. Nearly an hour had passed since I commandeered her office chair.

Niska wore a one-piece shamrock-green dress that didn't quite cover her handsome knees. I liked the freckles around her nose and the smile that said she was honestly happy to see me. Hanging from her left shoulder was a rather large buff-colored canvas sack.

"Hey, N. How you doin'?"

"Fine. I made brown-rice pudding last night." She swung the shoulder bag out onto the desk and opened it wide. Therein I saw her polka-dot blue-and-white purse, a few books, an exercise mat, a fine-toothed comb and an Afro pick, two brushes, a makeup bag, and a quart-size Tupperware tub. This last item she brought out and set before me.

"Want some?" she asked.

"Maybe later." I stood up from her chair and she moved to stand next to it.

"Were you looking for something in my desk?"

"No. Just getting a different perspective is all. Where's Tinsford? I don't think I've ever gotten in before him unless he was on a case."

"Uh-huh, excuse me, but I have to go to the restroom."

She went down the hall of offices to the door just beyond Whisper's. I pulled a guest chair from the far wall and set it before her workstation, still feeling the tremors from my mortal battle with demons of the past.

The phone rang once and I reached over to answer.

"WRENS-L Detective Agency."

"Easy?"

"Hey, Saul. Where you callin' from?"

"Niska didn't tell you?"

"She just got in."

"I'm up north. At the Oakland shipyards."

"Oakland?"

"The IC called last Wednesday," he said. "They've been underwriting a policy for Seahawk Shipping Lines. Too much cargo's gone missing over the past eighteen months and they want us to look into it."

The *IC* was actually the IIC, the International Insurance Corporation, an indemnity provider owned by Jean-Paul Villard, president and CEO of P9, one of the largest insurance consortiums in the world. JP's number two was Jackson Blue, a good friend of mine. The IIC had us on commission and so whenever they called, one of us answered.

"You ever hear of a group called the Invisible Panthers?" Saul asked.

"No."

A toilet flushed in the back offices.

"Who are they?" I asked.

"They say they're some kind of left-wing political group that don't want to be known."

Niska came out from the hallway and pointed at her ear with a query on her face.

"It's Saul," I said to her, and then I asked him, "It's a whole political organization?"

"I really don't know. Maybe paramilitary. Is Niska there with you?"

"Yeah."

"Tell her hello for me."

"Those radical groups up there are dangerous. Maybe you should have somebody with you. I could ask Fearless."

"No. At least not yet anyway. I'm just making some contacts buying black-market Japanese electronics. Nothing to worry about so far."

"Okay. But don't cut it too close."

"Don't worry. Tell Niska I'm saving the expense reports for when I get home."

"Okay. Talk to you later."

"Goodbye, Mr. Lynx!" Niska shouted before I hung up.

"He says he'll have the expense reports when he comes back."

"That's what he always says. Tinsford's gone too."

"Where?"

Niska started organizing her desk while answering my question.

"This older white lady named Tella Monique came in last Tuesday," she said. "She wanted for him to find her son Mordello because her husband had disowned him and threw him out when he had married a Catholic woman nine years ago."

"Nine years?"

"Uh-huh. But now that her husband died she wants her son and his family back."

"So where's Whisper doin' all this?" I asked.

"He's in Phoenix 'cause the son was mixed up with a motorcycle gang called the Snake-Eagles, somethin' like that, out there."

"A black motorcycle gang?"

"I don't think so."

"Damn. I hope he got his will up to date."

Niska grinned and said, "Nobody ever sees Mr. Natly. They won't even know he was there."

"Any news for me?"

"Not really. You got the check from Mr. Zuma?"

"Um . . ."

Charles "Chuck" Zuma was a millionaire who had a twin sister named Charlotte. It took Charlotte most of her thirties to run through her half of their sizable inheritance. Then she used a loophole in the family trust to turn Chuck's twenty-eight million into bearer bonds. After that Charlotte Zuma disappeared.

Her brother offered me two-tenths of one percent of as much of the money as I could return. I took the job because there was no violent crime attached. I was trying to take on easy jobs that didn't include, for instance, motorcycle gangs and left-wing paramilitary groups.

"Did you get the money?" Niska asked again.

"Technically."

"Technically how much?"

"The sister learned from her wasteful years," I said. "Her investment advisers increased Chuck's money to nearly forty million."

"That's an eighty-thousand-dollar fee." She did this calculation without using her fingers.

"The forty million is all tied up in funds that a whole army of forensic accountants have to disentangle."

"But all you need is eighty thousand."

"Chuck's broke. He's living with a rich cousin up north of Santa Barbara."

"So we don't get paid?"

"It'll take at least a year before he gets his and we get ours. But he gave me collateral."

"What kind of collateral?"

"A pale yellow 1968 Rolls-Royce Phantom VI." I might have grimaced a little while reciting the name.

"A car?"

"They only made a few hundred of 'em," I said. "And none in America. It's worth at least twice what Zuma owes."

"But you can't put a car in the bank."

"I could sell it."

"A car."

"Yeah."

"You parked it downstairs?"

"It's in the shop."

"A car that doesn't even work?"

"I'll be in my office."

2

I liked Niska. She considered every problem before offering an answer and therefore almost always did a good job. But I wasn't in the mood for good service or comradeship. That morning I had a yen for isolation. Just hearing her footsteps down the hall wore on me. When she went to the restroom a second time I had to put down the book I was reading because of the whining of the pipes and the sound of the door clicking shut. Even the faint whiff of her essential-oil perfume seemed to crowd my space.

By 10:17 I made a decision. It took a few more minutes to tamp down the unreasonable anger before going out to the front office.

Niska was typing at great speed on her IBM Selectric. She typed, organized, and filed away our notes, correspondence, and case journals. At seventy-five words a minute, the rapid-fire clack of the letter ball on paper set my teeth on edge.

"Niska."

"Yes, Mr. Rawlins?" She stopped the racket, looking up innocently.

Behind a forced smile I asked, "You like that Transcendental Meditation stuff, right?"

The surprise pushed her head back two or three inches.

"Um," she said. "Yeah. How come?"

"They have those two-week-long getaways where everybody does yoga, right?"

"There's some exercises but mostly they meditate. I went to two weekend retreats but the week-longs are very expensive. And I only get two weeks' vacation anyway. I was thinking of going to one around Christmas maybe."

"How expensive is it?" I asked.

"Hundred and thirty dollars—a week."

"What if I gave you two weeks off and enough money for the retreat—on top of your salary? You could call 'em and go right up there this morning."

"But what about the files and the phone?"

"Files can wait and I learned how to answer a phone before you were born."

This was something new for the receptionist/office manager. Her eyebrows creased and her freckled nose scrunched up.

"I don't get it," she said.

"I want to be alone, honey. That's all. Whisper and Saul are already out, probably for a while. I think it would be good for both of us."

"So you just want me to pack up and go?"

"Right after I draw the money you need out of the safe."

She hemmed, hawed, and argued mainly because there was little precedent for a boss letting employees off from work on a whim back in 1969. And two hundred and sixty dollars plus two weeks' salary for doing something you loved was unheard-of. But the offer was too good to pass up, and so by noon she was off and I could return to my office in solitude.

I leaned back in my ample oak throne and sighed deeply.

"Alone at last," I said aloud.

"Either for good or not for long," a bodiless voice intoned.

In life that voice belonged to an old man I knew only as Sorry. He was the wisest man of my childhood, whose advice would come to me every couple of years or so to remind me that I didn't know everything and so to watch out for banana peels and blind corners, jealous husbands and comely wives.

More than once I worried that that voice was an indication

of severe mental disease. But then I'd remember that we lived in a world filled with insanity; where war, nuclear threat, and the slaughter of children crowded every day with distress.

In the America I loved and hated you could make it rich or, more likely, go broke at the drop of a robber baron's hat. That's why I had a pile of cash hidden somewhere safe, no rent or mortgage payment, and no property tax either. And that was just the material of life. My true wealth was a small family, a few friends, and a phone number that was unlisted even to the police.

These were just normal precautions. One thing I never forgot was that I was a black man in America, a country that had built greatness on the bulwarks of slavery and genocide. But even while I was well aware of the United States' crimes and criminals, still I had to admit that our nation offered bright futures for any woman or man with brains, elbow grease, and more than a little luck . . .

There was a sound out past the hallway toward the front of the offices. One of the settling cracks of the foundation, most probably. But then again maybe there was no sound at all but just my intuition.

I looked up and saw the shadow of a man standing a few feet back from the doorway, the only exit from my office.

Go left or go right but never move straight ahead unless there's no other way, Mr. Chen often taught in his self-defense class. *Look for the upper hand instead of trying to prove that you are the strongest. The other man is always stronger, but you will best him from either the right or the left.*

The problem was that I was sitting in a chair at a desk with my closest pistol in the bottom drawer. Whoever had walked in was good; he hardly made a sound. Even if I fell to the right and grabbed at the drawer he could have shot me right through the wood.

He took a step forward. I could see that he was tall and lean with a pantherish gait, but still his features were hidden in shadow.

"Are you Easy Rawlins?" he asked.

With those words the unannounced visitor crossed the threshold. He was in his early twenties with very short sandy-blond hair and an ugly bruise on his left temple. He wore a peach-and-white checkered short-sleeved shirt over a white undershirt. His blue jeans were stiff, ending at silent white sneakers. I already knew he was a white boy by the spin of his words.

"You always just walk in on people like that?" I replied.

"The door was unlocked," he said. "I said hello when I came in."

He took another step and I sat back again. His empty hands hung loose at the sides.

"I'm Rawlins. Who're you?"

He took another step, saying, "Craig Kilian."

One more step. It felt as if he was going to walk right up on my desk.

"Why don't you take a seat, Mr. Kilian?"

The offer seemed to confuse the young man. He looked to his left, identified the walnut straight-back chair. After a moment he went through the necessary movements to sit himself down.

"You just out the military, Craig?"

"Uh-huh. You say that 'cause'a my crew cut?"

"Yeah. Sure."

There was a haunted look in Kilian's eyes that would have probably still been there if he hadn't been walloped upside the head. All through World War II I'd encountered soldiers from both sides of the battlefield who had that look, who had been shattered by the din of war.

Craig took a pack of True cigarettes from his shirt pocket. Plucking out a cancer stick with his lips, he drew a book of matches from the cellophane skin of the pack. He lit up, took in a lungful of smoke, and exhaled.

Then he gave me a quizzical look and asked, "Do you mind if I smoke?"

I did mind. I'd been trying to quit for a couple of years. But there was something about Craig's glower that made me want to give him some leeway.

Watching him suck on that cigarette, I was reminded of an early morning in October 1945. It was outside of Arnstadt, Germany, and I was on guard duty after a long night of heavy rains. The war was just over and so we weren't as sharp as we had been in battle. My brand was Lucky Strike. As I smoked I was wondering what it would be like to go back home to Texas after outflanking and outfighting the white man, and becoming friendly with his women too.

I don't know what made me look to the right—a sound, an intuition—but there I saw a German soldier in a filthy and tattered uniform bearing down on me with a bayonet raised high. I turned just in time to grab the knife-wielding hand by the wrist. In that instant we had seized each other, locked, almost motionless, in a struggle to the death. My cigarette fell onto his coat sleeve. I don't know what I looked like to him, but his gaunt face was desperate and, oddly, almost pleading. He pressed harder and harder but I matched him sinew for sinew. Probably the deciding factor in that brawl was the fact that I was well-fed and he was not. He might have been trying to kill me in hopes of getting a few rations.

The smoldering sleeve started to burn. Smoke got into my left eye. I winced and he pressed harder. We were both shaking under the exertions, literally on fire. I noticed a tear coming from his eye. At first I thought it was in reaction to the smoke, but then I saw, and felt, that he was crying. He shook harder and I was able to press him down onto the rain-soaked mud. There I got the upper hand, forcing the blade toward his throat. He was trying his best to protect himself while blubbering.

I could have killed him as I had a dozen others in hand-to-hand combat. Death dealing was second nature after years on the battlefield. But instead I pushed his bayonet arm to the side, slamming it down on the wet earth, extinguishing the fire. He released the dagger, curled into a ball, and cried for all he was worth. I sat there next to him for long minutes. When he finally sat up I handed him my rations and indicated that he could leave. I should have taken him as a POW, but lately our troop had been executing anyone they deemed a Nazi.

Craig Kilian reminded me of the soldier I spared. Shell-shocked by war and stunned in civilian life, he was living in a world of his own, still trying to find a way back home. There were thousands of young men like Craig coming back from Vietnam. Innocents, killers, and children, all rolled up into the war-hardened bodies of veterans who had no idea what they'd done or why.

I reached into the drawer that held my pistol and came out with an ashtray kept there for whenever my friend Mouse came by to visit. Placing the ceramic dish in front of Craig I said, "Knock yourself out."

He took another drag off the low-tar cigarette and then tapped a smattering of gray ash onto the white porcelain.

There we sat; him hunched forward, smoking, and me leaning back, wondering whether I should have taken the pistol from the drawer.

Maybe two minutes passed.

"Why are you here, Mr. Kilian?"

"I, I was told that, that you're a good detective and, um, um, honest."

"By whom?" I asked, using my best English.

"A man named Larker. Kirkland Larker."

"I don't know anybody by that name."

Kilian stared at me, a deer frozen in the headlights.

"Is he a vet?" I asked.

"Yeah."

"What war?"

"'Nam."

"I wasn't ever there. He a black man?"

"Can you help me?" Craig asked instead of answering the question.

"I take it you need somebody honest because there's something questionable that needs investigating."

"Why you say that?"

"The bruise on your head. You dragging your feet instead of telling me why you're here. The fact that you won't look me in the eye."

"I need somebody I can trust," he said, looking directly at me.

"To do what?"

The question could have been two live wires pressed against the hinges of his jaw. His face went through exaggerated contortions like a cartoon bad guy who, for all his brutish strength, could not crush Popeye to dust.

All of this was simply prelude to the sudden, thunderous aftershock of the explosion that reverberated in the room.

3

The windowpanes behind me rattled in their frames. I could feel the air bulging against my eardrums.

It was just another sonic boom, a military jet breaking the sound barrier. I'd heard it so many times that it meant nothing. But for the recent graduate from Vietnam University it was life-and-death.

In an instant Craig was flying over the broad desk straight at me.

I moved to the right, but not fast enough.

Craig's powerful left arm ensnared me and for a moment I believed that I was going to experience my last moments at the hands of a battle-hardened vet who had lost his sanity in the jungles of Vietnam. But instead of knifing, choking, or battering me, the young lion backed into the nearest corner, pulling me along as a kind of shield. He was shivering, and a low moan, almost a growl, emanated from his chest.

Pushing free, I turned to face him, to provide cover from the imagined attack. He had his head buried in his arms. A preternatural stillness set upon him.

"It's okay, soldier," I said calmly to the top of his head. "It's okay. It was just a sonic boom. A sonic boom. You're safe. Safe."

"How many, Sergeant?" he asked softly. "How many are there?"

"They're all dead, soldier. They've been dead a long time. You're safe, safe and sound."

I placed a hand on his right shoulder, causing him to jerk away and gasp.

"It's all right," I said. "They're all dead. Dead and gone."

When I laid my hand on him this time he didn't resist.

"I can hear 'em," he said. "I can hear 'em in the night when everybody else is sleepin'. I hear 'em."

I remembered the night terrors I had after liberating my second concentration camp; the animated skeletons of men and women dancing around the corpses of the Germans we'd killed.

"It was just a sonic boom," I said, and Craig raised his head.

He looked around in confusion. It was as if he didn't know how he got there crouched on the floor with some black man kneeling before him.

"What happened?" he asked me.

"Some fool broke the sound barrier and you had a flashback to the war."

He nodded and I held out a hand, pulling us both to our feet.

"One of my partners keeps a fair bottle of bourbon in his desk drawer," I said. "Why don't we get us a shot?"

Whisper always had a fifth of Cabin Still sour mash bourbon in his bottom drawer. He had glasses there too. I downed my first shot in one draft. Craig did the same. It made him cough pretty hard. I sipped the second shot but he downed that one too, this time merely gagging a bit.

He held out the glass for a third go-round but I shook my head and said, "First let's go back to my office and find out what you need an honest detective for."

We were seated again, silent again, with Craig looking everywhere but at me. After letting this go on for a while I said, "So what do you want, Craig?"

He made a sour face and turned away, fidgeting so much that for a moment it looked as if he might crawl right out of his chair.

Then he went still.

"Have you ever heard of Blood Grove?" he asked.

"Can't say I have. That some battle in Vietnam?"

"No. It's a, it's a orange grove out at the far end of the San Fernando Valley. They specialize in blood oranges."

"Okay. Is that your problem?" I wasn't impatient but Craig had to be spurred on or he would stall.

"I like, I like to go camping out there when the nightmares start coming even when I'm awake, you know?"

I nodded.

"Out there it's mostly just farms. And if you climb up to this place called Knowles Rock there's a cabin nobody uses and a campsite where you can build a fire and be so alone that it's like you're the only man in the world. I usually only go to the campsite because I like sleepin' outside. The cabin is maybe a quarter mile from there."

"And whatever problem you got has to do with out there?"

Craig blinked at me.

"Yeah," he said. "I was sound asleep in the early evening. It had been a hot day and it's a seven-mile hike from the place where I park my mother's car. I went to sleep early. But then I woke up all of a sudden at moonrise. There was this full moon staring me right in the face. And when I sat up I saw that there was a campfire goin' at the cabin."

"A quarter mile away," I said, just to prove that I was listening.

"Yeah. I looked at that moon and then at the glow of the campfire and it was like I was drawn to it; like some kinda moth or somethin'. And then I heard a woman screaming, 'Alonzo! Alonzo!' It was faint because of the distance and the trees, but I heard it. She'd probably been yelling and that's what woke me up.

"Before I knew it I was on my feet in just my long johns and T-shirt running for the cabin. The closer I got, the louder her screams. She sounded scared outta her mind."

Craig stopped to hold his right hand over his mouth and nose.

I thought I'd have to urge him on again, but then he said, "They were outside the cabin. The woman's clothes was all ripped. A big black man with long straight hair had tied her to a tree. He had a knife. The next thing I knew I was runnin' at him.' "

Craig stopped talking because he was remembering the events in the orange grove. He was mesmerized, panting too.

"What happened then?" I asked.

"I grabbed him. Tried to get the knife away. We fell to the ground and the woman, girl really, was shoutin', 'No, don't! Don't get in it!' "

"Don't get in what?"

"I don't know," he said, almost pleading. "I don't know."

That was a little break in the story. I was happy to have sent Niska away.

After a while I said, "Why don't you finish tellin' the story, Craig? Finish the story and we can get another drink."

"We were rollin' around on the ground, fighting for the knife, and the girl was shouting . . . and then I flipped him."

"Like a judo throw?"

"Nuh-uh. He was tryin' to get on top'a me but before he could get set I heaved up and fell on him. That's when I felt the knife sinkin' into his chest. His eyes got real big like a man when he knows he's got a bad wound."

Craig Kilian stood up and backed away, knocking the chair over. He got all the way to the wall, five feet behind. I believe he would have gone a mile if there was nothing there to stop him.

"I stood up over him and he was holding on to the haft of that bayonet, I mean that knife. The girl shouted, 'Alonzo!' "

"Alonzo?" I asked.

"I wanted to call a medic but then somethin' hit me." He raised his hand to the bruise on his temple. There were tears coming from his eyes but he gave no other sign of crying—no heaving or whine.

I could almost see the dying man laid out before Kilian's eyes. Behind him was the Vietnam War with all its dead, its carpet-bombing and heavy boots. In the distance, far behind that, I imagined Korea and Auschwitz, Nagasaki and ten thousand slave ships coming from the distant horizon over the African Sea.

"Mr. Kilian." No word had been spoken for some minutes. "Craig."

He looked up from the ground where the man named Alonzo lay dying. He saw me but I'm not sure that he knew why I was there.

"What?"

"What happened after you got hit?"

Judging from his face, the question didn't seem to make sense.

"After you stabbed Alonzo," I added.

"Knocked out," he said. "When I woke up it was morning. About six hundred hours. The sun was out."

"What about the girl and the man that got stabbed?"

"Nobody," he said, shaking his head. "Nobody but the dog."

"What dog?"

"A little black puppy lickin' my face. There was no white girl or black man. I didn't even see any blood on the ground."

"All gone?"

"Just the puppy and about a thousand white cabbage butterflies flitting through the grass."

"Was the white woman big and strong?" I asked.

"Nuh-uh. She was little."

"And how big was Alonzo?"

"A little taller'n me and full. You know, two hundred pounds or more."

"Come on," I said. "Let's get another shot of whiskey."

4

I sat behind Whisper's desk, leaving Craig the visitor's chair. I told him to sip this glass because that was all he was getting.

Some of his story had the ring of truth, maybe even most of it. But more than that I believed in the innate goodness of the shell-shocked soldier.

Goodness is a complex word in my profession. Good men and women can be guilty of terrible crimes, just as there are those with evil intent who can never be found guilty in a court of law. In a book I'd recently read, the main character, Billy Budd, was as good as a man can be, but he murders an evil man named Claggart. Good and guilt often go hand in hand.

"So what do you want from me?" I asked.

The veteran's first response was as if I had slapped him. His head jerked back and there was a flash of anger in his eyes. But somewhere along the way Craig Kilian had learned to conquer his hot temper. He took a deep breath and shuddered.

"You're a detective," he said. "A good one, I'm told."

"By a man I never heard of."

"I want you to find out if I killed that man and what happened to the woman. What were they doing there?"

"Which one?"

"You mean they might'a been there for different reasons?"

"No. I mean what is most important? If the man died or if the girl lived and is okay. Or why they were there."

"If I killed him is the most important thing," he said. "But I'd like to know it all. I feel like I got to know."

"Did Alonzo say her name?"

"No."

"Did she hit you or was she still tied up?"

This question caught Craig off guard. He thought for a minute, a minute more. It seemed as if the answer was a very important thing.

"She was tied up, yeah, with rope, but the rope was kinda loose; she might could'a pulled free."

I sat back and pondered. This was one of those cases that I shouldn't even have considered. But there was something . . .

"Why do you need these answers?" I asked.

"Because I can't sleep. I haven't had ten minutes since that morning."

"How many days ago did this happen?"

"Three. Three days."

"Look, man, you got in a fight, maybe stabbed some guy, and then got knocked out. You woke up and there was no body and no one who could have carried a big man like that outta there. He was probably her boyfriend and she helped him get away. That's the way it usually is. A man and woman get into a fight. He slaps her around and she screams bloody murder, but anyone gets between 'em and she will turn on them. Knock 'em upside the head with a stone."

"But why would she do that?"

"Why are young men like you killing women and children in Vietnam?" I offered.

Craig's eyes furrowed. He was thinking about something. Those thoughts didn't make it to words. Then he nodded. I felt that I had almost convinced him, almost dodged the bullet of feeling I had to consider taking up his cause.

"Um," he hummed. "I hear what you're sayin', but could you do me a favor?"

"What kind of favor?"

"Will you talk to my, my mother?"

"Your mother?"

"Uh-huh."

"Why?"

"I think she could explain it better than I can."

"Was your mother there?"

"No. But she knows me. She can explain to you what I'm askin' for."

"What can she tell me that you can't?" I really was flummoxed.

"Just call her. Call her and you'll see what I mean."

There I was, now as at 7:04 in the morning waiting to see when the hippie came out with his long-necked watering can. Something about Craig Kilian intrigued me.

"And how was it you found me?" I asked.

"I already told you. Kirkland Larker. He said that you were a good detective and that you were colored and could maybe get a handle on this Alonzo."

"But I don't know any Kirkland."

"He knows about you."

"How do you know him?" I asked, looking for a reason, any reason—one way or another.

"There's a bar on Western called Little Anzio. It's not official or anything but mostly only veterans go there."

"Never been inside but I know the place. This Kirkland hangs out there?"

"Yeah. Yeah, that's where I met him."

"You don't even look old enough to get into a bar."

"I'm twenty-three."

"How many tours of duty?"

"Three."

"What kinda missions?"

"The last two were seek and destroy." As he spoke of war he seemed to get more certain.

"And you met this Kirkland at Little Anzio?"

"He bought me a drink one day. We started talkin'."

"When was this?"

"Maybe four months ago. Something like that."

"And you told him about Alonzo and the white girl just a few days ago?"

"Yeah."

"And that's the first time he mentioned me."

"Yeah. I said that I got in a fight with a . . . a black man over a white girl. I said I was knocked out and wanted somebody to find out if she was okay. He made a call and then gave me your name."

He was going to say, *I got in a fight with a nigger.* I was sure of that. I stared and he fidgeted a bit.

"Nothing good can come from me finding this Alonzo—dead or alive," I said. "Do you want to end up in prison because you lost a few nights' sleep?"

Craig moved in his chair. It was what can only be described as an undulation; as if there was a creature that had been sleeping inside him suddenly came awake.

"So will you call my mother?"

"No."

The shock that registered on his face almost made me laugh. He was like an eight-year-old after baring his soul. There was no way in his imagination that I could turn him down.

"If we talk at all I need to meet her face-to-face," I said. "Can't trust some voice over the telephone line talkin' about murder."

"Oh, okay," he said. "Sure. That'd be fine. You want me to write down the address? I'll call her and tell her you're coming."

I thought, maybe he should also tell her that I was a fool. Maybe that too.

I took a sheet of paper and a yellow number two pencil from Tinsford's top drawer. Doing this, I realized he would know that I used his office as well as drank his whiskey. I hoped he wouldn't mind.

Handing him paper and pencil, I said, "Write it down. Tell her I'll be by later today. Gimme her phone number too. I'll call but just to tell her when I'm coming. While you're at it you might as well give me directions to that campsite too—just in case I decide to look."

"We could go see my mother right now."

"I got other business now."

"You're not going to the cops, are you?" Kilian tensed in his chair and I doubted if my self-defense training would be enough to handle him.

"And what would I say to them?" I asked. "That some white-boy Vietnam vet says he stabbed somebody named Alonzo in another county, got knocked out, and then, when he came to, the man he stabbed was gone?"

"I don't know. Maybe."

"Write down the directions and your mother's name, phone number, and address. Tell her I'll be by later on."

Craig's face said that he wanted to argue. Once again he was that eight-year-old boy intent on getting his way.

"Take it or leave it," I said.

After a moment or two he began to write.

The entrance to our offices opened onto a separate staircase that led up from the street. I walked Craig Kilian to the top of the stairs and watched his descent. Through the small window opposite the front door I kept watching as he crossed the street and climbed into an eggshell-colored Studebaker. Three minutes passed before the engine turned over and the car drove off.

After he was gone I went back inside, making sure the front door was locked. Then I washed Tinsford's glasses and returned them to their drawer. In the little toilet I did my business, then cleaned up. In the mirror there were the faces of many men: a middle-aged black man in fair shape but worn; a veteran not unlike Craig Kilian; a free agent who only took orders out of love, duty, or, far too often, as a consequence of guilt.

Maybe twelve minutes after my potential client had left I was walking south to Pico and then eastward. Upon reaching La Cienega I headed south again.

The whole time I was wondering about why I didn't turn down the vet's request. It would be nothing but trouble to go out looking for a man who got stabbed in the middle of an orange grove. A black man and a white woman that might have been hallucinations but, considering my luck, probably weren't.

I would have turned him down out of hand if it weren't for my understanding of the America I both love and loathe.

In America everything is about either race or money or some combination of the two. Who you are, what you have, what you look like, where your people came from, and what god looked over their breed—these were the most important questions. Added into that is the race of men and the race of women. The rich, famous, and powerful believe they have a race and the poor know for a fact that they do. The thing about it is that most people have more than one race. White people have Italians, Germans, Irish, Poles, English, Scots, Portuguese, Russian, old-world Spaniards, new-world rich, and many combinations thereof. Black people have a color scheme from high yellow to moonless night, from octoroon to deepest Congo. And new-world Spanish have every nation from Mexico to Puerto Rico, from Colombia to Venezuela, each of which is a race of its own—not to mention the empires, from Aztec to Mayan to Olmec.

I'm a black man closer to Mississippi midnight than its yellow moon. Also I'm a westerner, a Californian formerly from the South—Louisiana and Texas to be exact. I'm a father, a reader, a private detective, and a veteran.

I'm sure as shit a vet.

From the sand-strewn corpses of D-day (on that day my race, for a brief moment, was all-American) to the Battle of the Bulge with its one hundred fifty thousand dead, to the masses of skin-stitched corpses, living and dead, at Auschwitz-Birkenau. The explosions in my ears, the death at my hands, and the smell of gunpowder and slaughter made me brother to any man, woman, or child who ever raised arms or had arms raised against them.

Because of that bloody history, Craig Kilian was as much my brother in blood as any black man in the U.S. I had to help him because I could see his pain in my mirror.

5

It was just about Eighteenth Street when I made up my mind to go see Kilian's mother. That decision accomplished, I could then think about my destination.

The pale yellow 1968 Rolls-Royce Phantom VI was in the shop for its quarterly tune-up. I had in my possession a contract that said the car was under a yearlong lease to me for payment of one dollar. If, at the end of that time, Chuck Zuma couldn't pay at least sixty thousand dollars, I would assume ownership of the automobile.

A block past Sawyer on the western side of La Cienega was the slender entrance to an auto mechanic garage with a red-and-yellow sign that read EXOTIC CAR SERVICE AND REPAIR above the roll-up chromium door. Past the entrance was a workspace that bulged out to accommodate three hydraulic lifts surrounded by deep shelves stacked with automotive parts and tools. The business was a two-man operation. The first of these was fifty-four-year-old Lester Pineman, the original owner, who now spent most of his time sitting on a backless metal stool in a little nook of an office at the entrance. Short, he was fat around the middle with powerful hands and usually had a cigar clenched between his teeth.

"Rawlins, right?" he asked in a gruff voice. I imagined that his larynx was coated with thirty-weight car oil after all those years in the garage.

"Yeah," I said brightly. I'm always happy when the decision is made and the job is before me.

"Lihn!" Lester shouted.

"What?" came a definitely feminine voice from the bowels of the repair shop.

"It's that guy about the six."

From behind a concrete pillar came a short figure wearing a teal-green jumpsuit. She was pulling heavy canvas gloves from her hands and shaking her head so that her thick black hair would fall back. This was Vu Von Lihn, a thirty-seven-year-old refugee from Vietnam. Her story was that, from 1965 to 1967, she had worked for Nguyen Van Thieu and his staff. The distribution of labor between Lester and Lihn was that he chewed the cigars, collected the money, and pontificated while she repaired the fancy automobiles.

Lihn was slight and sleek, sultry and strong—she had a scar like a lightning strike down the right side of her face that had left that side's eye a useless and pale blue orb. Her lips were thick and sneered naturally, telling you there were some teeth behind any kiss she might bestow.

"Hello, Mr. Rawlins," she said, walking right up to me and holding out a hand.

"Ms. Vu Von," I said.

"You can call me Lihn," she said, almost as if in song.

"How's my baby?"

She turned away and walked toward the back of the garage. There she, and I, came upon the Rolls. Its long snout and classic cabin just about yelled elegance. It had a rolling chassis and a black hood and roof, with pale yellow sides. Just looking at it took my breath away.

"It's in perfect shape," Lihn said. "I did some work on the engine so it will keep its calibration longer than most of these V8 disasters."

Nodding at the car, I was thinking about the mechanic.

"Tell me something, Lihn."

"What's that, Mr. Rawlins?"

"Easy."

She gave me that dangerous smile and said, "Easy."

"If you're only a year or two out of Vietnam, how come your English is so good?"

"My mother sent me to the American school in the mornings in Saigon. My father taught me auto mechanics in the afternoons."

"Oh. Anything else I need to know?" I asked.

"Don't let Lester try to charge you. Everything I did was part of the maintenance fee we got from Mr. Zuma."

I wandered around the car imagining kicking the tires. Then I jumped in behind the wheel, moving my butt around to get comfortable.

"You sure you can manage a right-side drive?" Lihn asked through the open window.

"I once drove an ice delivery truck that had the same setup."

This explanation made the mechanic smile.

"You talk to Raymond?" she asked me.

When I took delivery on the car I had to bring it down to the garage. My good friend Raymond Alexander followed so he could give me a ride home. When he and Lihn looked at each other, something happened—something deep; kindred souls meeting for the first time. Mouse, that's Raymond's nickname, told me I could take his car because he'd be getting a ride with the lady mechanic.

"He was fine the last time I saw him," I said. "As a matter of fact I can only remember about five times in the forty-two years I've known him that he wasn't glad and happy."

"God doesn't make many like him," she said with forceful objectivity.

"And he only made one Ray," I furthered.

She smiled again and I was a little bit jealous of my perfect, murderous, maybe even psychopathic friend.

Driving my little piece of heaven up to the front gate, I told Lester that Lihn said I did not owe the three hundred and fifty dollars he demanded. He frowned and chomped on the cigar but I managed to drive away without him swinging a crowbar at the best car I ever had.

I decided to take La Cienega up toward Sunset before heading west for my new home. The car felt like driving a yacht down the street—it was that smooth. The secret ecstasy of finally having arrived at success filled the cab of that Rolls.

I passed Pico and Olympic, finally crossing Wilshire into Beverly Hills. I had even made it a block or two past that when the flashing red lights appeared in the extra-wide rearview mirror. It was one of those wake-up calls that happen in the lives of black men and women in America when they mistakenly believe they have crossed over to freedom.

I pulled to the curb, put both hands on the steering wheel, and sat patiently awaiting the rendering of the calculation of my situation. That equation was a matter of simple addition: Rolls-Royce + black man without driver's cap + any day of the century = stop and frisk, question and dominate—and, like the solution of pi, that process had the potential of going on forever.

The cops used the classic flanking maneuver. One came to the driver's-side window while the partner moved up along the rear, making sure that I wasn't hiding an army in the back seat.

The cop facing me gestured that I should crank the window down. I did so, feeling the pressure of the other cop's eyes on the back of my head.

"License and registration," the man outside my window demanded.

He was tall and slender, thirties and tan.

"Aren't you an LA cop?" I asked instead of obliging.

"So what?" His name tag read L. Bowen.

"This here is Beverly Hills."

"We can make arrests outside our jurisdiction if we're in hot pursuit." He allowed himself a smile.

"Pursuit of what?" I asked, thinking of the Bill of Rights.

"The report of a brother who stole a Rolls-Royce."

Our eyes met over his lie. Then he recognized something.

"Say . . . you're that nigger, right?"

O America, my America.

"Which one did you mean?" I asked, even though I knew the answer to his question. He recognized me as the sometimes special adviser to Commander Melvin Suggs—the third-highest-ranking cop in the LAPD rank and file.

"Don't you get smart with me," L. Bowen said.

I had license and registration on the dashboard. There was also the legal-ownership document signed by Charles Zuma in my breast pocket. These I handed to a man who had somehow managed to despise me with no personal knowledge whatsoever.

L. Bowen and his partner, E. Simmons, pored over the documents while discussing my fate. I didn't hear what they said but I imagined that they were considering whether or not they could roust me without incurring the ire of the LAPD brass. Finally L. returned my papers.

"You were three miles over the speed limit, but we'll let you off with a warning this time," he said.

"The Beverly Hills limit or the hot pursuit one?" I asked. I shouldn't have.

They had me get out of the car and put my hands on the roof of the Rolls while they patted me down. They gave me a ticket, knowing I'd never pay it.

The whole process took about half an hour. If I added up all the half hours the police, security forces, MPs, bureaucrats, bank tellers, and even gas station attendants had stolen from my life, I could make me a twelve-year-old boy versed in useless questions, meaningless insults, and spite as thick as black tar.

6

I made it to Sunset Boulevard without further incident. Driving west down the Strip was slow going, but I liked the streets filled with hippies, head shops, and discos. There was what they were calling a cultural revolution going on among the youth of America. They wanted to drop out and end the war, make love for its own sake, and forget the prejudices of the past. These long-haired, dope-smoking, often unemployed wanderers gave me insight into what my country, *my country* might be.

There was an extra added benefit driving by the hippie hoi polloi that day. The young people ogled my fancy ride. Some of them, most of whom were white, gave me the black power fist and even mouthed, "Right on, brother."

I liked that car way too much.

The crowds ended after five or six blocks, and I was speeding along the boulevard, now lined with mansions and big trees, vast green lawns and no pedestrians to speak of. The speed limit picked up and hardly anyone noticed my car because I was going deeper and deeper into the land of wealth.

After about three miles there was a northbound, nameless turn-off that became a dirt road in six or seven minutes. That slender lane went another seven or eight miles with a solitary yellow Rolls-Royce its only traffic.

After twenty minutes or so of deep ruts and hairpin turns over wooden bridges across dry streambeds and past a pond or two, I pulled up to a high iron gate. A man came out from a bamboo hut set before the barrier. He was maybe five nine, hirsute, with ocean-blue eyes and swarthy skin that had been kissed by the long-suffering sun of Sicilian history. Under curly black hair and a generous mustache one might have thought him to be in his forties, but I knew that Cosmo Longo had just turned thirty-two on May third.

The sentry broke into a big smile and walked toward me as I exited the car.

"Easy!" he announced to the woods and earth, sky and a far-off sliver of the Pacific Ocean that could be seen between two westerly crags.

"Cosmo. How you doin' today?"

The Southern Italian immigrant wore heavy black trousers with a button-up fly and a white T-shirt, the fabric of which was quite a bit thicker than its American cousins. His bare feet were bigger than most shoes.

"Carving a crucifix for my aunt in Cefalù." He pulled out the moderate-size red garnet stone that he was slowly fashioning into the religious icon. It was both ornate and primitive, something reminiscent of another homeland, one I had never known.

"Beautiful," I said.

The manly sentry grinned and nodded; then he said, "She got here about fifteen minutes ago."

He produced a key from a dark pocket and used it on the man-size gate contained within the larger metal structure. He ushered me through and we came to a nearly vertical granite mountain-side that supported a funicular. The right side of the double-car conveyance was made from brass-tinted glass, polished copper, and ebony wood. It was beautifully detailed, which was fitting for its destination.

I looked up at the hillside to our left and said, "I bet Gaetano is in that big oak halfway up."

"Not even the right hill," Cosmo said, gleeful at my bad guess.

There were always two Longo guardians at Brighthope Gate. One sat in the bamboo hut waiting for tenants, visitors, workmen, and, of course, unwanted guests. Another of the brothers hid somewhere in the surrounding hills with a high-powered rifle guarding his blood and the entrance.

Cosmo pulled open the sliding door to the funicular and ushered me in. Once I was safely bunged inside, he engaged the mechanism that pulled my car up while the counterweight, the leftward chamber, came down again.

The angle was steep, one hundred degrees, and the view through tobacco-tinted windows was magnificent. To my right sprawled the Pacific Ocean, a sleeping giant at the end of the world. To the left lay the ever-growing landscape of LA, spreading out toward the distant hills so far that the borders faded into a smoggy haze.

At the top of the rise was Brighthope Canyon. Not actually a gorge, Brighthope was a shallow bowl carved out of the top of a coastal mountain, a lush depression that contained six houses connected by cobblestone pathways laid out three-quarters of a century before. You can't see most of the buildings, as they are hidden behind and under trees and other vital vegetation. Only a stunning blue-and-white Victorian mansion is apparent. This baronial home was the capital of the little village, where sixty-three-year-old Orchestra "Sadie" Solomon lived with her gay soul mate, Reynard Khan, a man of seventy-one years. Though Reynard never touched Sadie, he stayed at her side for decades.

They, or I should say she, owned the entire property. Sadie, and her father before her, gave out free "ninety-nine-year-until-death" leases to all the tenants. The previous occupant of my place had been named Norman. He died at the age of one hundred and two. Norman lived there for so long that no one remembered his surname.

I inherited his house after being introduced to Orchestra by the minor real estate mogul Jewelle Blue, my friend and Jackson's wife. Reynard, who kept his sexuality a secret back then, was being black-mailed by a young man with a camera—George Lund. George, in concert with a beautiful young man named Laurent, got Reynard on his knees. It was my job to help him back up again without making my involvement known. It was a complex coordination, but my police contacts, Melvin Suggs and Anatole McCourt, were more than happy to bust, and bust up, the extortionists. As far as Reynard was concerned, the problem merely went away. Orchestra was extremely grateful for my sensitivity. I also think she could imagine turning to a man like me for assistance from time to time.

So she decided to offer me Norman's house, which had been abandoned for six years.

I accepted Sadie's offer because I'd been worried about my daughter's safety in some run-of-the-mill house on the city streets of LA. My job as a detective could be byzantine and even, at times, downright deadly. It often felt that I passed through life like a mad surfer negotiating a monstrous tsunami. Living on the mountaintop, protected by five Sicilian bodyguards, at least Feather could feel like she was living a normal life—smelling the flowers and considering the thoughts of Euclid and Shakespeare from classes at school and W. E. B. DuBois and Sojourner Truth from my library and that of Jackson and Jewelle Blue. And besides, no other neighborhood that I could afford would allow a man to raise a garden in his front yard and on his roof too.

The exit at the top of the vertical railway was a large irregularly shaped concrete platform studded aplenty with semiprecious stones, iron discs stamped with the shapes of dozens of wild creatures, and various religious emblems rendered in every metal from copper to zinc to gold.

A long, curved, and sloping path of blue brick led down from the platform to the cobblestone walkway that meandered between the half-hidden houses. Under the shade of three cypress trees I came upon Oktai Lorenz, a Spaniard with coppery skin and black, mildly Asiatic eyes. Oktai was in his fifties, a professor specializing in the history of war at UCLA, and a collector of butterflies. He stood six foot four and was built to practice the subject he taught.

"Mr. Rawlins."

"Señor Lorenz."

"How go the hostilities down below?"

"Simmering, but nowhere near a boil."

"Very good," he said as I passed.

The Bowl of Brighthope was in many ways as eccentric as the little black shantytowns I had known in my days wandering around East Texas and southern Louisiana.

7

A few minutes after leaving Oktai I came to the house that would be in my name and then my daughter's name for the next ninety-eight and a quarter years.

It was three tall stories high and cylindrical, painted mission white, and sporadically draped with ivy and passion fruit vines. There were windows, both large and small, at odd intervals and of different shapes. The path leading to the front door was paved with white marble tiles flanked on one side by nine five-foot dwarf peach trees and on the other by plum. The lawn that once ran around the structure was now made up of rolling rows of beans, tomatoes, yams, potatoes, onions, garlic, the beginnings of an asparagus patch, and Louisiana hot peppers. I puttered in the garden every morning I could. And if I was away, one of the Longo clan made sure that the weeds were tamed and the plants and trees watered.

On the roof of the house, in large terra-cotta pots, I was cultivating twenty-seven different types of rosebushes.

Coming home never failed to make me smile.

I walked up to the plain-faced and thick ironwood door like it was an old friend welcoming me in.

My friend was ajar.

The foyer of our home had no walls but was simply a dais that stood three feet above the rest of that level. The entire first floor of our turret house was without partition, just a supportive pillar here and there. It was a kind of rambling living room that broke down into sections according to how the furniture was arranged. If we gave a party the entire level came together. But most times there were little areas where Feather entertained her friends and I mine.

The most amazing thing about this room, and the whole house, was a stream that ran a crooked path across it. The creek bed was rudely hewn out of mountain stone. The water originated from an underground well in a higher, neighboring mountain. It was fresh enough to drink and the stream itself was quite slender until it reached the koi pond near the open-air terrace at the far wall.

I followed the twisted pathway for its forty-one steps. This led to the sunlit verandah and the circular seventeen-foot-wide and three-and-a-half-foot-deep pond. There were more than eighty koi frolicking in the water. The fishes were white, black, blue, yellow, cream, orange, red, and many combinations of those colors. The huge bright-colored koi sashayed and flitted through the water like angels of a more primitive, more sophisticated time. Some were well over a foot long. My shadow reminded them of food so they crowded the surface near my feet.

The little yellow dog, Frenchie, toddled up to the edge of the water imagining a wriggling fish between his teeth. But Frenchie was too old and not big enough for that. At one time he hated me, but the years had mellowed him, and while he rarely greeted me, he no longer snarled at my scent.

Beyond the koi pond was the outer terrace, which was larger than my first apartment when I was fourteen and living on my own in Houston's Fifth Ward. It, the patio, was paved with blue and red tiles from Mexico and walled by a thick green-glass barrier that stood about four and a half feet high.

She was standing there wearing a pale pink dress that came down to just about the middle of her well-developed calves. With one hand on the ledge of green-glass brick wall she was gazing down along the coastal mountains where they tumbled into the ocean.

"The door was unlocked again," I said.

She turned her body without moving her feet, smiled, and said, "Hi."

That one movement cinched it. The daughter of my heart was becoming a woman.

"The door," I insisted.

"Daddy, we're on a mountaintop and we know all our neighbors. If somebody knocks, I don't ask, Who is it? I just open up."

I was thinking about Craig Kilian and the door to our offices, which we kept unlocked during business hours. I remembered him jumping across the desk at me.

"Sometimes our neighbors have guests," I said, "and even though we know the people around us, that doesn't mean we know everything about them."

"You're just being paranoid."

"That may very well be, but I still need you to respect me and do what I say."

Feather turned fully around, taking my words seriously.

"I do respect you," she said.

"But you got to lock the door behind that."

"What happened today, Daddy?"

I took in a deep breath. Both my adopted children, Jesus and Feather, were in many ways more intelligent, definitely more mature than I.

Jackson Blue, who had read and retained every important book the central library had to offer, once told me that when a child is orphaned at an early age a large part of his psyche remains fixated there.

"It's like the boy just turns into a man instead'a growin' up into one," he said.

I'd been on my own since the age of eight.

I told Feather about Craig Kilian and how he had a breakdown from hearing a sonic boom. When I finished she smiled and said, "I'll be sure to lock the door from now on."

It took a minute for the fears and anger to settle, then another to appreciate that Feather saw it as a duty to calm me when I worried about her.

"You want me to make you some orange tea?" she asked.

I nodded.

"Let's go upstairs."

All the staircases in Roundhouse, as we had dubbed our domicile, ran along the curved outer walls. Twenty-four-inch steel-braced snakewood stairs jutted out from the white, adobelike walls, accompanied by curved brass banisters that were anchored twice—on one floor and then the next.

The second floor was our kitchen/dining room area. The eight-burner stove had two-foot-wide slabs of oak on three sides, creating a table of sorts. The whole structure stood in the center of the cooking area. There was also a huge utility oven and broiler embedded in the central wall.

I sat at the stove-table while Feather puttered with the kettle, loose tea, and cups.

"What you do today?" I asked her, recovered from my fear of an open door.

"Matteo drove me down to Dawn Westerly's house. Her dad put in an Olympic-size pool so we did laps for an hour and a half."

Matteo Longo was, among other things, chauffeur to the residents of Brighthope. Exceptionally tall, he was a pale-skinned man who had the scars and craters of adolescent acne spread across his face. He loved telling jokes and so had a better understanding of English than his father or any of his brothers.

Matteo had driven me to work that morning.

"How many laps?"

"We didn't count."

"How you gonna win the gold medal if you don't count?"

"Daddy," she said in faux exasperation.

She put a pot of the steeping tea and a white ceramic diner mug in front of me and said, "Let it sit for six minutes."

"I'm supposed to count that, right?"

She rolled her eyes and took the stool next to mine.

"So what are you dressed for now?" I asked the thirteen-and-a-half-year-old brown-cream-colored girl.

"Don't you remember? You said I could go over to Anita's house tonight."

"Which one was that?" I asked, trying my best to sound as if I didn't recognize the name.

"You know. Anita Kolor. Her parents have that house on Malibu Beach."

I knew Anita, her mother, Mary-Margaret, and her money-manager father, Keith Kolor. Saul Lynx did a background check on them when it became clear to me that Anita and Feather were becoming friends.

"Oh, right," I said. "You know I'm a little nervous you hangin' out with all these wealthy kids from that fancy school'a yours. I mean, I don't want you thinkin' that we're rich just 'cause'a this house."

"It's an expensive school, Daddy. That's where rich kids go. That's why you sent me there."

"They got those kids with scholarships and grants," I offered as a possible alternative.

"Five," Feather said, holding up the full complement of fingers on her left hand. "Six including me. Kenisha Richards, Bob Cho, Lana Sizeman, Bic Roan, and Pookie. I know them all. I hang out with two of them. So are you saying that they should be my only friends?"

"I thought you played tennis with Anita," I said, rather than having the argument, which belonged in my head.

"Yeah," she agreed. "I do. But we're supposed to have an early dinner and then I thought maybe you or Matteo could drive me over to Aunt Jewelle and Uncle Jackson's house after. I'm baby-sitting and spending the night. And maybe I could talk French with Uncle Jackson."

The cowardly genius, Jackson Blue, was fluent in eight languages—not including computer binary and pure mathematics. There was a time when I wouldn't have turned my back on Jackson, but, in spite of common logic, some people do change. His wife, Jewelle, once married to my deceased property manager, Mofass, was one of the strongest-willed and most brilliant people I had ever known. Jackson made something of himself through love of Jewelle and depth of mind.

"I took on a job today," I told my daughter.

"The one where the guy had the mental breakdown in your office?"

"He's a vet and I feel for him. But that means I might not be able to pick you up." This simple refusal saddened me.

"That's okay. I already asked Matteo and he put it in the book. I was gonna ask Uncle Jackson if he'd take one Tuesday afternoon a week to do French with me and Pookie."

Michelle "Pookie" Fontelle had been born in Lafayette, Louisiana, and came to Watts with her mother, Morona, at the age of nine. Pookie was a math savant and maybe an even better artist. Morona had survived situations that would have destroyed most men, just to get her daughter into that school. And it was obvious that Feather wanted to get her fourteen-year-old friend in a dialogue with her "uncle."

I sighed and shook my head slightly.

"What's wrong? You don't want me to go?"

"Why are you wearing that dress?"

"You don't like it? Aunt Jewelle picked it out for me."

"It's just kinda grown-up for a girl your age."

"I know, right?" She smiled, stood up, and twirled for me. "But the Kolors are having a cocktail party and Anita asked me to wear something pretty. She said then she wouldn't feel funny."

When I was a young man in Houston, women could wrap me around their fingers. All a girl had to do was whisper my name and I was ready to throw down. Feather had that impact on me, but I was sure she'd rather die than lie to me. All this instilled a feeling that I couldn't exactly describe.

I was trying to put that feeling into words when the phone rang.

My demure and sophisticated daughter leaped up from her stool again and ran for the wall phone yelling, "I'll get it!"

I could relax. For the next little while Feather would be a child again and I would be released from the parts of my mind that were shrouded in fears for her safety.

"Hello? Connie? Uh-huh. Yeah, girl. He did? I mean, why would he even think she would go out with him?" She broke into hysterical laughter. "My daddy would say that he couldn't help it. But I think he needs somebody to help him help it . . ."

Her words, tone of voice, even the way she stood was different. I shook my head again and took the second stairway to the third floor, where our bedrooms were. Then I scaled the straight-up fireman's ladder through the portal to the roof.

The circular crown of Roundhouse contained my twenty-seven rosebushes in their simple clay pots. From the moonlight-colored Musk Rose to the deep red Maiden's Blush, from pale coral Bourbon blossoms to the passionate yellow Molineux.

I visited my rosebushes every day. They glowed for me, sang in colors for me. And they offered me a place and time where I could smoke my one cigarette of the day. Lucky Strike, LSMFT, the finest cigarette a workingman could hope for.

The added benefit of a single smoke a day was that the first cigarette is by far the best. That first deep drag is both elegant and ecstatic. Mmm.

The rose-garden roof of Roundhouse was the place I felt most comfortable. At the highest point in Brighthope Bowl, the sky above it was almost always blue. The rosebushes rustled against one another in the upper breezes and I was alone. For me there's a deep satisfaction in solitude.

I leaned over the turret edge and saw the sire of the Longo clan, Erculi, ambling toward Orchestra's blue-and-white manor. He looked fifty but was nearer seventy and always dressed in gray gardener's clothes. He and his four sons worked on the property, holding simple titles like groundskeeper, machinist, housepainter, and chauffeur. But the Longos were anything but simple. In Sicily they had gotten into a beef with a rival clan. Reynard told me that there were thirteen deaths among the Longos and the Trifilettis before Erculi decided to migrate his immediate male kin to America. Reynard said that in his lifetime Erculi had killed thirty-one men.

Thus far I had kept Erculi and Mouse away from each other. No reason to tempt fate.

Returning to the kitchen a good half hour later, I saw that my daughter was still on the phone. "Are you still on that thing?"

"It's Aunt Jewelle," Feather said, holding her hand over the mouthpiece. "I think she wants to talk to you."

"JJ," I said into the receiver.

"Hey, baby," the real estate mogul murmured, almost shyly.

Jewelle loved men but she didn't trust ninety-nine point nine-nine percent of us, including both her husbands. I was one of the few she believed would be there for her on her own terms—even if she didn't know what those terms might be.

"I hear Feather's tryin' t'make your house into a hotel."

"Daddy!"

"You know we love having her, Easy," Jewelle said. "And her friend sounds like she should know a man like Jackson."

"Take her if you want her, but she will empty your refrigerator and your cupboards. That girl and her friends are bottomless pits."

"Daddy, stop."

"Okay then," Jewelle said. That was code. Maybe she didn't know it, but whenever she said *Okay then*, that meant there was trouble on the horizon.

"What's up, girl?"

"Nothing."

"Oh yeah, it's sumthin' all right."

"Um . . . well. I have been having this little problem since I bought an empty lot on Flower downtown. Jackson says that it's a perfect place to start a research center."

"Researchin' what?"

"You know, computer stuff. He says that because of the mechanics of computers they need to keep the memory cold so that it won't catch on fire or melt. And there's what he calls a stone substratum under that property that would be perfect for the refrigeration units and also pretty much earthquake-proof."

Grinning, I remembered a time when Jackson and a friend of his named Toto would burglarize liquor stores for spare change and cheap wine.

"That all sounds aboveboard," I said.

"It should be, but there's this white man named Oliver Shellbourne. He owns a lotta the land down around there. He likes to see himself as a tough guy and so doesn't want some black chick getting in the way of his future sweatshops and shopping malls."

"He's blocking the sale?"

"No. I bought the land from a friend of Jean-Pierre. Shellbourne couldn't go up against the head of P9, but now he's getting somebody to make threatening calls to my office. I don't want to tell Jackson because he'll go to either JP or somebody like Mouse, and you know what'll happen then."

While in the French Resistance, Jean-Paul Villard once executed a Nazi sympathizer. He left the man's corpse, detached penis in mouth, in the town square. Mouse was somewhat north of that.

"He doesn't call himself?" I asked.

"No. It's just some other rude white man."

"What's he say?"

"I can't repeat it."

"Oliver Shellbourne?"

"Yes."

"Okay. I'll take care of it," I said. "I can't tell right when, but soon."

"Thank you, baby," she said, and that was all I needed to smile.

I traveled with Feather down to the base of our mountain and saw her off with Matteo on her busy adolescent life. After they had driven off I stood there for a while girding myself for the transition from domestic bliss to wartime.

Little Anzio was not the kind of place that someone in a fancy Rolls-Royce had ever frequented. The ad hoc veterans club was down on Western in the middle of a block where there were two forbidding alleys, a strip club with no bouncer out front, another bar next to a liquor store, and a seven-story sweatshop that hired Chinese and Mexican women to do some kind of labor from 6:00 a.m. to 9:00 p.m.

The bungalow that housed Little Anzio wasn't designed to be a bar. There were large picture windows across the front obscured by full-length battered green-and-ocher window shades. The front door, at the left side of the one-story building, was made from metal and painted rust red. You could feel the heft of that hatch when pulling it open.

The barroom smelled equally of sweat, old skin, and the fumes from more cigarettes than Nat King Cole had smoked in an entire lifetime. The fluorescent lighting was bright, almost blinding, and there were twenty or so customers—all men. Most of these were from about my age upward to eighty, but there was a scattering of youngsters too—ex-servicemen who had spent their time in Korea, Vietnam, and other, less publicized campaigns. They were of all races, an unusual detail for gatherings of military men in the turbulent sixties.

"Who the fuck are you?" a man barked. He was standing with his back to the waist-high oak bar—a good nine paces away.

He was glaring at me. I glanced back.

"I asked you a question," he said. He wasn't really shouting, but his voice was both focused and sharp.

He was a white man, in his middle forties and a decade or so from peak shape. But I imagined he remembered the dance well enough.

Still, I didn't answer.

He pushed himself away from the bar and took the first few of the nine steps. The five or six other men standing at the bar watched his progress.

"You deaf?" he asked, his voice still gruff and definitely threatening.

"No, I'm not."

The vets turned their attention to me, wondering, I supposed, if a fight might break out.

"It's just that," I added, "my mother taught me that I am not required to reply to rudeness."

"Your mother?" he said, taking three more steps.

I let my right foot move back half a span so that my left shoulder pointed forward. That would make him think I was retreating and allow the best torque for a right hook, should the need arise.

But before the blowsy barfly could take steps seven and eight, an elderly gentleman moved spryly between us. The dance was becoming more social.

"Hold up, Bernard," the older man said, gesturing with the point finger of his left hand. I got the feeling that our interrupter was right-handed and so was using the same ploy as I.

"Outta my way, Cletus," Bernard said.

"This man is a guest in our little club and he hasn't done nothing to you."

Cletus was also white, somewhere between seventy and eighty. That could have made him a survivor of World War I, what they once called the Great War.

"He won't answer my questions," Bernard said.

"I wouldn't answer you neither, you talked to me in that tone."

In 1969, even in California, it was still an unusual experience for a black man to be defended from a white man by a white man.

I squared up my shoulders and said, "My name is Easy Rawlins. I was a master sergeant for most of the last big war. I went in under Patton and came out with not one mark on my body or against my name."

The spite in Bernard's fat face showed that he was stymied. I added further insult by holding out a hand in friendship.

"Go on, Bernard," Cletus urged. "Shake the man's hand."

Reluctantly Bernard grabbed my hand and then let go.

"Let me buy both you men a drink," I said.

The malice in Bernard's visage leavened somewhat with this offer.

The bartender was a sallow lad named Meanie. He supplied our drinks with a professional air.

"Yes, sir, I went to war August 1, 1914," Cletus Brown was telling me after we were served. Bernard, whose last name was Michaels, sat on the other side of him brooding over his rye.

"But I thought we didn't declare war on Germany until 1917," I said.

Cletus Brown smiled at me. The few teeth he had left looked strong enough to tear military-grade beef jerky.

"That's right, son," he said. "That's right. I had to go over to France and enlist there. I learnt the language, picked up a Bergmann submachine gun, and never looked back."

We were standing at just about the center of the bar, which was little more than a big oak box. On the other side of sulky Bernard, at the far end of the drinking table, a shaggy-haired white man was leaning against the wall and conversing with a light brown Negro— both of whom were on the young side. The two were talking but the white one was giving me furtive glances now and again.

". . . the Germans hated freedom," Cletus was saying, "and my people, all the way back to the American Revolution, have fought for *liberté, égalité, fraternité.* The war for freedom is a calling that not everybody hears . . ."

A tall, olive-skinned man walked up and put a hand on Cletus's shoulder.

"That's our Lieutenant Brown," the new visitor said. "Oldest, bravest, and most honorable man in this room."

The older man's chest pushed out.

I appreciated the new player's respect while suspecting his motives.

"Easy Rawlins." I held out a hand.

"Norman Toll." He took the offer and gave me a hearty shake. "What you doin' here, Master Sergeant?"

It was the same question Bernard had asked and it came from the same place—an innate distrust of newcomers.

"I was asked to come by a young man named Craig Kilian. He

said I could get some information from a guy name of Kirkland Larker."

"What kind of information?" Norman Toll was a few years older than I and certain of himself the way white men in America had been ever since they identified themselves as the master race of this magnificent land.

"Craig's business."

The veteran impresario was not happy with my answer but he accepted it.

"Corporal Larker," he called to the white man watching me from the end of the bar.

"What?"

"This man wants to talk to you. He says it's got something to do with Private Kilian."

Kirkland Larker stared at me about three seconds longer than was civil. Then he pushed away from the wall. I honestly thought he was going to run. But after a sniffle and snort he walked my way in more or less military fashion.

When he reached us Cletus went down to the other end of the bar and Bernard, after ordering another rye and Coke on my tab, made a crablike move a few feet away.

"Corporal First Class Kirkland Larker," Toll said, "I'd like to introduce you to Master Sergeant Easy Rawlins."

We shook hands and Toll wandered off to a distant table.

"Drink?" Meanie asked Larker.

"On me," I added.

"Tequila straight up," Kirkland told Meanie.

"I'll stick with bourbon," I added.

Alone the corporal and I studied and sipped at our drinks. I was in no hurry and he seemed worried. The whiskey wasn't bad. And the bartender hadn't charged me as yet.

I liked Little Anzio. It was just another of LA's ten thousand hidden jewels. But more, it seemed welcoming. If you overlooked Bernard's need for confrontation, it was an ideal spot for a man like me—on an off day.

But this was no Sunday afternoon.

"You know my name?" I asked the afternoon tippler.

"I never met you or anything."

"That's not what I asked," I said. "Craig Kilian came to me and said he needed my help. I wanted to know where he got my name and he gave me yours."

Kirkland stood up a little straighter. He was in his early thirties and lean. Maybe he played basketball or something to maintain a modicum of muscle tone, but violence did not appear to be his first instinct.

"Did you talk to Craig?" he asked.

"I'm here."

"Are you going to help him?"

"Help him what?"

"He said he got into some, you know, fight or altercation or something and it was with this black guy. It sounded like he needed help."

"What kinda help?"

"He didn't say specifically, just that he had this fight or something and he needed to find out if the guy . . . I don't know, maybe if the guy was gonna cause trouble."

Kirkland seemed a little shifty, but that didn't reveal what he did or did not know or, for that matter, what his motives were.

"The question is," I said, "how did you know to give him my name?"

Kirkland looked into my eyes, hesitated, and then said, "Chris . . . Christmas Black."

My idea of the perfect private detective was a man who never let what he was feeling or thinking show on his face. This goal wasn't difficult for someone like me because that was business as usual for black folk reared in the South. No matter what you learned, you were never to let it overwhelm what your job was, what your responsibilities were. But the name Christmas Black put a weight on my mind. He was the soldier's soldier. In his days in the military they dropped him hundreds of miles behind enemy lines, where he killed who needed to be killed and then lived off the land till he was back in his barracks.

Christmas Black was a warrior and so anything having to do with Craig Kilian had the potential to be war.

I am proud to say that even though I was thrown off by how Kirkland had gotten my name, I was still aware enough to notice that my witness was leaning back from me.

I stepped quickly away from the makeshift bar, only an instant before Bernard Michaels swung an empty Coke bottle at my head. He put his full weight behind the cowardly attack and so tumbled off-balance, hitting his head on the hardwood edge of the bar. He fell to the floor in a heap, bleeding from the scalp and out for the count.

"I saw everything," Norman Toll said as he ran up to us. Other vets were looking after Bernard.

"He was trying to hit you from behind," Toll added. "A coward and a sneak."

I heard the words and shared the sentiments, but my eyes were on Kirkland.

"Did you see him?" I asked the corporal.

"Yeah, but, um, I thought he was just gonna join us," Larker lied.

9

I expected to go home after Anzio's. There to consider what I'd learned and decide whether or not to see Craig Kilian's mother. Instead I drove farther downtown to an address on Wilshire Boulevard, which was at that time the North American headquarters of P9, the insurance behemoth. In the late sixties P9 owned the second-tallest building in LA.

It was after 5:00 but the company was at least partially open twenty-four hours a day because of the international money markets. The guard came to the locked glass doors and let me in without resistance. I'd been to the offices pretty often because my good friend, Jackson Blue, was senior vice president in charge of both data processing and general planning.

"How can I help you, Easy?" the guard, Philip Channing, asked. A gray-headed white man who was almost retirement age, Phil was part of corporate security and therefore well aware of me.

"Asiette in?"

"Still up in her office, I think."

When I first met Asiette Moulon she worked in a small office behind the first-floor admissions desk. She was in her early twenties. Now, just a few years later, she had a big office at the end of a long hall on the third floor. She was in charge of all admissions, with more than a dozen people reporting to her.

Asiette stood five three in stocking feet with black hair that further accented her shocking violet eyes. A Frenchwoman from Burgundy, she would be considered lovely in any language or clime, class or time.

That day she was wearing a bright orange minidress that flared out a few inches above the knee.

"Easy!" she squealed, then ran to my arms and kissed me on the lips.

The first time she ever did that I almost pushed her away. I'd known black men in Texas and Louisiana who'd been lynched for even puckering their lips upon seeing a white woman.

But times were changing and Asiette and I had been seeing each other on and off for the past year.

"How are you, honey?" I asked.

"Come on in," she said.

She led me into her bright yellow office and pulled me until we were both sitting on top of her strawberry-colored desk. She took my hand and laid her head on my shoulder.

"You 'ave come to see me?" she said to our hands.

"I came to see the security boss but I'd never drop by without saying hello to you."

"Just hello?" she said, pouting only a little.

The late sixties were the cream-filled center of the sexual revolution. Asiette and I had done things together, and with others, that I would never have imagined just five years earlier.

"It's a job, baby," I said. "You know we all have to pay the rent."

"Do you want to take me home after the rent?"

I was forty-nine at the time. And so I knew that a question like that was never just about tonight.

"It might not be till tomorrow," I said. "I mean, if you're not busy or anything."

I expected the reply to get her to smile, but instead she frowned and stood.

"I," she said to my knee, and then she looked up. "I've been seeing a man."

Like I said, that was the sixties. There was a lot of *seeing* among a certain crowd.

"And you like him," I said, trying to help her out.

"His name is Stefano Lombardi."

"Okay."

"He's the head of sales in P9's Rome office."

"Good salary. Wonderful country. I passed through on my way to France during the war. Even then you could see the beauty."

Asiette was looking me right in the eye.

"He has asked me to marry him," she said.

I felt something. Actually it was quite a few things. I liked Asiette's company and I'd learned a lot from her. She was young and I cared for her at least partly the way I felt for Feather. These thoughts logjammed in my head and I found that I had no words to say.

"Well?" the Frenchwoman demanded.

"Honey . . . it's not my call."

The World War II survivor's nostrils flared before she said, "You better go on upstairs, Easy. I wouldn't want to get in the way of your job."

The main office of North American security for P9 was on the thirty-sixth floor.

The president and CEO of the company, Jean-Paul Villard, once offered me the top security position, but I turned him down because of a recent windfall and a lifelong distaste for being answerable to anyone.

I did, however, have a suggestion of whom he might hire.

The double glass doors had the words SÉCURITÉ POUR L'AMÉRIQUE DU NORD stenciled across them in gilt and scarlet lettering. Through the glass I could see the burgundy carpeting and dark wood shelving along the walls of the large reception area. At the center of the room was a big mahogany desk. Behind this sat a young man who was studying the pages of a slender, drab green file.

I didn't knock but the young man sensed me and jumped to his feet like the soldier he was, ready for action.

I smiled and waved at the hale specimen in the thirty-dollar Sears suit.

He approached the door, took out a large ring of keys, and used one of these on a small silver disk at the far end of the left-side entry. Then he pulled that portal open maybe four inches.

"Yes?" he asked, as if talking to a stranger.

"Is he in, Edmund?"

"Major Black is working."

"Here or elsewhere?"

"Do you have an appointment?"

"I don't need one."

Resentment filled the veteran's eyes.

"I'll check if he wants to see you," Edmund Lewis said.

He closed and locked the glass door, turned away, and walked to another door at the back of the reception room. There he knocked and then passed through. No more than half a minute later the military receptionist returned and admitted me to his domain.

"He said to show you in," Edmund informed me.

"I know the way."

Edmund moved to block my passage and said, "I'm supposed to take you."

"Did the major actually say that?"

This question stymied Lieutenant Lewis.

"No," I continued, "he did not. You just think that when I enter your space I have to take your orders, and that's just not true. So why don't you step aside?"

I don't know why I was so angry or, for that matter, why I was trying to pick a fight with a combat soldier who had been active in Vietnam as recently as Craig Kilian. Luckily for me our face-off was interrupted.

"You better listen to him, Ed," an assured voice said. "You might defeat Easy hand to hand, but he's like the VC; if you don't kill him he'll keep coming back at ya."

Christmas Black was standing at the back doorway. When I didn't come immediately in, he understood that our conflicting natures were escalating in the outer office.

"Yes, Major," Edmund said, standing straighter and yet with greater subordination.

"Mr. Black," I said, mostly to show Edmund that I wasn't bound to military nomenclature.

"Come on in, Easy," the major said.

Without direction we went to our preassigned seats.

Christmas's office was smaller and more Spartan than Edmund's room. The floor was light pine and the one painting on the wall was of a black soldier pressing forward against nebulous, seemingly insurmountable odds. His desk was a table made from cherrywood. My chair was crafted from the same material.

Over the years the eternal war hero (retired) had learned to respect me, hence the comparison to the VC. I knew that he respected the Vietcong and their North Vietnamese allies as the greatest soldiers in the greatest army thus far in the twentieth century.

Christmas was a big man; six four in bare feet with the shoulders of a giant. His skin was medium brown and his eyes a lighter brown than you would have expected them to be. He had scars here and there and no sense of humor whatsoever. His seven-year-old adopted daughter, Easter Dawn Black, was a Vietnamese refugee. Christmas had killed her parents on a secret government raid. She was an infant and so didn't remember. But that one act made him quit the profession that almost every male member of his family had been in since before the Revolution.

"What can I do for you, Easy?" asked the man I had recommended for the job of North American coordinator of P9 security.

"Corporal Kirkland Larker."

The name sparked something in the soldier's eye. He considered me, weighed where the discussion might lead, and then changed the subject.

"You're looking in pretty good shape, Master Sergeant," he said. "You been working out?"

"Used to be working out was what I did from the minute I woke up to late that night with my, or my best friend's, girl."

There wasn't a thing I could say that would make Black crack a smile.

"But to answer your question," I continued. "I have been visiting your martial arts recommendation. Son Chen's got me doing sit-ups and push-ups and he taught me that it is only a fool who believes they can overcome any foe by direct conflict."

Christmas smiled at that phrase, which I was sure the eighty-two-year-old Chen had taught him when he was a younger man.

"Larker's a fuckup," the government bona fide killer of men, women, and children said. "He drank before missions and stole from the PX."

"He says that you gave him my name in order to help one of his friends."

The major looked up at a point somewhere above my head. I took this as a glimpse at something in the past. And, because there was a hint of distaste at the corner of his mouth, I supposed he didn't like what he was seeing.

This reverie went on for some seconds before he said, "Corporal Larker was in my squad in 'Nam. That was nine years ago, at the beginning of the American intervention. I was going to have him transferred at the first of the next month. We were on furlough for two weeks so I didn't have to worry about him causing shit in the field.

"But then Lieutenant General Reeves got the report that there was a VC weapons depot that had been set up only twenty miles outside Saigon. They didn't have an exact location, so an airstrike was out of the question. If Reeves sent out a regiment, the news would travel and the timing for whatever strike had been planned could have been sped up. So . . ."

I was wondering how Black's account was going to bring me back to a straight-haired black man named Alonzo who might or might not be dead.

". . . I told my little squad to pack up and we went out on a seek-and-destroy." There was little joy in Christmas. "I made Larker the radioman." He looked directly at me for the first time since the tale began. "I mean how much trouble could he cause on a radio no VC could hear?"

I hunched my shoulders.

"We were air-dropped at twenty-four hundred hours and by three hundred we'd located the nest," Christmas continued. "We had the munitions to take 'em out. All we needed to do was get close enough. You could tell this was the start of a major offensive because they had maybe a hundred men spread out, ready to repulse any attack. But they didn't reckon on a small group of well-armed men coming in down the middle of the Ben Hai River.

"It was deep jungle so we made it to maybe seventy-five yards from the target. The shoulder-fire missile launchers were setting up when I tripped a net trap. Motherfucker fell on me and set off this gook gong-alarm. Gunfire came from all sides. They had me. I yelled for the rocket launchers to fire. I got hit in the right arm and left leg. Then something, someone fell on top of me and started shooting. He shot everywhere at once. He kept it up till one of the rockets hit the sweet spot in the VC arsenal. The explosion was like a goddamned blockbuster come with his sister the firebomb. When the explosion happened the shooting stopped and my rescuer cut me out of there."

Christmas was sweating. This was something I'd never seen before.

"It was Larker," the major said. "He called in an airstrike, then jumped on my back and opened fire, cut me free, bound my wounds, and dragged me back to the river."

The stillness in the room held the reverberation of explosions and death, the scent of gunpowder with a hint of blood.

"A malingerer and liar, sneak thief, and cheat. Kirkland Larker is everything I despise, but he saved my life that night. His actions were . . . heroic."

"So he told you that his friend needed somebody to find out what happened after a fight in the woods," I concluded.

"Not even that, Easy. He said a friend needed to find someone, a black man. I asked him if it had anything to do with revenge and he said absolutely not. So I gave him your name."

"Why didn't you call me?"

"I wanted to give the man a chance. He hadn't gotten in touch with me since I gave up my commission. Maybe he'd changed. Anyway, I knew you would see any trouble he represented for what it was."

I sighed and stood.

Christmas Black looked up at me.

"Is this going to be a problem for you, Master Sergeant?"

"Probably, but problems are my meat and potatoes."

"If you need anything, all you have to do is call."

"Thank you," I said and then let myself out.

10

I stopped at Edmund Lewis's desk. He'd returned his attention to the slender file that engrossed him before I entered.

"Yes?" he asked.

"You mind if I use your phone?"

"This is a business line."

"Okay. Then ask your boss if I can come back in his office and use his."

I'm not quite sure why Lewis didn't like me. It wasn't a race thing because Christmas was black and Lewis idolized him. I'd fought in some of the biggest battles of World War II, so it couldn't have been disdain for some ignorant civilian.

"Is it a local call?" he asked.

"Probably not."

He snorted and I picked up the receiver, took a slip of paper from my pocket, and dialed the number.

"Hello?" she said after seven or eight rings. Her voice was what I can only call voluptuous. It also sounded as if I had interrupted her nap.

"Am I speaking to Ms. Lola Thigman-Kilian?" I asked, reading Craig's scrawl.

"When is it?"

"Say what?"

"When is it?"

"It's a little after six," I said.

"No, no, no. What day is it? Tuesday?"

"No, ma'am. It's Monday."

"Oh. So this is Mr. Ezekiel Rawlins?" Her clarity was shocking after the fuzzy start to our conversation.

"Yes. Yes, it is."

"CK told me you were calling but then I fell asleep and I thought it was tomorrow already."

"Well, ma'am—"

"You have my address, right?"

I read the numbers and street name aloud.

"Bring some coffee, will you? I'll be waiting."

Driving a bright yellow Rolls-Royce Phantom VI while wearing black skin in the late light of summer—all that through a working-class, mostly white neighborhood—is an experience not meant for the faint of heart.

I parked by the curb next to the three-story, twenty-seven-unit, pink-plaster-coated apartment building. In order to get to apartment 2G I had to go around back and climb a flight of external stairs. People had been watching since I pulled up. As I passed apartments along the way, curtains swayed open and heads appeared behind screens to witness the black man who had pulled up in a Rolls.

I got to 2G and knocked.

A woman of great beauty and shimmering gold hair pulled the door open and said, "Come in, Mr. Rawlins. Come in."

It was a relief to be away from the gawkers, though I thought that I might be safer with them than with the forty-something bombshell named Lola.

Five eight or nine, she was swathed in a red-and-black wrap that was something more, and less, than a housecoat. Her face, both heart-shaped and handsome, had reached a level of perfection that had spelled trouble for her since childhood; trouble for her and anyone else she happened upon.

"Come have a seat in the nook," she offered.

We were standing in one of those modern all-purpose rooms. It was a kitchen, a dinette, and a sitting room all in one. The dinette, which she called the nook, was a small round table set next to the refrigerator with two bright chrome and blue vinyl chairs.

There were two bottles of beer set out for company. I handed her the brown paper bag containing a paper cup of coffee and then sat down.

"Ms. Kilian?" I said.

"Mr. Rawlins," she replied, rummaging through the small bag. "Didn't you bring some coffee for yourself?"

"I thought I'd stick with beer."

She smiled while lowering onto the utility chair with as much grace as any princess or lady-in-waiting. I think I might have been a little too obvious noting this style.

"I used to be a dancer," she explained.

It was my turn to say something, but every reply that came to mind had nothing to do with my mission.

"Um," I said and then cleared my throat.

Craig's mother's features were of natural, and maybe even a little careless, feminine perfection. Only the slightest details indicated her age. She sipped her coffee and watched me with dark, dark eyes that had a glittering of yellow at their centers.

"Do you need an opener?" she asked.

"What?"

"For the bottle."

"Um, sure . . . I'm here about Craig."

The use of her son's name muted the smile and caused her forward shoulder to shift from left to right, approximating the flow of a wave. This image reminded me of the Ben Hai River, which made a hero out of a malingerer and nearly cost a good soldier his life.

She handed me a bottle opener and said, "Yes. He told me you'd be calling."

"Do you have any idea why?" I popped the top of my Hamm's beer.

"I was a stripper in Lexington, Kentucky, when I met George Kilian," she replied, as if this was an answer to my question. "He was helpless, wanted to save me." She pursed her lips, looking into the paper cup like it contained something precious, but flawed. "I took pity on him."

She smiled again and I understood that she was performing and I would have to wait for the recital to run its course.

"No one, man or woman, should ever start a thing with someone they feel pity for, Mr. Rawlins; leaves a bad taste.

"I woke up with that bitterness in my mouth for seven months and then I left Kentucky with the clothes on my back, my natural talents, and a baby in my belly. The only thing I ever got out of that whole affair was Craig."

"So maybe old George was worth it," I observed.

Lola considered my words but deigned not to comment.

"When Craig was still little I stripped for our daily bread. I even turned tricks for the right attitude and the right price. We stayed afloat but I never did learn how to deal with money. I think that's why Craig thought he was joining the army. He figured he'd make enough to support me through the GI Bill."

"That's why he *thought* he joined?" I asked.

Smile completely gone, Lola studied the question. The realization slowly dawned that I was now a part of the old dance.

"I helped him make up his mind," she said with guilt-ridden certainty. "Some men think that every word a woman says was his idea first."

"Even your son?"

"Especially him. But I would have stopped him if I knew what war did to some people." She leveled those yellow-jacket eyes at me, expecting . . . something.

"Why did Craig tell you that he wanted us to meet?"

"Homicide." She said the word as easily as one might have said *dishwater*.

"You think there was a murder?"

"Maybe not murder. If Craig is lucky maybe not even a killing. But my son is not a lucky man and something happened; something that even if you have to use the word *attempted—homicide* will follow."

"Craig's got a lot of problems," I agreed. "Loud noises put him in a completely different state of mind. I talked to him less than half an hour and found that out."

Lola studied me a little closer. If I was a dog I would have either bit or submitted.

The decision made, she stood abruptly and went through a door that revealed a small section of what might have been the bathroom. She rummaged around in there and came out with a wadded-up cloth. Coming back to her chair, she dropped the lump on the table between us.

I knew what I was looking at. I didn't want to touch it, but that was not the time to be squeamish.

The yellow-and-red tie-dyed T-shirt was about six ounces heavier than it should have been—because of the blood it had soaked up. It was still a little damp and also crusted black from the drying bodily fluid. There was that faint metallic smell mixed with the equally strong odor of some kind of incense oil. I had to concentrate to keep from gagging on the contradiction.

"This is your son's?"

"He came to me the morning after it happened."

"Why didn't you influence him to go to the police?"

"You know what it's like, blood." She said *blood* just like one of my soul brothers hanging out on the corner at Florence and Central, 138th and Broadway, or any of a thousand other places from the Southside of Chicago to Selma, Alabama. "Craig was the kind of kid that always got into trouble. At school, after school, before school started in the morning. The only time he wasn't in trouble was when he was asleep."

I imagined that the young man she was describing would have had turmoil in his dreams too.

"What kind of trouble, Mrs. Kilian?"

"Call me Lola, Ezekiel."

"They call me Easy," I said. "What kind of trouble did Craig get into, Lola?"

"Disturbing the peace, public drunkenness, assault, assault with a deadly weapon . . . that was only a rock he threw. They got him on GTA but that wasn't even him. His friend Pickles gave him a ride in a car he said belonged to his uncle. They put Craig in juvenile hall on a nine-month sentence for the one thing he didn't do. That just made him angrier. I struck up a friendship with the deputy warden, so it wasn't as bad as it could have been. After that I made Craig think that it was his idea to join the army. I thought it would make him into a man."

"Did it?" I asked because, even though I thought I knew the answer, I wondered what she would say.

For the first time Lola looked like an honest woman trying her best to tell the truth without defense or manipulation.

"No," she said. "It only broke him down more. He doesn't get into trouble too much now, but . . . but it's all my fault, Easy."

I could feel the creases in my brow and eyelids.

"What, Easy?"

"We just met, right?"

"Yeah. So?"

"So you don't know me. I'm just some guy off the street and here you dump, right down on the tabletop, evidence that might could get your son the gas chamber."

A smile slowly spread across Lola's generous mouth. That grin contained all the certainty of a mountain goat atop the highest peak. She inhaled deeply and then began to speak.

"A woman like me has to be able to read a man"—she snapped the fingers of her left hand—"like that. It's not a talent as much as a survival thing, instinct.

"Craig's a white boy and you can see that he don't come from nuthin'. And when I say nuthin' I mean me. I don't know much, but after a long life of hard knocks I can tell you that most soul brothers will not call a cop unless they absolutely have to. Craig says that you're a detective. He met you at your office. This could just be a roll of the dice. Maybe you can't help us. But things *will* go bad if somebody don't try somethin'."

"Why not just let it be?" I asked. "From what Craig says there's no evidence."

"That might be fine for you or me, Easy. But Craig is losin' his mind over it. He can't sleep. He calls me in the middle'a the night cryin' and talkin' nonsense. Two nights ago he said that he was gonna go out and find . . . and find that nigger."

She reached into the right-hand pocket of the black-and-red house gown and took out a thin fold of a few bills. At least the top one was the hundred-dollar denomination.

"Save him this one time and I will be a better mother from now on. I swear."

She was looking me in the eye. There was no carelessness there. So I dropped the bloody shirt and took the cash. Six hundred dollars. All brand-new bills.

After counting I looked back up into eyes that encompassed a vast plain of darkness. I expected to see stars if I looked too long, and so I said, "Okay, I give."

"You'll help him?"

"I'll look into what did and did not happen. In the meantime you should burn this shirt."

11

It was twilight when I rounded the corner from the back of Lola's apartment complex. My Rolls was still there but a police car had pulled up behind it. I almost turned around to see if maybe there was some fence I could jump over. I did not come from the kind of background where you willingly walked up to cops obviously wondering about you.

"A black man could get shot for sneezin' too hard," my aunt, who was not my aunt, Hattie used to say.

"Uh-huh," her mother, my great-not-aunt Ball, would always echo. "They shoot first and aks questions after."

But I was a property owner, an independent businessman, and I hadn't committed any kind of serious crime in months. So I walked up to that Rolls-Royce as if it was what I did every day.

I had unlocked the door and cracked the handle before the officers exited their prowl car, hands on the butts of their pistols. They had a whole raft of questions, needing me to prove my identity and ownership in triplicate. The question-and-answer period lasted maybe twenty-five minutes, but it's all been said before so I won't go through it again right now. They didn't arrest me so I drove far enough east that only the car was an anomaly, not the driver.

John's bar was housed on the third floor of a nondescript building at 114th and Central. Most of the rest of the businesses on that block were still boarded up and charred from the riots four years before.

One store had a hand-painted sign that read MICHELLE'S HAIR AND NAILS. It seemed to be open for business. There was another place with no sign but it had been freshly painted and gussied up some. Passing by in my noteworthy vehicle I caught a glimpse of what might have been a barber's chair at the back of the outer room.

Driving around to the alley that ran behind the new generation of black businesses, I parked the bright yellow car in John's garage. From there I ascended the rear stairway and pressed a black button next to the double-thick, triple-locked rear door. Nine minutes passed before I was identified through some method I couldn't define and the door came open.

John the bartender was a better version of me. Taller by at least a quarter foot, even darker-skinned, and an inch or two more broad, John was a friend from Texas; from a time when liquor was cheap and life cheaper still.

He got in the whiskey business and ran a series of unlicensed bars around LA, one after the other. The new one, like all the rest had been, was called John's and you could gain admittance only if he wanted you to.

"Easy, what you doin' comin' up the back stairs like some sneak thief?"

"Sneakin'."

"What you need?" He had already turned around and was walking down the slender, dimly lit corridor toward a distant red door.

"What do most people need when they come to a saloon?" I asked, following in his wake.

"Most of my customers come to drink alcohol."

"Drink's only the primer. They really come to be with other fools and talk to you about their foolishness."

"Any problems Easy Rawlins got is beyond a poor brother like myself," John opined. He passed through the red door into a bright blue hallway that was half the length of the first.

I laughed and followed until we exited the blue hall through a yellow door leading to the area behind his bar. The drinking room we faced was quite large, brightened by a wide skylight gathering the little sun left in the sky.

There were only three customers. All of them black men intent on their libation. I didn't recognize anyone.

"Where's Tiny?" I asked.

Tiny was the three-hundred-pound bouncer who was usually perched on a high stool behind the green, metal-jacketed, third-floor front door.

"Tiny don't come out till the sun go all the way down," John said like he was Moses delivering the Eleventh Commandment from on high.

I made my way to the other side of the bar and sat on one of the tall oak stools.

"What's your pleasure?" John inquired.

He might as well have asked me to explain the theory of relativity. I sat there counting scars the barman's face had accrued over many years of doing business.

"What's wrong, Easy?"

"How many years we know each other, man?"

"Might be as much as thirty. Near 'bout anyway."

"Have I ever given you anything?"

"One or two tight spots and some good laughs."

I took the keys to my Rolls and put them on the mahogany.

"That's the ignition and trunk key. You can't keep it. At least I don't know if you can. But there's a right-side-drive yellow Rolls-Royce locked up in your garage out back. Why don't you hold it for me a couple'a months?"

That was the first and last time I ever saw a boyish gleam in my friend's eyes.

"What I got to do for that?"

"Lend me your Pontiac for a few days and try not to bang up mine too bad."

"Bang it up? Brother, the only thing I'm ever gonna do with a car like that is go sit in it, drink a flute of champagne, and smoke the biggest, blackest cigar I can find."

"Can I use your phone?" I asked.

"You know where it's at."

It was nearly 8:00 but both Edmund Lewis and Christmas Black were still at work, making sure that P9's billions were secure.

"Security," Edmund announced.

"Easy Rawlins for Christmas Black," I said.

Edmund had given up stonewalling me and passed the call right through.

"Black."

"You said call if I needed help."

"Name it."

"I could use a good operative to meet me at the end of Filomena Road in the hills above Orange County at six hundred hours tomorrow."

"Done."

"You need any directions for your man?"

"If a man can't get there on that, I got no use for him in my army."

12

I was in my broad bed by 9:30 and up six hours later. My first waking action was to go to Feather's door and look in. I did this every morning of our life together. I forgot that she was staying over with Jewelle and Jackson. The bed was made and everything else was neat enough.

I wandered around the third floor feeling odd. It wasn't that I missed my daughter but rather that I felt her absence. It occurred to me this gentle awareness was not as painful as but even deeper than heartache.

By 5:29 I was at the end of Filomena Road in far eastern Orange County. He was already there, leaning against a black Harvester Scout 800. Despite his clothes the man looked more military than the Jeep knockoff. He wore a short-sleeved dark blue flannel shirt and rugged black jeans. The beret adorning his head was at a rakish tilt, the only true vestige of a military career.

"Chris," I said. "I wanted a grunt, not a general."

"I could tell you were in trouble at the office," he reported. "I couldn't trust getting a man paid a salary to back you up and I sure didn't want to send that man to his death."

He said these words in a neutral tone but I heard the strain of hardship that lay underneath. And he was right. We were, I and almost all of my friends, men and women, living on the wrong side of the danger line.

* * *

I gave Christmas Craig's directions to Knowles Rock and he led the way, forging ahead like a bloodhound.

We ascended at a pretty good clip. On the way I told Black about Craig and his problems.

"You think it was in his head?" he asked. "You know a lotta these army pups today smoke dope and take LSD."

"I think it's more shell shock than chemical."

"I don't believe in battle fatigue. If you light a man's bed on fire he'll remember pretty quick where he is and that he wants to live."

I didn't argue because like any good soldier, my friend needed to believe that he could conquer any enemy—including fear.

It took about an hour and a half to cover the seven miles to the camp. Mostly we passed through blood orange groves but at the end there was a pretty steep rise where pine nuts took the place of citrus fruit.

The campsite was in a clearing and there was a cabin, just like Craig said. It was a crude affair constructed from uncured pine boards topped off with a tin roof. There had been a fire in front of the place; not so much a campfire but more like a trash burning. A few wisps of white ash still clung to the ground around blackened earth.

Christmas was already scanning the grounds when I headed for the lodge.

It was a simple room, sixteen feet by eighteen. The only furniture was a gray-and-white-striped wadded-cotton mattress on a single bed frame. The shelves held no larder. The floor was swept and maybe even washed down. There was no evidence of who might have stayed there and nothing of value or intelligence.

When I came out, Christmas was down on one knee using a twig to sift through the meager detritus of the fire.

I joined him.

"What about the cabin?" the security expert asked. He was looking down, his face enveloped by shadow.

I told him what I didn't find.

"Motherfuckers," he said. "Goddamned motherfuckers. Pieces of shit is what they are."

"They?"

He looked up. Believe me when I tell you that you never want man, woman, or beast to cast that kind of gaze in your direction.

"Three sets of footprints, not counting your client. They swept the motherfucking ground. Cleaned it out the way we did it in 'Nam when the brass didn't want evidence for a UN review." Part of the rage was that he was angry at himself. "They got rid of almost everything. That poor kid never had a chance."

"Three?" I said.

"The woman probably and two men. One of the men was wounded. He could have died and they just wiped out the signs, but I don't think so. A man and woman left together, then you got two sets of men's footprints walking through the dirt and grass. Not together. No. The woman and a man left first, then the other two—first one and then the other."

Looking down, I saw a half-burned red, green, and black business card. No complete words were evident, but there was a curved green line indicative of some kind of snake or lizard that might have inhabited the burned part of the card.

"Motherfuckers!" Christmas's muted yell was both a threat and a curse.

He stood up violently and stormed over to the outer edge of the clearing. I let him simmer there, not wanting to get in his way.

I was trying to think about what that card meant. It was familiar, but not from some other card. Something else . . .

"What are you gonna do about this shit?" Christmas was standing over me. It was shocking that he could get so close without me noticing. This reminded me of Craig Kilian silently invading my office.

"What's the matter?" I asked, climbing to my feet.

He stood there looking through me. Then he started to talk.

"I was in nearly every big blowup they had in World War II and Korea. And I was in 'Nam too, in the early days; major under Lieutenant General Jared 'Quick' Johnston, a white boy of the Alabama persuasion. I don't think he liked colored people, as a matter of fact I know he didn't. But I was the best and he knew he had to have the best with him. We threw our men on conflagration like dry twigs on white-hot flame. That's what these motherfuckers did to your boy. Killed him but left him breathing and walking, a dead man in so much pain that it'll live on past him."

I wasn't exactly sure what the soldier meant, but I knew that as the restraints of military order eased in Black's mind his anger grew. I didn't see him that often, so this was the first time I had noticed the degree to which he was fraying around the edges.

Something about the distaste in the ex-soldier brought to mind a debauched club named the Dragon's Eye.

"How's Easter doin'?" I asked.

The question had the desired effect. His breathing evened out and an almost smile brushed his lips.

"She's a good kid, Easy," he said. "Fast and strong and smarter than any other kid in her grade—boy or girl. She only takes orders if they make sense to her. Better than me by about a mile."

That card had struck a memory. It revealed something about Craig's situation that I wasn't about to share with my partner. Christmas had to work through his rage before he could go out on the playground with the other kids.

On the way back to the cars I took a plastic bag from my back pocket and collected maybe a dozen oranges.

13

John's 1958 dark green Pontiac Bonneville was roomy and rolled along like a young man walking down the boulevard—steady but with a little swagger.

I reached the office a few minutes shy of 10:00.

The outer door to our private stairwell was sturdy but rarely locked. There came the scent of burnt tobacco as I crossed the threshold. The threat was clear, but those were my stairs and so I mounted them, three at a time. When I turned at the first half flight I detected an added hint of patchouli oil blending with cigarette smoke. Three more turns and I saw him, perched at the top of the stairs, listening to my approach. He stood only when I came into view.

"Mr. Rawlins?" he asked hopefully.

The young man's foot-and-a-half-long hair was deep brown against pale white skin. Upon standing he proved to be quite tall. I'd seen his features in two people I'd known, and also, if I wasn't mistaken, I had met him once a dozen or more years before. His scant facial hair made him look younger, but I put him at about twenty-five.

"Milo, right?" I said.

Surprise registered on the young man's face. He made a sound that was also a question.

"I met you at your parents' house in 1956. You answered the door and then called for your mother."

His eyes tightened as he tried to remember. There was a glimmer of recognition, but the details were lost.

"I came to you to find my sister's daughter," he said. "Robin's little girl."

By then we were standing toe-to-toe on the platform before the front door of my office. He was half an inch taller but I had the weight advantage. I wanted to fight him but he made no threatening gesture. His tone was respectful.

In the corner he'd leaned a large nylon backpack that had once been bright yellow but by the time it got to my door it was well used, torn, mended, and generously soiled.

"Your mother send you out here?" I asked him.

"No."

"Then how did you find me?"

"Can we go inside?"

I looked from him to the sad pack and back again before saying, "Sure, but leave the bag out here."

I took out the key and unlocked the door, pushed it open and gestured for him to walk through.

"Keep going down that middle hall to the end," I said. "That's my office."

Remembering another young white man, I locked the front door and followed in the footsteps of Milo Garnett.

He was standing in the middle of the office awaiting further instructions. The hippie wore blue jeans and a threadbare multi-colored, tie-dyed T-shirt. His frame was thin but carried the strength of youth.

"Take any chair," I said and then went around the desk.

I sat down and Milo was still considering the three chairs as if his future depended on the right choice.

"What's her name?" he asked, still contemplating.

"Sit."

He went to the chair at my left.

"What's my niece's name?" he asked again.

"Answer my question first."

"Um, I forget."

"How did you find me?"

His first response was to sit up straight, probably something he learned in grade school. When an adult asks a question part of the answer is represented by posture.

"I went to college in Rhode Island but couldn't hack it so I got a job on a farm but that was hard and I got sick."

"Sick with what?"

". . . and my mother and her husband came out and brought me to his house," he said, passing right over the question. "I was there when you called and Mom got so upset. She always told me never to mention my sister, but then her and Lambert were fighting about it. You know . . . arguing without raising their voices."

"Lambert is your mother's husband?"

He nodded and gulped down some air. "He's the one that said your name. My mother told him that you were a Negro detective in LA. After I got better I hitched out here because, um, um, that little girl is my blood no matter what color she is."

"You just climbed up on the freeway in Boston and put out a thumb?" I asked. "You didn't even know where to find me but you bummed across country for thousands of miles?"

"What's wrong with that?" Milo said, showing his first glimmer of backbone.

"Her name is Feather and she's been with me—"

"Did you name her that?" he asked, cutting me off.

"No. Your sister did . . . before she died." The last three words caused Milo to blink.

"She's my blood, not yours," he said, against tears.

"But I'm her legal guardian. I got the papers in a file cabinet at our home."

This testament slowed the young man's passion. His eyes softened and he said, "I want to see my niece."

My breath became deadly shallow and I could feel my body tensing, seemingly of its own accord. The violence I was feeling must have shown on my face.

"Look, man," the hippie said. "I just want to meet her. I want to know my family. I don't care if she's black. It's my mother that's racist, not me."

I had my own opinions about that.

"I understand," I said. "But you can see that this is a big thing, right? Feather is still just a child and I'm the only family she's ever had—me and her brother, Jesus. I have to tell her that you're here and then ask her what she wants to do."

"But I'm her blood," Milo countered.

"And your blood, your mother, refused even to talk to her," I said. "Your blood, your father, murdered Robin and Feather's father rather than have it known that his daughter had made a black child. Don't talk to me about blood, son. It's not blood that sat up with her through nights of whooping cough and fever. It's not blood that put food on the table and clothes on her back."

Milo listened. He really did. He knew about his father and sister. His mother knew about it and lied to the white world they lived in.

"Okay," he said after one nod and then another. "You're probably right. I can't just walk in and say I'm her uncle. I can wait."

"Where are you staying?"

"Nowhere. Just got in last night. I found your office in the yellow pages and came over about nine."

"You slept on the steps?"

He nodded and I pondered.

"I know a good guy," I said. "Longhair like you, lives up above the Sunset Strip. He has a big house and lets people stay with him most of the time. Why don't I bring you over there? Then I'll know how to get in touch after I talk to Feather."

"All right. Yeah."

The decision made, we sat in the aftermath staring at each other.

"Look," I said. "I got to make a call. Why don't you gather up your things and go downstairs? I'll be there in a few minutes."

Milo stood up and went about the tasks assigned. I picked up the phone to take care of a task of my own.

"Hello," she answered on the first ring.

"You soundin' sour, Etta."

"Hey, baby," she said. "That friend'a yours like to get on my last nerve. He didn't get home till after three in the morning. Three! Come in the bed drunk and kissin' my neck. It's only deep religion kept me from killin' him in his sleep."

"He still asleep?"

"I'll roll him out for you."

I'd been holding the line for a few minutes when Mouse said, "Hello," his voice thick with sleep.

"Raymond," I said. "What you doin' this afternoon?"

"Sleepin'."

"I might need a hand and both'a my partners are outta town."

"What kinda hand?"

"I gotta go ask some questions over at the Dragon's Eye. You know what it's like in there."

"The Dragon's Eye? Damn. You right, that could get kinda strenuous. An' you know I need me some exercise. I gained three pounds in the last two years."

"You remember what time they open?"

"Four . . . Uh-huh, yeah, they open at four."

"I will see you there at five."

"You got it," he said and then he hung up.

*　*　*

". . . I mean," Milo was saying as I drove up San Vicente toward Sunset, "straights like my mother and her old man are what's holdin' everybody down. They're the ones cause this war and racism and private property bullshit. That's what's holdin' everybody back from their potentials. It's meditation and mind-altering chemicals can bring us to another level completely . . ."

Sitting in a moving car turned him into a different person. At the office he was brooding and dour, but in the passenger seat he climbed up into the pulpit of his mind and preached. He'd been talking ever since we left the curb. The only time he'd stop was either to light a cigarette or suck on one.

". . . take you and me, for example," he said. "We're the same. Blood and bone, history and heart. We got the same problems and we all need the same answers, ask the same questions. It's just—"

"Hold up, youngster," I said, intent on stopping the flow of palaver.

"What?"

"You think we're the same, you and me?"

"Yeah," he asserted. "Marx and Lenin, Jesus too. They all—"

"It's my turn, Milo. Let me talk a minute, okay?"

"Yeah," he said, "sure."

I got the feeling that people didn't usually get to speak once he started on a tear.

"I hear what you're sayin', but I see it a little different," I said.

"You mean you believe in this capitalist bullshit?" There was actual disdain in his words.

"The way I see it is that you'n me were both in a shipwreck and we got washed up on opposite shores. Not far apart, maybe only a quarter mile or so, but the waters between us are shark infested. It looks like we're in the same place; lotsa sand and maybe a palm tree or two. Sun is hot like hell and the saltwater so blue. We're both stranded but there's one big difference."

"What's that?" Milo Garnett asked.

"I'm on a desert island, and even though it looks like you are too, really where you washed up is a peninsula." I glanced over at Milo and saw that he was listening again. "If I set out on my way looking for food and water, company, or just a different view, all I'll do is walk in a circle and end up back where I started—looking at you. But you take the same walk on your side, you will end up back in the bosom of America; hot dog stands, beautiful women, and enough drugs that you'll forget that shipwreck and the time it seemed like we were in the same jam."

"You really believe that?"

"Test it out."

"What do you mean, get marooned?" He had a vocabulary.

"Naw, man, you don't have to go that far. Just shave your face, get a crew cut, put on a gray suit and red tie. Then go out there and see how much they compare you to me."

Milo eyed me suspiciously. He sneered a bit but then faltered in his resolve.

"But that's wrong," he said.

"You right about that," I replied.

I pulled to the curb outside of the hidden domicile of the young millionaire Terry Aldrich, a block or two north of the Sunset Strip. The holly hedge surrounding the property was so high that you could see only the upper floor of the mansion, which, I knew from past experience, was a four-story hodgepodge of conflicting architectures and styles.

"Go through the path cut in the hedge and knock on the front door," I said to Milo. "Whoever answers, tell 'em your name, my name, and then say you're there for Terry to give you a place to stay. Even if he's not in town they'll open up and give you a corner to curl up in."

Milo was concentrating on me. Maybe he was still thinking about the desert island versus the peninsula.

"Remember," I said, "your name, my name, and that you're

there for Terry. I'll talk to Feather and then get back to you in a few days at most."

The young uncle nodded and climbed out. He pulled his dirty yellow pack from the back seat and went to and through the hedge wall leading to the hippie manor.

I drove off wishing that *he* was now on that island, with me on my way to safety.

14

It was just shy of noon and I had some hours to kill, so I drove out to Hollywood, had a chili cheeseburger with fries, then went out to see a movie for the first time that year. A few days before, they released one called *Butch Cassidy and the Sundance Kid* with Paul Newman and a new guy. It was good because there was action and you could laugh too. I'd forgotten how much I love a big dark movie house with the sound so loud and the world somewhere far off.

The Dragon's Eye was a club a bit deeper into Hollywood. It was on a street named Gantner with a big parking lot out back that was surrounded by a fourteen-foot-high brick wall that had a dozen or so little inlets along the sides. The entrance had a double-door system and a camera that monitored everyone coming through the first portal. Passing the first door, you went through a gaudy red-and-black hallway and encountered the second gate. This was pulled open by an exceptionally tall man wearing a red tux and tails. If you were to ask me his race, I'd've said *albino gator* because his false smile resembled the many-toothed predator's grin.

"Easy Rawlins?" Razor-mouth asked.

I'd never met this particular bouncer but I wasn't surprised that he knew my name, because of my oldest friend, Raymond "Mouse" Alexander. Mouse was a remorseless killer, a criminal from sunup to sunup, and one of the five most dangerous men I knew of in Southern California. But he was more than that. Raymond was connected to organized crime because of his predilection for committing high-yield heists. Due to this affiliation even those establishments that usually turned away black skins were more likely to leave the door ajar.

"Yes, I am," I said.

"Come right on in, sir."

Sir.

The dining room of the Dragon's Eye was a perfect circle with maybe eighteen round tables taking up the main floor. There were semi-secluded booths along the wall. The *waitresses* wore variously colored thin silk slips with nothing underneath. The Eye was not a strip club but rather a high-end gathering place for sensualists of all genders and persuasions. I'd never been above the first floor, but it was rumored that there were bedrooms and other chambers nestled there where clients and their guests could enjoy all kinds of pleasure, pain, and euphoria.

The champagne was very good, starting at a hundred dollars a bottle, and the steaks well aged. The ladies serving were nice but you couldn't press them—the management needed their servers smiling and friendly. You could, I'd been told, negotiate with the serving staff—I was relying on that.

The only thing wrong with the Eye was the smell. Not a powerful odor, but just a whiff of something too sweet, with, at the same time, somewhere at the back of the nasal wall, a hint of rot.

Raymond was sitting at a round table at the very center of the room. He wore a dark green suit with the same color vest over a lime shirt, all topped off by a deep brown, short-brimmed Borsalino cocked on the side of his head. Two women, one brown-skinned in pink and the other white in black, were talking with him, laughing loud enough that I could hear them across the nearly empty room.

I walked up to them. The tabletop was a swirl of different pastel colors, making it and its cousins resemble pirouetting dancers endlessly, gracefully in motion.

"... I told Benny that he had to pull up his pants before he could tie his shoe," Mouse was saying.

The women seemed genuinely entertained.

"Mouse," I said.

"Easy!" Raymond's grin was gated in gold and there was a glittering yellow diamond embedded in his left upper front tooth. "Ladies, this here is my lifelong friend, Mr. Ezekiel Rawlins."

"Hi," the lady in pink said. "Desdemona."

She held out a hand and I shook it, gently.

"I'm Priss," said the girl in black. She smiled and nodded. No touching for her.

I pulled out a chair and Desdemona asked, "Should we bring over the champagne now, Mr. Alexander?"

"All the way, baby."

The women departed and I settled in, wondering about the word *lifelong*. This was not a Mouse word. I'd never heard him use it or any other word in that category. He was an intelligent conversationalist and most certainly a raconteur, but his language was stripped down and bare like our hardscrabble lives had been in the Fifth Ward.

But this meeting was not about vocabulary.

"You didn't have any trouble at the door?" I asked.

"Trouble? There better not be no trouble. Shit. I fuck trouble in the ass and send him home to his mama."

I laughed and said, "I thought that since you're retired you might have lost touch with some'a the made men."

"Lost touch? Retired? No, baby, that's not it. I mean, I don't do as much as I used to, but ever since Dearborn I get to run jobs ..."

He went on to explain that he agreed to go with one of their heist bosses to Michigan to plan a hit on an armored car company.

"Mothahfuckah said he needed twelve men, three specialized

cars, a mothahfuckin' bulldozer, and on top'a that he wanted at least four months to plan the job. They were going to kill a few guards too . . ."

Somewhere in the middle of that our five-hundred-dollar bottle of Brut arrived. Mouse had a sixteen-ounce T-bone and I got a Caesar salad to offset the street chili.

". . . you know me," Mouse was saying. "I just stood back and listened 'cause it wasn't my job. But then one day when we was scoutin' I noticed this hale-lookin' black janitor . . ."

Hale?

". . . I called the overboss and told him that I could do the whole job for a tenth the cost in two weeks' time. All he had to do was bring in a good-lookin' woman from East Europe know how to talk good English. Three-and-a-half-million-dollar take and the whole thing took sixteen days with four men and Natasha."

"Why a woman from Eastern Europe?" I asked.

"You know, Easy, a white woman from America try to be talkin' like she liked a brothah but he might could see that she lookin' at a niggah in her mind. And I needed our inside man to feel trust. Those European girls, especially if they wantin' to move west, be happy for that dark meat."

I laughed and Mouse appreciated the respect.

"So that's why I call it *semiretired* nowadays," my killer friend concluded. "But why you wanna know, anyway?"

"Etta seemed uptight, that's all. And I know she wanted you to give the heavy shit up."

Mouse's eyes tightened a bit, making it feel as if a shadow had fallen across our pinwheel table.

A moment or two passed before he said, "Lihn. Vu Von Lihn. That girl make me feel sumpin'. I think I do her too."

"Like you're in love?" I couldn't keep the surprise out of my voice. In his nearly half a century of life Mouse had professed love only for his mother, now dead, and EttaMae Harris.

"Is all you wanted was some salad?" he asked. "Or is there a job for us?"

"We should go to the barroom if you're finished eating," I answered. When Mouse changed directions you either cut bait or lost the pole. "I need to find out if anybody here knows some people I'm lookin' for."

"White people?"

"One is, one isn't."

"And what you need me for?"

"First, just to get in the front door."

Mouse's grin glittered at that.

"Then," I went on, "there's the chance I might get what I wish for."

He smiled again and the threat of love moved into the background.

"You got any names?" he asked.

"Alonzo's the only one I heard so far. That and where he was last seen at; a place called Blood Grove."

Mouse was back on track with me. He nodded and said, "I know seven niggahs named Alonzo."

"He might just be one of them."

Our early dinner, including tip, cost just under eight hundred dollars. This wasn't the kind of job I expected to get paid for. Instead it was my dues for turning in time to see that German soldier before he could stab me in the back.

The big white alligator, whose name was Rudolf, showed us to another door under his purview and ushered us through. We descended a spiral staircase for sixty steps or so. The well opened into a jazz bar with a black trio playing for more than a hundred patrons.

The Dragon's Eye bar area was twice the size of the dining room. The male patrons, except for the trio, me, and Mouse, were all white, as were most of the women. The bar was an enormous dragon carved from a hard, mottled-brown boulder. The stone was highly polished and the coiled myth's head rose at least eighteen feet above the three bartenders. There was a live flame flickering in the beast's left eye socket.

"I see a couple'a people I know, Easy," Mouse said. "I'm'a go over there and ask if they could help us with your man."

As Mouse walked away through the tide of white, I watched and wondered about him. For more than four decades I had been sure of the smiling killer. He never altered his path in life. But now he was becoming a different man—and change for the personified threat of death was not a welcome incarnation.

"Hi," a young woman's voice chimed.

15

I turned to see a lovely straw-haired woman with rich brown eyes and a small scar at the tip of her chin. The scar was reminiscent of some kind of foreign punctuation mark.

"Hi," I replied.

"What are you thinking about?"

"Uh . . ." I uttered, reluctantly.

"You wanna buy me a drink?" She was happy to change the subject.

The second question took me away from Mouse and that German soldier.

"Sure do," I said.

The young woman looked deeply into my eyes. I appreciated the attention.

"What's your name?" she asked.

"Easy Rawlins."

"Easy? You could call a boy Easy, I guess, but a girl would suffer under a name like that."

I grinned and said, "It's short for Ezekiel. What's yours?"

"Montana."

"For real?"

"Can I help you?" a man's anything-but-helpful voice asked.

Swiveling my head to the left I saw the bartender, a beefy and pink-skinned specimen with a scowl for a mouth. His hands were working on drying a tall glass with fingers swollen from muscle.

He was maybe thirty and only five eight, but if he ever clamped on with those mitts, that would have been the end of whoever got grabbed.

"What's your pleasure, Montana?" I said to my bar date.

"I didn't ask her," the pink bartender said as he put down the glass.

I considered grabbing the tumbler and smashing it around the vicinity of his eyes.

"Rudolf says that Mr. Rawlins should be considered a platinum guest," Montana informed the barman.

I didn't look at her because he could have used that glass on *my* eyes.

Absorbing this intelligence, the bartender went through an amazing transformation. Across the wasteland of the pink man's broad, flushed face, glower turned to grin.

"Sorry, sir," he said. "Monty always has the same. What would you like?"

I made my order and he moved away.

"My father was born in Cleveland but he always wanted to be a cowboy," Montana said with a bit of nostalgia in her voice.

"Say what?"

"Instead he named me Montana and I turned into a saloon girl."

"I'd probably name you Platinum."

Montana grinned and bowed her head, only slightly. "*Platinum* means that if Cunningham made you mad he might could get fired."

"It's more like I made him angry."

"Yeah," she agreed. "Sometimes the band brings in a guest. They could sit at a table but the rules are they can't stand at the bar. That's for white customers."

"The story of my life and my father's and his father's and his."

Montana reached over to pick up a glass filled with red liquid. My drink was there too. Cunningham had stealth capabilities rivaling Craig Kilian's and Christmas Black's.

"Did Rudolf ask you to follow me?"

"To take care of you," the daughter of a would-be cowboy corrected.

"Oh."

"What do you need, Easy?"

She sipped the red drink and I considered my position. I wasn't used to people offering to help me without the use of subterfuge on my part. Most often I had to cajole them with some circuitous chitchat for a good while before they let up on what I wanted to know.

"I'm looking for a man, or the girlfriend of a man named Alonzo."

For the first time Montana had to consider her words before replying.

"Um," she said, the answer in mind but still wondering if it should come out of her mouth. "What's the girlfriend's name?"

"Don't know."

"Is this Alonzo a black man?"

I nodded and sipped on my orange juice.

"I don't know if it's the man you're looking for but there's a guy named Alonzo that's kinda like a talent scout for the Eye. The waitresses have a pretty big turnover rate."

"And this Alonzo reps women?"

"Yeah, you could put it like that. I didn't get here through him but a lotta my girlfriends did."

"He have long straightened hair?"

She had to think a minute. It didn't look like she was stalling.

Montana shook her head and uttered, "No. Just normal. A short Afro."

One of the most questionable things in my line of business is an easy answer with nothing at stake. I considered that truth a second too long.

"What's wrong?" asked the blond woman who studied men up close and often.

"I walked into this place expecting to spend the rest of the night asking my question. And here, the first person I meet has the answer tied up with a bow."

When she wasn't thinking about it, Montana's pretty smile turned beautiful.

"I like you, Easy. You pay attention. Most men I meet expect the world to bend over for them. They ask a question and think you have to tell them the truth. You ask the question and know there's no one answer. I like that."

She was the kind of woman you wanted to like you. But I was on the job.

She smiled again and touched my wrist. "Ask anybody who works here, Easy. They all, or almost all, know Alonzo."

"But this one doesn't have straightened hair," I added.

"Not the last time I saw him."

"And when was that?"

"A couple of weeks. He usually comes in in the daytime and talks to the floor manager."

"And who's that?"

"Another drink?" That was Cunningham, doing *his* job.

"Put three rounds on my tab," I said, glancing at him.

"Be back after a while," was his reply.

"You've been to clubs like this before," Montana observed.

"Management here tonight?"

"Upstairs. One floor past the dining room."

I was considering my next move. Montana studied my contemplation.

"What now?" she asked.

"I was thinking that if I wanted to give you the two twenties in my pocket, would it be bad manners just to put them in your hand?"

"There's these little red envelopes at this end of the bar," she instructed, gesturing at the wall behind me. "Put whatever tip you want in one, write my name on it, and drop it in the slot on the other side."

"That doesn't seem like a reliable system."

"Only Rudy has the key to the box, and he empties it every night."

"Okay," I conceded. Then I gestured to Cunningham that I wanted my check.

"You want to go look at the parking lot?" Montana offered.

"Say what?"

"Forty dollars won't get you to the top floor. But it's nice out back. They got padded benches in the recesses along the wall."

It proves how engaging Montana was that I was surprised at her suggestion. She saw what I was thinking and took it as a compliment.

"No, no, baby," I said. "You already gave me all I need."

She pouted prettily. "Everything?" she said.

At that moment Cunningham put down a half tumbler with my paper bill stuffed inside. I picked out the check.

"Is it because I'm white?" she asked, just fishing.

"Certainly not."

"You don't think I'm pretty?"

"Come on now, girl, when was the last time you looked in the glass?"

"Then what?" She was going to ride that horse into the ground.

I counted out the outrageous cost of drinks and sighed.

"I'm a detective."

"A cop?" She pulled her head back an inch or so, a tiger cub reacting to a king cobra's threat.

"Private. I got a client who wants to talk to a man named Alonzo. Maybe it's your talent scout, maybe not."

"A black private eye?"

"One day they'll have black astronauts too."

Montana smiled for me again.

"I'll be right up there with you, my brother," she said and then moved close as if to kiss.

The fact that our lips didn't touch was more powerful than if they had.

She walked off into the growing crowd and I took in a lungful of air.

I talked to seven other Eye employees. Five of them knew of the black talent scout named Alonzo. None of them remembered straight hair.

After a couple of hours talking I pressed through the jazz and bodies toward a corner table where Mouse had been sitting most of the time. His company was two older guys who looked like they'd been drained of everything vital, including their souls. One of the mummies wore a blue suit, the other gray.

When I approached the table, two young men with faces that somehow resembled scars stood to block my passage.

"Hey, Kikkino," Mouse said. "Tell your boys not to get their breaths on my friend."

Blue Suit said something that might have been in English and the thugs parted like as if Moses had spoken their names.

I wondered if I should sit but Mouse stood up before I could decide.

"Good to see you guys," Raymond said to the dead souls. "We'll talk about that job later." Then to me: "Come on, Easy."

We achieved the dining floor and walked toward where Rudolf was standing. When I realized that we were headed for the door I put a hand on my friend's shoulder and said, "I need to get an address before I leave. They tell me the club manager got it."

"You mean for Alonzo Griggs?"

"You got his last name?"

"Name, phone number, address, and the smell'a his pits. I know who you lookin' for and I know where he say he live at. On top'a that I know where he stays when he needs to hide out."

16

I followed Mouse's Caddy from Hollywood to Inglewood. At that time of evening in 1969 there was not a great deal of traffic. It was about a quarter past ten when we turned into an alley off Coeller Street. The unpaved lane went by the back doors of a few warehouses and then abruptly stopped at a tall steel mesh fence with barbed wire nested across the top and a huge BEWARE OF DOG sign hung about midway. Above the warning was another, smaller sign that read CAFKIN'S JUNKYARD.

"Cafkin," I said. "Who's that?"

"He the man that owns the place where Alonzo go when he wanna stay hid," Mouse explained.

My friend had a long and slender crowbar in his right hand and a grease-stained brown paper bag in the other. He set the bag down, then threaded the crowbar through the hook of the big padlock holding the chains that kept the front gate from opening.

"You take one side and I will the other and we'll twist," Raymond said. "Somethin' gotta give."

"What about the dog?"

"Dogs," he corrected, his smile glittering. "You got your gun, right?"

I sighed and we started turning the steel fulcrum. At about nine turns I heard the metal scrunch. At eleven one or more of the thick chain links cracked. By sixteen the chain fell away and the gate swung in a few inches.

I was thinking about the plural of *dog* when Mouse walked across the threshold of danger.

It was an old-fashioned junkyard. A few cars, some refrigerators and stoves. There were boxes, areas, and entire aisles that specialized. One little canvas-covered walkway had only pants. Old jeans, corduroy, khakis, discarded slacks done in wool, nylon, cotton, and even silk. There was a kitchenware corridor with cast-iron pots, chipped but otherwise fine china, plastic ware, cutlery, and cooking utensils from measuring cups to garlic presses. There was even a little lane that hoarded discarded electronics. There you could find electric lamps, toasters, flashlights, and a whole bin filled with tiny defunct transistor and crystal radios. These organized places and containers were Cafkin's little store. Farther on, beyond the sorted materials, tarp-covered junk was piled high with no particular order imposed.

Mouse led me down a curved pathway dimly lit by a string of low-watt bulbs hanging from whatever the electrician could find to tack on to. It was a dark night and the thought of canine fangs had me on edge.

We turned a sharp corner defined by the sleek side of a once-orange tractor that teetered by itself near the back fence.

That's when the dogs started to bark and howl, bay and snarl.

To my shame I jumped back and went for the .38 in my pocket.

"Easy, what's wrong with you, man? If they didn't jump us at the gate you know they not doin' they job. So they prob'ly locked up."

Probably was the word I chose to highlight, finger on the trigger.

Then I saw the kennel with its high fence. Two of the three mongrels were bouncing off the wire barrier in between canine exhortations. The third dog just stood there growling, showing its most prominent teeth.

Next to the dog enclosure was a tin shack that abutted the wall of a larger structure. It could have been an office, bedroom, or outhouse.

"Hey, boy. Hey, boy." Mouse was talking to the enraged dogs. "Here, look what I got for ya."

From the greasy paper bag he pulled three steaks. With these he enticed the junkyard guardians until there was almost no complaint whatsoever.

"You just pulled some steak out your ass?" I asked.

"Naw, man. I got these from Arnold, the cook over at the Eye. Had him take three rib eyes cooked rare out to my car."

"We go in here?" I asked him.

Ray walked up to the hatch that had been cut into the side of the tin shack.

He slammed on it mightily and then called out, "Alonzo! Hey, Griggs!"

One of the dogs barked a little but soon gave up.

Mouse tested the door handle.

"Do's unlocked."

I reached forward and pulled the portal open.

"Anybody in here?" I called. "Alonzo?"

Mouse found the light chain and a cluster of five or six two-hundred-watt bulbs flooded the squalid room, giving off a concentrated yellow glare. The space was larger than it seemed from the outside because the occupant had broken through the wall of the larger building.

There were crowded workbenches and junk piled on the floor. Nothing was painted, papered, or tiled. You could see motes of dust rising and falling on the air, illuminated by the garish light.

There was a bunk in the farthest corner.

That's where the dead man lay.

"Shit," Mouse muttered upon seeing the naked black corpse. "I guess the story about his dick was true."

He was well endowed.

Other than the single maroon sock on the left foot, he was naked. There was a hole in his chest a little to the right of where his heart should have been. The grin on his lips was insincere. Maybe, I thought, it was a grimace he made trying to stay alive. His right eye was shut, as if he was winking at one last joke, but he didn't die laughing. It was a fact that he tried to live. I could tell of his struggle by the fallen, wadded-up pillow he'd used to try to stem the flow of blood. There were pints of the vital fluid on the thin mattress and down on the concrete floor below.

"He a stupid mothahfuckah." Mouse shook his head, sneering at the dead man.

"Why you say that?"

"He in the business like me, you know? But he do all this cowboy shit without information or any real kinda plan. You know a clean job should have no gunplay at all and at least enough for a year's salary for every man in the crew. Griggs and his boys'd knock over a bank for twenty thousand dollars. Less."

"He was a bank robber?"

"Not only banks."

"Raymond, why didn't you tell me all this before?"

"You said it was about a fight. I didn't wanna put a live man's business in the street. You know I'd kill somebody did that to me."

I tried to think of something to say, some criticism, but he hadn't failed to tell me anything that I could complain about. I wasn't looking for a heist man.

On a rough pine wall above his death cot were tacked dozens of pictures of him being entertained by many, many naked women. Nine or so feet from the dead man was a thirty-five-millimeter Nikon camera on a tripod. A wire led from the camera to a place very near the dead man's blood.

"Damn," Mouse said. "I guess after fuckin' all them women all he had to do was look at a picture and bust a nut."

My friend was the kind of man who cracked jokes with the noose around his neck.

"I don't think he'd given up on the flesh," I said. "From the looks of it he was with a girl just before he got shot. He was about to snap a photo but instead caught a bullet."

"You think she shot him while he was fuckin' her?"

"That would be a difficult move," I surmised.

"Maybe she had some help."

This notion sent me to the camera, but its back had been pried open and any film was gone.

"Well, at least you fount your man," Raymond said. "I hope he didn't owe you no money, though. You'd have to collect it with a dump truck."

"I don't think this is the guy I'm lookin' for."

"Why not?" Mouse said. It was almost a challenge.

"The Alonzo I was hired to find had long straight hair and he'd been stabbed pretty bad a few days before—in the chest."

"Maybe he was shot but whoever had the story figured it was a knife man done it."

"The person who hired me was the one that stabbed him."

"Oh."

There was a desk beyond where the empty camera stood. It had a flex desk lamp, stacks of blank paper, and also pages with notes on them. I turned on the light and started going through papers, looking for some clue. There was a journal filled with men's names and addresses (mostly PO boxes) along with what they liked: *in the ass, regular, big titties, long dicks,* and many combinations of these and others—including *race, sex, size,* and *hair color.* There was a box of nine-by-twelve envelopes on the floor addressed to men all over California and, to a lesser degree, the country.

There was an overabundance of information but nothing that

resembled a hint as to why a man who should have been Craig Kilian's victim was not.

I'd spent nearly half an hour going through the office looking for something that would connect Craig and this Alonzo. I say *I* was looking rather than *we* were because Mouse had gone outside to play with the dogs. He let them out of the pen and roughhoused with them while I searched.

I found a pair of trousers that Alonzo must have shucked off before climbing into the cot. In the right back pocket there was a thin ostrich-skin wallet that contained twenty-seven dollars, his driver's license, three Social Security cards under different names, and a few business cards. There was also the snapshot of a young white woman in a demure pose. On the back of the photograph, in what I suspected was the dead man's scrawl, was written *DD*, with an AXminister exchange phone number.

Donning a pair of cotton gloves I found in the dead man's desk, I dialed the number on Alonzo's phone. No one answered.

Mouse and I parted ways in the alley.

"Easy, your life is way harder'n mine and I'm what they call a career criminal," he said before opening the door to his chartreuse Caddy.

"Thanks for helpin', Ray."

"Call me if the reaper at the do', man. I like the way you do business."

17

I stopped at a twenty-four-hour gas station on Sepulveda. The attendant filled the tank and checked the oil. He washed my windshield too. It was 12:47 in the morning but I didn't hesitate to make the next call from a phone booth at a far corner of the lot.

"Hello?"

"Hey, Jackson."

"Easy." You could hear his smile over the phone.

"You up?" I asked.

"You know I am, brother. Between midnight and five a.m. is the only time I get for my personal studies."

Jackson's "studies" consisted of an in-depth examination of dozens of professional scientific and social-psychological journals that wrote about the latest research, inventions, and theories concerning their particular subject of interest. I once asked the cowardly genius why he'd spend so much time studying things that scientists around the world got paid for.

His answer was, "Capitalism."

"So now you a communist?"

"No, Easy, I like my money like any other niggah do, but it's the way we get it fucks with the flow'a knowledge."

It always tickled me when Jackson started talking like a ghetto professor. I was reminded that understanding was not the property of any race or class, religion or revolution.

"How does an economic system fuck with what you know?"

"The production line, brothah. Man, woman, or child, you work on the production line. And when you on that line you only know your one specialized task. Attach the left front tire to the Ford; put the doodad in the big box. You a blind man strokin' a elephant. And it's not just Detroit puttin' a car together. You work for *Psychology Today* an' you prob'ly don't know shit about the latest breakthroughs in quantum mechanics."

Another thing I loved about Jackson was that he'd reel out some very complex notions and expect you to keep up.

"So?" I asked some years ago when we had this conversation.

"People know mo' and mo' every day, Ease. It's exponential. And that mean that there's things out there like jigsaw puzzle pieces that if you see where they connect, then you will know sumpin' that nobody else in the world do. It's like gold jus' layin' around waitin' for somebody to pick her up."

Jackson could give a great lecture, but that early morning I had more immediate things on my mind.

"Feather still there with you?" I asked.

"She sleep in the second guest room. You know that girl is a balm to Jewelle's heart."

"One of the drivers over my place will pick her up around ten," I offered. "That okay?"

"No problem, man. Question is, are you okay?"

"Why?"

"Christmas Black dropped by my office today. He asked if I had been keepin' up with you."

"And what'd you say?"

"I said I'd rather chase a tornadah. I got the feelin' that you and him were kinda mixed up in sumpin'."

"I hope not."

"Excuse me, mistah," a strained voice said.

Standing outside the booth was an old black person. I wasn't sure if it was a man or a woman. Whatever, they had their worldly belongings in a rusty supermarket cart.

"Talk to you later, Jackson."

"You got a dollah, mistah?" the vagrant asked when I cradled the phone.

His or her skin was darker than mine and they were a full six inches shorter. The world had come down like a sledgehammer on the street drifter's life. I recognized the damage because I'd been dodging that blow from the time I was a child.

After giving the urban nomad five bucks I called another night owl—Anatole McCourt.

The big, brawny, and beautiful Irishman was the special assistant to Melvin Suggs, who was, in turn, the real, if not the acknowledged, number two to the chief of police. Anatole stayed in the office late every night and then had his private line forwarded to his home phone after that.

"McCourt," he answered on the first ring.

"Lieutenant."

"Mr. Rawlins. I've been hearing a lot about you. Something about a stolen Rolls-Royce car."

"You doin' GTA now, man?"

Anatole didn't like me very much. His early experiences as a uniform in South Central gave him the idea that the citizenry there were the enemy, in opposition to the invading army that he represented. But I don't think he was racist. He just didn't trust anyone who knew how to profit from flaws in the system. It was natural for him to feel that it was his job to block my progress.

"What can I do for you, Rawlins?"

"There's a junkyard in Inglewood called Cafkin's. I was out at the Dragon's Eye in Hollywood and I heard somebody talkin' 'bout how there's a dead body out around there."

"Murdered?"

"Dead is what they said."

"Who said?"

"I don't know, Lieutenant. Some white guys. I was out in the parking lot with one of the girls. We went into this little crevice she use and the men gathered round just outside and started talkin'. They didn't see us and we waited till they were gone before coming out."

"Did you hear a name?"

"Griggs. They said the name was Griggs."

I liked the idea of shaking things up at the sex club/restaurant. Maybe that would help me later on. Also I wasn't happy about leaving a murder victim moldering in his own juices.

The last call was to Asiette.

"*Allô?*" she said.

"Hey, baby. Did I wake you?"

"Where are you?"

"On my way home."

"I'll meet you at the funicular."

Gaetano Longo stood at the base of the mountain that was my home. He was a bearish man, big and seemingly lumbering. Seemingly. I'd seen him move quick enough to catch a dancing rooster with just one grab.

"Signor Rawlins," he said in a rumbling voice that sat on top of a growl. "It was too cold and so she stayed in the car. Feather doesn't come."

"She's with her godparents."

The Sicilian grunted and gave me a nod. He didn't want Feather to be in trouble and he didn't want me to bring wanton women home when the child might see or hear.

* * *

Asiette was sleeping under a blanket behind the wheel of her indigo Citroën. When I knocked on the window she opened her Liz Taylor eyes. She emerged still wrapped in the blanket. Then she opened the cloak, showing me that she wasn't wearing anything other than a smile.

In the house she dropped the cover and pulled me to her. She looked at me with intensity and said, "I am so sorry, Easy." Then she kissed me.

"For what?" My throat was a little constricted by the osculation.

"I was trying to make you jealous with Stefano."

I lifted her in my arms, kissed lips and neck, shoulders and breasts.

We didn't make it upstairs. There was a large sofa near the verandah and the koi pool. After her next campaign of kisses I tried to return the favor but was too weak to go on. She rose up over me, kissed both eyes, and said, "*Dors, ma cher.* I will wake you in the morning."

But I awoke first. Lifting the blanket she brought along I looked at her body. She was a strong woman, slender but solid. Her skin was the color of cream with a few drops of vanilla extract blended in.

Asiette Moulon taught me new ways to see the world when I had thought I'd seen it all. But she was too young despite this gift of wisdom.

"Easy," she said. "Do you want to kiss her now?"

18

Later in the morning I saw Asiette down to her French car and kissed her lightly on the lips.

"Do you forgive me?" she asked.

"Ain't nuthin' to forgive," I said, reaching down into the roots of my language. "Man like me got to be ready when the woman is."

"I love you," she said. I don't think she'd ever said those words before—at least not to me.

"And I you. More than you know."

I took that bittersweet moment to drive down to the third address Craig Kilian had given me. It was an apartment house off East Olympic that had once been a mansion. There was an immense dark-needle pine tree growing in the yard and a porch that completely surrounded the front and sides of the four-story structure.

The portico was inhabited by three souls: a man of about fifty years with sixty extra pounds of belly, a sharp-featured woman who looked older than she probably was, and a girl of nineteen or twenty sitting on the banister wearing jean shorts and a tight red blouse. They were all what America calls white people.

I ascended the stairs, nodded at the congregation, and then moved toward the fancy glass-and-hardwood front door.

"Can I help you?" the man asked. He stood up from a redwood lounger and took a step in my direction.

"No," I said honestly.

It's too bad that frankness is not an asset in American race relations.

The man frowned and asked, "What are you doing here?"

The woman, who was short and wiry, gazed at me like a small bird eyeing an oversize grub.

"You ask everybody walks up your stairs about their business?" It would have been easier to explain the circumstances, but Easy is my name, not my nature.

"I'm asking you," the man claimed.

Now the teenager was watching. I swear I saw her nostrils flare.

"I'm gonna walk through that front door and go to apartment three fourteen to have a friendly chat with Craig Kilian. If you wanna try and hinder me in any way I welcome the distraction."

That set his head up straight, like a puppy dog that had just got his first whiff of wolf.

I passed through the front door without further conversation.

The building must have once been a fabulous mansion, but the job of breaking it up into apartments was necessarily jerry-rigged. The hallway on the first floor started out wide, but then, when it turned abruptly to the left, it became a slender passage with only two apartments. The stairs had been halved in some way, making me wonder how anyone moved their furniture in. The second-floor hall consisted of two left turns. The second of these revealed a group of little kids playing various games under the watch of a woman who should not have looked that tired so early in the morning. There had been quite a bit of noise before I walked by, but silence reigned as the brood of children watched mutely until I passed. They started howling again when I turned the first tier of the third-floor stairs.

The next floor was one great empty space with eight apartment doors along the encircling walls. No one was out and there was only one door open. Intuition told me that that door belonged to Craig—intuition was right.

* * *

I knocked on the open portal and called out, "Craig?"

Taking a step inside, I saw him at the end of a longish passage. He was just standing there, barefoot, in the middle of the sparsely furnished room, staring at the floor.

"Craig."

He looked up as I approached. When he saw me his eyes tightened. At first he was wondering if I was friend or foe, but then there came a glimmer of recognition. A wavering smile crossed his lips.

"Mr., Mr. Rawlins," he said.

I entered the room and was immediately assaulted by a seven- or eight-pound brawny black puppy. The beast struck my shins with its paws and tongued my fingers for every lick of salt it could find.

"Get down from there, Sammy," Craig said in a completely human tone.

"This the dog you found up at Blood Grove?"

The question soured the young man a bit.

"Did you talk to my mom?" he asked.

"Didn't she tell you?"

Craig winced, not giving an answer.

"That Lola's something else," I said.

"What's that supposed to mean?" The anger rose in his voice like a river on a cloudless day overflowing its banks due to a faraway cloudburst.

In an imperfect world I do believe a man could get himself killed saying good morning in the wrong key.

"That she's fierce," I said. "That she'd protect you no matter what the danger was."

Craig listened to my words closely and then nodded.

"She knows me," he agreed. "When I can't explain myself she's got the right words."

"I went out to the campsite with a Green Beret." I changed the subject so as not to say something wrong again. "He agreed with part of your story. But he thought that there were four people there including you and the girl."

"Four?"

"You, the two you saw, and the one that hit you," I said. "It was his opinion that all four walked away under their own power."

Craig's eyes sifted through the images my words presented. His breath picked up its pace, slightly.

"Did you?" he asked and then stopped. "Did you find out their names or anything like that?"

"Nothing. They didn't leave anything on the ground outside and the cabin was laid bare too."

"But nobody died?"

"Not then. Not there."

"Nothing about a guy named Alonzo?" Craig asked.

"No. Nothing." I was a fountain of negatives.

The bad boy turned sad soldier studied his bare feet a moment.

Sammy kept leaping up on me, ecstatic that he had found such a sturdy playmate.

There were sounds of radios and TVs playing in other apartments. Somewhere a man and a woman were yelling. The air was very still.

"There was one other thing," I said finally.

Craig looked up, wishing, no doubt, that his mother was there to carry the conversation.

I took out the photograph I'd found in the real Alonzo's wallet and showed it to the boy-soldier.

"Do you know who she is?" I asked.

One of the symptoms of shell shock is that the victim of the trauma sometimes loses themselves in thought. Craig stared at that picture a good long minute. He turned it over, saw the phone number, and then turned it back again. He waited a bit longer before saying, "No. No. I don't."

He didn't ask where I got the photograph or why I was asking him about it. In short, he was lying. The question was—did he know he was lying?

"There was no body, no blood, no evidence of a life-and-death struggle at the campsite you sent me to," I said in my professional voice while tugging the little photograph from his fingers. "If I went to the cops with this they'd say, 'No evidence, no case.' So my advice is to consider yourself lucky, love your dog, and forget all about Blood Grove. Don't go up there again."

Craig gave a smile that was also a grimace. He nodded, shook his head, and then nodded again.

Sammy the dog was leaping up and down between us, whining happily.

"I guess you're right, Mr. Rawlins," he said. "I guess you're right."

"Hey, mister?" the girl in the short shorts hailed when I came back out on the verandah. She was the only one left out there.

She walked up to me both shy and bold.

"Yeah?"

"Hinder was all mad that you didn't stop and explain yourself. He wants to think he's the super but he's just another tenant."

"His name is Hinder?"

"Uh-huh. Why?"

"Nothing. People like to think they have control over what they see as their own territory. They try and protect it like a bear or a dog."

"A dog with no teeth," the girl said with a sneer. "My name's Shirley."

"Easy," I replied, pressing three fingers against my chest.

"Easy, do you think I should try and be in the movies?"

I'd come up the stairs into this young woman's life and showed her that the rules she felt oppressed by didn't necessarily apply.

Now she just had to ask the question that burned in her mind both day and night.

I conjured a contemplative look and nodded.

"You know you're a pretty girl because there's a mirror in your bathroom," I said. "And you're old enough to know what a pretty girl can expect from men between the ages of sixteen and sixty-nine."

She smiled, telling me that I knew how she felt.

"That's both a blessing and a curse," I went on. "As long as you remember that you can try anything you want because the only real thing a young woman like yourself has is her dreams."

After saying this I hustled down the stairs so as not to incur feeling in myself, herself, or Hinder, if he happened to be watching.

19

On the far side of Brighthope Canyon there's an odd-shaped but generally Olympic-size swimming pool. Erculi Longo kept it clean and an underground engine warmed the water to just about seventy-two degrees.

Orchestra Solomon, wearing a yellow dress under a pearl-gray wrap, watched the grotto-like pool as my daughter swam back and forth with intention and steady speed. My sixty-something landlady smiled down on the amphibious child, pleased as many older women are at the unconscious strength of youthful femininity.

I sidled up next to one of the wealthiest women in California and said, "She could be the best in the world if she applied herself."

Without turning toward me Sadie replied, "A long time ago my mother told me that the best is never the best."

"That's a truth," I said, and a kind of melancholy settled on me. "I met Joe Louis in Vegas once. They called him the best and he paid for it in more ways than a poor black man could imagine."

"You're a good father, Ezekiel. That's better than being a good man. But you're a good man too."

"I just keep the flies off."

"She comes straight out of your heart."

"Daddy!" Feather called. She swam for the closest edge to me and Orchestra, emerging from the water in a fluid motion like a seal or an otter.

"Hey, baby," I said, hugging her wet body and bathing suit.

"Hi, Miss Sadie," she said to our landlady, shivering just a bit.

I pulled a towel from a cherrywood dowel installed on the side of a cedar tree. When I tried to drape the cloth around her shoulders she pushed it off.

"You're cold," I complained.

"I like to feel cold after a swim," she said, looking off into the distance.

"You want to come inside?" I suggested. "I could warm up some gumbo."

"Let's sit out here for a while."

We sat on a bench of stacked gray slate stone.

I turned to invite Orchestra to join us, but she was already walking back toward her home.

"What you do today, Daddy?"

"I went out and picked some oranges for Erculi." I sat as close as I could to the swimmer, hoping to impart some of my warmth.

"You see anybody?"

"Christmas Black."

"How was Easter Dawn?" Even though Christmas's daughter was much younger, Feather liked the little girl's company because of her ability to pay attention.

"She wasn't there," I said. "I saw him at work. I saw Raymond too, along the way."

The hint of a shadow crossed my daughter's brow. Not a darkness so much as an undigested memory.

"A long time ago when I was eleven," she said, leaning a little against me, "I was staying with Aunt Etta and Cousin Peter. But then Mama Jo called up and told Aunt Etta that she needed help because this man had pneumonia and Mama Jo wasn't strong enough to move him around like she had to . . ."

I tried to imagine how large a man would have to be to need both Jo and EttaMae, the two strongest women I knew, to drain him of fluids by witchcraft and gravity.

". . . so Aunt Etta told me to stay with Cousin Peter . . ."

Peter Rhone was a young white man I once proved didn't commit a murder. He'd been blamed for slaughtering the young black woman he loved. After the case was over he left his wife, deciding to live with Mouse and Etta as a kind of atonement. He slept on their screened-in porch, cleaned, cooked, shopped, and, I suppose, took care of my daughter when EttaMae had errands to run.

". . . but then Uncle Mouse came and told Peter that he was gonna take me to the park . . ."

Peter would have been sorry to let Feather go, and he would have called Mama Jo to tell Etta, but Jo's only means of communication was a phone booth about half a mile from her Compton home.

"Did Mouse take you to the park?"

"Uh-huh, yeah. He met this man named Maxie and they talked about somethin' I didn't understand. But there was these other girls there and we played jump rope and talked about boys and school and stuff. And then this big man came up and said something I didn't really hear, and Wanda, one of the girls, said he should just leave. And the next thing I knew Uncle Mouse was there. He told the big man to go over with him to the other side of the park and Maxie bet us that we couldn't do a hundred skips with double skip ropes. He said that he'd give us two dollars each if we could."

Feather sat there remembering the contest for a moment.

I was about to ask her what happened in the park when she said,

"We won and everybody got a two-dollar bill from Maxie and then Uncle Mouse came back and we went to his car."

"What about the big man?"

"I didn't see him again, but when we got to the car Uncle Mouse took a rag out of the glove compartment because he had a cut on his finger and he wanted to wipe it off. And that reminded me that Wanda said Mouse was probably gonna kill that man because he wasn't nice to me."

We sat there for a few moments.

When I put my arm over her quavering shoulder she asked, "Do you think Uncle Mouse would have killed that man?"

"Never," I said.

"How come never?"

"He just wouldn't do something like that." What I meant to say was that Mouse wouldn't murder somebody in a crowded place in the daylight, but those details weren't important to make clear to my child.

I was considering the talk I'd have to have with Mouse when Feather said, "I was thinking that maybe I'd change my name."

"Change your name to what?" Some years earlier I'd legally adopted Feather, giving her my last name. I feared she was about to reject this christening.

"Genevieve." She pronounced the name in the French way, using all four syllables.

"Why Genevieve?"

"I like the way it feels in my mouth and it's French and I speak French and my good friends could call me Ginny."

"Why don't we go inside and get warm?"

I made long-grain white rice and heated up a pot of frozen blue crab gumbo thickened by both gumbo filet and fried okra. Feather loved that stew and I did too. We ate for a while and she explained how geometry defines the old universe while Mr. Einstein's theory of relativity described the new one.

"So could there be two different universes?" I asked the chomping child.

"Of course. Maybe even a billion of them. Maybe we could live in a completely different place by just thinking about it."

She was coming to the end of the bowl.

I was just about to tell her to go up and take a shower when instead I said, "Your uncle, your real uncle, Milo Garnett, came by the office yesterday."

"Who?"

"Your mother's brother from back east."

Feather put her spoon down and leaned back.

She already knew the broad strokes of her mother's life and death. More than a year before, she'd asked if we could find her grandmother and any other family, but this was the first real chance she had at meeting her blood. I told her that Milo had heard about her and come all the way to California to meet her. And, oh yeah, he's a hippie.

"How tall is he?" was her second question.

I told her.

"What do you want me to do?" she asked.

"He seems like a nice young man," I said after a bit. "And he traveled almost three thousand miles to meet you."

"Why didn't him and his mom try to talk to me before?"

"I think he was a kid and his mother was heartbroken over the deaths of her daughter and husband," I said delicately.

"But why's he here now?"

"I guess he grew up enough to make up his own mind."

"Where is he?"

"Staying with friends."

"Do I have to see him?"

"Not right now. Not until you're ready. If you don't want to see him, you don't have to."

"What do you think I should do, Daddy?"

"Sit with it. Think about it. And know that I will always be there with you and you will be safe."

"Could he make me go with him?"

"Absolutely not."

20

That afternoon bowl of creole stew felt like an end point of sorts. I called Milo and told him that his niece needed a little time; that I'd call back in a few days. I guess he'd settled in pretty well at the hippie house and so voiced no complaint.

Niska was working her mantra in Redlands. Their own cases kept Saul and Whisper out of town. And I stood at my back office window a couple of early mornings watching bare-chested Stache carrying his watering can out to the greenhouse.

On Friday Feather was off with some girlfriends at a swimming event and I was at the office reading a slender text on the theory of relativity so I could keep up with her junior high school classes.

"Anybody home?" a gravelly voice called from the front office.

I had decided that I wouldn't allow Craig Kilian to make me so fearful that I'd start locking doors.

"Back here!" I called.

I could hear his footsteps, heavy and hard soled, as he marched toward and then into my office. He wore a gray suit that had the mildest of pink patinas running under the surface, a shirt white enough to shine, and a bloodred tie that had been woven at the neck into a perfect square knot.

He was short for a man, five seven or so, and had once been fat. When I met him he was a homicide detective in South Central LA. After solving a couple of high-profile cases, with my help, he was now the number two or three cop in the city, depending on how you judged influence versus rank.

This last detail was what surprised me about the unexpected visit: a man in Melvin Suggs's position did not make house calls.

"Easy," he said. "You're looking prosperous."

"And I can see that Mary Donovan is keeping your shit together. Have a seat."

Melvin didn't hesitate. He grabbed a chair and pulled it close enough to my grand desktop that he could rest his beefy fingers on the ledge.

"Why you say that?" he asked.

"No wrinkles on the suit or shirt, a tie that the king's butler could have knotted, and fat gut still gone the way of the steam engine."

Mel didn't want to smile but did anyway.

His live-in girlfriend, called Mary Donovan for at least the past three years, was a con woman, thief, bank robber, and, if you scratched deep enough, I'm sure you'd've discovered that she'd been involved in crimes that would get a person hanged. But in spite of all that, she and Melvin were deeply in love. Their love story was like a fairy tale finished in San Quentin just before the author was due for execution.

"She's been taking me to these fancy parties lately," the cop confessed. "Congressmen and senators, billionaires and movie stars. Says that I could move on up and become an important man in California."

Their relationship was a disaster waiting to happen but you couldn't tell either one of them what was in store.

"Looks good on you," I said, telling the truth.

Pleasantries over, Melvin caught my eye and said, "Anatole found a murdered man at the back of a junkyard in Inglewood. Tells me that you're the one told him about it."

"I told him that I overheard some people talking at the Dragon's Eye and that they said a man named Griggs was dead. Nobody said anything about him being murdered. And all I stumbled on were the words."

"What people spoke these words?"

"I told Anatole. I was in a clench with a young woman around a corner from them. I didn't see anybody and nobody mentioned any names but Griggs and Cafkin's."

I was lying of course. From the look in his beautiful taupe-colored eyes I could see that Melvin knew it.

"There was a lot of pornographic material on the scene," he said. "He was found in a tin shack—did you know that?"

"Why are you here, Mel?"

"Griggs frequented the bar where you heard about him. He was what they call a talent scout."

"So?"

"The night you told Anatole about what you heard, you were seen with Raymond Alexander at the Eye."

"I already told you I was there."

"But you neglected to mention Alexander."

"I *neglected* to mention I took a piss too. What's your point?"

"Griggs was shot." It was a statement intended to indicate my, or my friend's, culpability.

"Was he shot with a forty-one-caliber shell?" This was Mouse's weapon of choice.

"Some people said that both you and Alexander had been asking about Griggs."

He had me. There was no reason to continue that particular lie and so I took another tack.

"All right, all right. I was tryin' to be professional but you got me. The day I went to the Eye a woman came to my office. She said her name was Charlotte Nell and that her daughter, Portia, had been seduced and turned out by Griggs. She wanted to find him to buy her daughter back. I asked around, found that he showed up at the Eye now and then. I asked some questions and a little guy in a green suit told me that he'd heard Griggs had been killed. I found out where the cat stayed at and called Anatole. Just a citizen doing his duty."

"The man who told you," Suggs said, "what's his name?"

"Said it was Tom."

"Tom what?"

I shrugged and Melvin snorted.

"White guy?"

"Yeah," I said.

"How do I get in touch with this woman, this Charlotte Nell?"

"She said she'd come by the next day. . . . She didn't."

"You got a number?"

I shook my head and said, "I figured that with Griggs dead the daughter came back on her own."

"Maybe the mother killed him," Suggs suggested.

"If she did I wasn't the one who told her where to find him."

Melvin knew when he was being played. He also knew that when he once lost Mary I brought her back home.

"Sounds pretty slim," he said after a bit.

"Am I under arrest?"

"The coroner says that he'd been dead for two days. That means you were asking about him after the killing."

"I guess I could'a been creating an alibi. But why would I do that when I could just let someone else find the body on their own?"

"If I had that answer," Suggs said, "you'd be in cuffs right now."

"You want I should give you a description of the client?"

I made up some features and he jotted down a few notes. Charlotte Nell had nothing in common with Lola except her age and race. When I told Melvin that was all I remembered, he stood straight up from the visitor's chair, told me that unless they found the killer someone would be back to ask more. I said that my door was always open and he left through it.

* * *

By noon I had migrated up to Niska's desk. I'd spent an hour or two trying to think of how the LAPD could charge me with the pornographer's death. It seemed unlikely and so I traded in Einstein for the *Herald Examiner.*

21

Somewhere just after 1:00 I heard the door downstairs slam shut. This gave me time to take the .38-caliber snub-nose from my pocket, place it on Niska's blue blotter, and cover it with the newspaper. Some seconds passed and there came a knock on the upper door.

Someone might think that this friendly request represented a more sophisticated kind of visitor rather than some shell-shocked vet or hard-bitten cop. But I knew that the safest way to enter a room was to knock first—so as not to get shot.

"Come on in," I called.

The man who pushed the door open was remarkable; maybe an inch taller than I and white like aged ivory. The one and only descriptive adjective that defined him was *blunt*. From the extra-broad shoulders to his helmetlike bald head, from his hammer hands to the hairless and protruding eyebrows. Even the color of his suit, a waxy crayon blue, made you think of some bad guy who just walked out of *Dick Tracy* in the funny papers.

"You Rawlins?" he commanded.

"And to whom am I speaking?"

"You Rawlins?"

"I'd like to hear your name before I answer that question."

Mr. Blunt's eyes were the color of pond scum, wavering between dark mud and coagulated algae. He took a bellows breath to keep from jumping across the receptionist's desk and said, "Eddie Brock."

He was as much an Eddie as I was a bee-size Helena hummingbird that sometimes inhabited the southern swamps of Louisiana.

"Have a seat, Mr. Brock. I'm Rawlins."

It took a moment for Eddie to tamp down his rage. The request for civility was not a common event in his life. Brock lifted a heavy oak chair and then dropped it back down in the same place. Then he sat, heavily of course.

"I wanna hire you," he said. It was less a request and more a fait accompli.

"To do what?"

"On retainer."

"Retainer for what?"

Eddie Brock was definitely not a man used to being questioned.

"For whatever I need done," he said.

"I don't provide that kind of service, Mr. Brock. People come to me to find out if their spouse is cheating. They want to know if their employees or clients are stealing from them. I'm not a bodyguard, bouncer, or leg breaker. Operators like that don't have offices with front doors."

Eddie could make his eyes very small. I imagined that I looked like a distant marksman's target. The stare lasted no longer than four seconds but they dragged by like an anvil being hauled by a rusty chain through half-dry cement. Then, suddenly, he broke out into a grin.

"Let's start over," he said. "My name is Eddie Brock and I need a detective to do some work for me."

I smiled, showing no teeth, and nodded.

"The first thing I need," the big man continued, "is for you to find a woman I'm looking for."

"She have a name?"

"Donata Delphine. I have her picture right here."

"Why do you want her found?"

This question actually made Mr. Brock blink.

"Excuse me?"

"What is your interest in Miss Delphine?"

"Your job is to find her," he said. "Mine is to talk to her once you've done that."

"Your job," I stated. "Who pays you?"

"Don't you want a job, soul brother?" The waters were getting choppy. "I mean here you are sittin' on your ass in this big place all alone. Looks like you could use gettin' paid."

"What I can use is not trying to find some woman for an angry boyfriend intends to do her harm." I was beginning to enjoy the banter. For some time I had been practicing grabbing my .38 and pulling the trigger. I figured that, if it came down to brass tacks, I had the edge.

Brock grinned again. If a smile had a sound his would have been a death knell.

"Who said anything about hurtin' her?" he growled. "I just want to talk."

"About what?"

"That's personal."

"Don't get me wrong, Mr. Brock. I like money just as much as the next guy, but I don't know you. I don't know you and you want me to find a woman that might not want to be found. If a crime comes from that I could be charged as an accessory. At the very least they might pull my license."

Eddie reached into his too-blue jacket's breast pocket. The fingers of my right hand twitched an inch closer to the *Herald*. He noticed the movement, smiled again, and took out a three-by-five photograph.

"This is her," he said while handing me the picture and staring into the depths of my eyes from the swamp of his.

Between the gun I wanted to draw, the picture I didn't want to see, and the man-boulder's smirk, I was nearly frozen . . . almost so.

With my left hand I reached for the proffered photograph,

plucking it from his forefinger and thumb. I held it far enough away not to lose sight of where my pistol lay.

That's when everything changed.

Donata Delphine was a natural redhead wearing just the right amount of makeup and hardly any clothes at all. She was sitting on a high stool that her legs curled around like two golden snakes mated for life. Her smile was alluring and her eyes managed to connect even from out of that two-dimensional medium.

She was gorgeous and she was also the woman in the photograph I found in Alonzo Griggs's wallet, the photograph of the woman Craig Kilian purported not to know.

"She looks like a whore. I know that," Brock apologized. "But a man can't help who he falls in love with. We dated a couple of times when I paid for it. And a few more times just like friends. Then something happened. I think it was the people she worked for. They moved her to another location and told me they didn't know where she was."

I nodded at the lie and began to wonder about the steps that had brought me to this crossroads. There was the German soldier I didn't kill and a dozen others I had. There was Craig Kilian, who was either the unluckiest white boy I'd ever met or, more likely, a client who was playing me.

Deceitful clients are nothing new in detective work. A PI can't afford to be too picky. But a man like Eddie Brock was beyond the range of, excuse the term, a few little white lies. If I had known the trouble I was getting into, I'd have turned Kilian away—I might have thrown him out a window.

But the time to cut bait was gone. Taking Craig's case brought this great white into my office and so I had to assess the damage.

"These people know where she is but won't tell you?" I asked, reasonably.

"Believe me when I tell you, Mr. Rawlins, these are not people you want to question."

"If you tell me I can't talk to them, then why should I believe you?" I said after rejecting two or three more civil replies.

"What?" Eddie managed to pack a good deal of threat into the word.

"I'm a damn good detective, Mr. Brock. I find people, stolen property, and the perpetrators of crimes that the police are too lazy to chase down. You'd be a fool to hire me if I didn't ask any questions."

He bristled at the word *fool* but I had to make a point—before I changed it.

Eddie hunched his shoulders and held out his hands—palms up. He was the kind of dangerous that made police shoot first.

"I don't get it, Rawlins. It's like you're interviewing *me* for the job."

"What if I were to say that I'd find this girl, this Donata, but before I told you where she was I'd ask her if she wanted to see you?"

"I could have made up my name," he said, finally falling into the false banter of our two-sided interrogation.

"You couldn't make up the way you look, man."

Once again his eyes turned into pellets. I was reminded that even if he looked blunt that didn't mean he was stupid.

After a moment his visage softened and Eddie Brock told me this: "I just wanna talk to the girl. She has information I need, that I have to have. If you can get her on a phone with me I'll pay you a hundred dollars."

"Five hundred and you have a deal."

I didn't want his money. I doubted that he'd pay me even if I could get the good-time girl on a call. No, I didn't want his money, but he had to think I did.

"No more questions, then?" Brock inquired.

"Not about what I'm gonna do but maybe a little about her," I said. "I mean the name doesn't sound real and the picture's great but I don't think it'll help that much. With that I could range around the exotic clubs, but that'll take time."

"Go to the Dragon's Eye," he said, and then he rose, an impossibly white hippopotamus from an opaque and stagnant pond. "Go to the Dragon's Eye. Someone there might know something."

"If you know where to look, what do you need me for?"

"She doesn't work there anymore and people start to act kinda squirrelly when I come around asking questions."

"You?"

"No one likes a smartass, Rawlins."

"How do I get in touch with you?"

This simple question stymied Eddie. He frowned a moment and then said, "I'll get back to you on that."

22

Eddie was gone but he left a sour resonance in the room; like a low-frequency hum putting pressure on the inner ear. Craig claimed to have stabbed a man, sent me to follow after the man's name, where I found a man who was dead—but shot, not stabbed. That man was a pornographer and a robber. And then there was Eddie Brock, whose middle name might have been Murder. There was a girl who didn't mind getting naked in public who all three men had some relationship to.

And then there was Lola.

She showed up at a few minutes before 3:00. I didn't hear her footsteps until just before the door opened. The .38 was back in its pocket. I looked up wondering if maybe Niska's desk was the place I was destined to die.

Lola's two-piece dress suit was the color of scarlet roses and over-ripe Meyer lemons. I figured that she'd spent two hours or more preparing for this visit. She was both ravishing and devastated.

"What's wrong, Lola?" I asked, rising to my feet.

She glanced at me, saw nothing it seemed, took a single step, and then crumpled to the floor. For a moment it felt as if I was in one of those forties movies when the one important witness walks in and then falls dead from a knife in the back.

But Lola had only stumbled. I rushed to her side, helped her up and into the chair Eddie Brock last sat in.

"Are you okay?" I asked.

"What?"

"Are you hurt?" I pulled another chair up next to hers.

"I, I need your help, Mr. Rawlins."

"What kind of help?"

She looked into my eyes as if maybe the answer to the question was there. That search brought her to the edge of a deep and dark abyss. Questions alone would not get to her fears. And so I took her right hand with both of mine. The fingers were cold.

I think it was my warmth that gave her courage.

"I haven't heard from Craig in two days," she said. "I've called him a dozen times. He's talked to me at least every other day since he got out of the army. Something's wrong."

"Did you go to his apartment?"

"I, I, I . . ."

If she could have found the words she would have told me that what I asked was a man's job and, for lack of anyone else, I was that man.

"You could have just called me to tell me that, Lola," I said, trying to slow the locomotive I felt bearing down on me.

She looked into my eyes, wondering at the statement like a cat might when you give it a name. It occurred to me that Lola had been performing for an audience for so long that her life had become that ritual.

"I need you," she said.

It would have been the easiest thing in the world to say no; no, you do not need me and furthermore I wash my hands of you and your son. That's what any sensible modern man or woman would have done. But I'm anything but modern and she knew it.

"How did you get here?" I asked.

"Taxi. It cost nine seventy-five."

I gave Lola a double shot of whiskey, called her a taxi from a nearby service, and sent her home promising that I'd call as soon as I found her son.

"Security," Edmund Lewis said on the first ring.

I told Edmund to tell Christmas I'd be picking him up at the office, that we were going to check on my client.

"When?" the war hero/receptionist asked.

"As soon as I can get there," I said and hung up.

I shouldn't have been rude to Lewis. He was just doing his job the best way he knew how. But my problems were piling up while the solutions side of the scale stayed empty. Christmas Black was sounding a wee bit unstable, but I'd need him if Craig was going through another of his episodes.

By the time I got to P9 it was almost 5:00. I couldn't have explained why I stopped by Asiette's office on the way; now I think that I was looking for a moment of respite before heading off to war.

She was just disengaging from a gentle kiss delivered by a quite handsome and well-dressed olive-skinned gentleman who might have been European.

"Excuse me," I said, making to back away from the door, which, in my defense, had been open.

"No, no, Easy," Asiette said. She rushed toward me and touched my hand. "This is my friend Stefano Lombardi. Stefano, this is Easy Rawlins."

Stefano had wavy black hair and an angular face that exuded extreme confidence.

He looked down his Roman nose at me and then smiled, reminding me a bit of Eddie Brock.

"You are the janitor?" he asked.

I was dressed in black jeans and a gray T-shirt. My shoes were cotton topped and rubber soled. He might have thought that I was the cleanup man. But to think something is not the same as saying it.

The Italian's rudeness would have bothered me if I hadn't had so many other issues to deal with. Asiette, on the other hand, turned her head toward him as if she had just been slapped.

"You got a connect to Christmas Black's private line, baby?" I said.

"Three six seven," she answered, still looking at the man who shared her kisses.

I went behind her desk, sat down, and pressed the numbers.

"Hello," Christmas said on the second ring.

"I'll be down at the entrance on the Wilshire side," I said and hung up.

"You let him sit at your desk?" Stefano asked Asiette.

"I got to go," I said to the Frenchwoman.

"I'm sorry," she replied. "I will call you later."

I drove.

Christmas wore a military-like dark blue suit with a tan dress shirt that was underscored by a tight red ascot nestled behind the open top button.

"What's up?" he asked after we'd gone a block.

I told him about Lola's visit but not Eddie Brock. Compartmentalization is one of the indispensable bulwarks of the detective game.

"Jackson Blue told me that you talked to him about me. What do you think of him?" I asked the question because I didn't want to speculate about the job at hand. Sometimes you just have to wait until you get there.

Christmas seemed not to have heard the question. He stared out the windshield, scowling at the world.

"It's like Kirkland," he said after a minute or two.

"What is?"

"Your friend Blue. Really he's worse. He's a coward, scared of his own shadow. I looked up his record. Do you know that he's been arrested thirty-two times—in Los Angeles alone?"

"For half that number he went to trial," I bragged, "and every time he was his own lawyer. He's seen the inside of the county jail often enough but he's never gone to prison."

"Yeah," Christmas allowed. "And he knows more about the history of warfare than my grandfather Moses Black did."

"Did you go to Jean-Pierre with Jackson's record?"

"It's my duty to report to the boss."

"What did the big man say?"

"He said that all a soldier was responsible for was to do his job. I could never be friends with Blue but I can't fault him either. Given his limitations he has been an extraordinary asset."

A few minutes after he said these words I pulled up to the curb in front of Craig's blowsy apartment building.

There were no tenants on the broad porch. The front door wasn't locked. Along the hallways and staircases children and mothers laughed, shouted, and yawped. I smelled hamburgers frying and spaghetti sauces simmering along with sweet concoctions and bread baking. There were all types of music from Dean Martin to Bob Dylan playing on phonographs. Many doors were open but Christmas and I had little interest in the lives therein.

We reached Craig's door in the big vacant space and stopped. Colonel Black made a hand gesture telling me that it was my choice. So I knocked and waited, then knocked again.

"Should we look for the super?" my by-the-book friend asked.

I tried the doorknob. It didn't surprise me that it wasn't locked.

The black dog, Sammy, leaped at me, battering my knees with his paws and licking at my hands. Sixteen paces in we found Craig. He'd been shot at least five times. Once in the right eye and the rest in his chest. He hadn't bled as much as Alonzo because death came quickly. He was lying on his side on a short sofa. I thought that he'd probably been moved because his back pocket was turned out, likely to get at his wallet.

Sammy started whimpering. I suppose the fact that his master didn't engage us proved to the creature that he was abandoned once again.

I lifted Sammy in my arms while Christmas swiveled his head, studying the room, exercising his expert scouting skills.

"What you need, Easy?"

"Not this," I said.

I don't remember what, if anything else, Christmas and I said. Craig Kilian was dead; had been that way for a while. There was a white phone on a tall side table against the far wall. I dialed Anatole McCourt's number and he answered. Within fifteen minutes the same number of men were swarming throughout the four-room apartment.

There was a Detective Nelson who wore a cinnamon-and-black checkered jacket, pale green trousers, and rose-colored sunglasses. He had a partner who I think was a sergeant but I don't recall the name. He wore a sports jacket that was light blue. Ten of the rest were in uniform and there were a couple of paramedics too, all of them male and some shade of so-called white.

Before Anatole arrived the gendarmes' attitudes were unpleasant.

"What were you doing in this neighborhood?" Nelson asked me.

"Waiting for you."

"Don't get smart with me."

"Detective, we're the ones that called Lieutenant McCourt."

"And how would you know to call him?"

"I'm a PI. I work for the LAPD now and again."

Sergeant Whatshisname was interrogating Christmas. I didn't hear what he asked, but my friend never uttered more than a short burst of three or four words to answer.

* * *

After another quarter hour Craig was moved from the sofa to a gurney. They laid him out all stiff and dead. One of the paramedics whispered something in Nelson's ear, causing the lead officer to look closely at the corpse and then at me.

Sammy the dog had curled up behind my ankles. He didn't like all the commotion.

"You say you were here to make some kind of report?" Nelson asked me.

"Mr. Kilian hired me to find a woman that he only knew as Dee Dee," I lied, for the third time. "I came here to tell him that he was wasting his money."

"Have you ever been here before?" There was a gleam of anticipation in the detective's eye.

"A couple of days ago."

Gleam came to grin.

Nelson turned to a uniform and said, "Put some cuffs on this man."

Dutifully the twenty-something officer pulled the cuffs from a holster on his belt. The young cop was my height and build.

He looked me in the eye and said, "Turn around."

"Who's in charge here?" a beautiful baritone brogue inquired.

Anatole McCourt was at least a head taller than any other man in ninety-nine percent of the rooms he entered. His skin was almost true white and his red hair was brighter and healthier than a human's hair should be. His suit was the color green that an artist would assign to a primordial forest. The emerald of his eyes belonged to the deity whose duty it was to oversee that domain.

"Lieutenant," Detective Nelson said as the uniform grabbed my right biceps and tried to twirl me around.

"What are you doing?" Anatole asked my would-be jailer.

The unnamed officer released me.

"I'm arresting him," Nelson replied.

"Arresting him? This is the man who called in the death."

"But he was here two days ago. The medic says that's probably how long the victim's been dead."

"And that makes enough sense for you to arrest the man?" Anatole asked. "Did the attendant give you an exact time of death?"

Nelson had no reply. Most likely he had never been questioned about the arrest of a black man. *He could have murdered him* was excuse enough to put me in jail for months, if not ever.

"What were you doing here?" Anatole asked me point-blank.

"Mr. Kilian had hired me to find a woman named Dee Dee. He had a description and a place, the Dragon's Eye. I looked but didn't find anything. After that I followed up on some leads of my own but they didn't work out. I came here to tell him that."

"The Eye is where you heard about Alonzo Griggs."

"Yeah."

"Is there a connection?"

"Not that I'm aware of, Lieutenant."

Anatole stared sabers at me. He would have never treated me the way Detective Nelson would—but that didn't mean he didn't want to.

Then the cop turned his attention to Christmas Black.

"What are you doing here, Mr. Black?" the Irishman asked.

"Mr. Rawlins asked me to come along. He told me that this boy was ex-military. Thought I might be of some help."

"Help what?"

"The private had trauma from the war. Sometimes a superior officer is useful in grounding an unstable soldier's mind."

"Was Mr. Rawlins worried about the boy being injured?" Anatole asked, showing Christmas great deference. This didn't surprise me; both officers judged men by rank and attitude.

"No," Christmas said. "He was not."

146 • WALTER MOSLEY

Detective Nelson was not happy with all the respect and calm language. His idea of an investigation had more to do with conquest than it did with intelligence.

After this brief interrogation Anatole began looking over the crime scene. He paid special attention to the dollops of blood on the sofa and the floor.

After that was over he told Nelson to carry on and indicated that he'd walk Christmas and me to the street.

I picked up Sammy, who squirmed around so that he could lick my face.

"What are you doing with the dog?" Detective Nelson challenged. I think his manhood needed it.

"My dog," I said.

"You got papers?" the detective asked.

"Drop it," Anatole ordered.

"Second murder in only a few days, Mr. Rawlins," he said.

"You know what they say about California, Lieutenant, nothing but bad luck and sunshine."

"I don't expect to hear from you again anytime soon," the Irish cop warned. Then he walked away.

When he climbed into a dark sedan halfway down the street I asked Christmas, "How you know him?"

"Jean-Pierre has a relationship with the police. He put me in touch with Commander Melvin Suggs and Suggs introduced me to McCourt as a kind of go-to if we needed it."

Sammy and I went to Culver City directly after dropping Christmas at his office. Lola was smiling when she opened the door, but the moment she saw us the ex–exotic dancer lost her equilibrium, stumbled backward, and fell on her butt. That was my mistake. I brought Sammy with me because I didn't want him befouling

John's Pontiac. But I forgot that Lola would have known about the dog. She talked to her son at least every two days.

Putting Sammy down, I went to Lola and lifted her by the armpits. The bad news she'd been expecting for more than twenty years left her limp as a rag doll. I dragged her to a dinette chair while Sammy barked, happily leaping around our feet.

Once seated, Craig's mama stabilized—at least she didn't slide back down to the floor. I went to the cupboard and pulled out a fifth of gin that I'd seen on my last visit. I poured a stiff shot in a grapefruit-colored plastic tumbler and brought it to the table.

Not one word had been spoken.

I sat down facing Lola. Sammy jumped in my lap, dancing for our attention.

"How?" she asked.

That one-word question could have been Lola Thigman's entire character profile. She was a realist. Nine hundred and ninety-nine out of a thousand mothers would have asked, begged for me to tell them if their son was still alive. But Lola knew.

I had these thoughts while staying silent because I didn't want to answer the question.

"Tell me," Lola demanded after her second swallow of cheap liquor.

"Somebody shot him."

She scrutinized me and then said, "In his apartment?"

"Yes."

"Did he shoot back?"

"It doesn't look like it. Did he own a weapon?"

"He brought back a rifle and a pistol from Vietnam. One time, when I had this boyfriend wouldn't let go, he offered me the pistol—for self-defense."

"You still have it?"

"Never took it," she said, shaking her head. "There's not a man alive could reduce me to that kind of fear."

"I'm so sorry, Lola."

For a dozen beats of a fast jazzman's drum she was on the edge of tears. Then she took in a deep breath and asked, "Did somebody call the police? Is that how they found him?"

"I found him. He'd been dead two or three days."

"And nobody heard it?"

"If they did they didn't call the cops. Maybe, maybe whoever did it used a silencer. You know the more I looked into the case the more it looked like there was mob activity around the edges."

There was something going on behind Lola's dark eyes. Already I'd seen the despair and regret, but now there was a hint of guilt.

"I don't have any more money, Easy."

"I'm not asking you for it."

"Yes," she said. "But I have something to ask you."

"What's that?"

"In all the work you've done, have you come up with anything that would identify my son's killers?"

Sammy had fallen asleep in my lap.

On September 19, I'd be entering my fiftieth year. Age doesn't teach much, but the years leave enough breaks and bruises to cause a man to take a moment before leaping. Lola appreciated this fact, silently. She waited for my answer because she'd made more leaps than any Olympic gymnast or common grasshopper.

"Have you ever heard of a man named Eddie Brock?" I asked.

"No. Why? Who is he?"

I reached into a pocket for the photograph that Brock had given me, waited a moment, then pulled it out and laid it on the table.

"That's Donata, Donata Delphine," Lola said. "What about her?"

"Your son had me looking for the guy he might have killed. He said the name was Alonzo."

"Did you find him?"

"I found a man named Alonzo."

"And was he dead?"

I nodded.

"So Craig did kill him. Maybe this was revenge."

"I doubt that."

"Why?"

"Craig said he stabbed somebody. The man I found was shot."

"I don't understand."

"The dead man had a photograph of the woman you call Donata in his wallet. Another guy, Mr. Eddie Brock, gave me this picture today. He wanted to hire me to find her."

Lola blinked rapidly three times.

"Craig liked her," she began, "but only as a friend. She needed help."

"What kind of help?"

"A boyfriend she had to get away from. Her and him liked rough sex but he had gotten too wild. She'd been to the emergency room twice."

"You think she'd ever been out to Blood Grove in Orange County?"

"Craig took her out there a few times."

"*He* took *her*?"

"Yeah. Of course. A long time ago, when Craig was a child, I had this boyfriend whose family once owned the orchard. He'd take us up there for picnics. I didn't walk around much but Leonard showed Craig all over the place. That boy treated the whole property like it was his."

"Why didn't you tell me that before?"

"I didn't think it was important."

"That's where Craig said he stabbed the man named Alonzo."

"He just told me that he'd gotten into a fight over a woman and that the man was stabbed. He didn't mention Blood Grove or Donata. I would have said something if I knew."

"Do you know how I can get in touch with her?"

"We weren't friends or anything. Craig brought her by for dinner one day. I think he thought she'd like me because I did the circuit in my day like she is now."

Life is one long side street with about a million crossroads, Sorry used to tell me when I was a boy. *Every hour, sometimes every minute, you got to make the choice'a which way to go. Some of them turns don't matter but don't let that fool ya. The minute you start to think that one way is just like t'other, that's when the shit come down.*

The shit was definitely coming down. Somewhere I'd started to believe I could survive any path set before me. But right then Lola was that passway and she represented a journey filled with ruts and vipers and highwaymen too.

"Is Lola your real name?" I asked.

"No," she said. "It's Clementine."

"Clemmie, do you want this dog?"

"I can't take care of a dog. I know Craig loved that little beast, so me taking him would not be good. He'd escape through a hole in the screen on Tuesday and I wouldn't remember to realize he was gone until the weekend. Maybe you know somebody with a kid would like it?"

"Yeah," I said. "Pack up some stuff like you were going away for a week."

"Why?"

"Bad people are after your son, at least they were. They think he possessed something important to them. I have no idea what that something is, do you?"

"I swear I don't."

"I kept your identity from the police but enough people know who you are and where you live. So the best thing for you is to be somewhere else."

"You think that Donata was involved?"

"I think you should pack a bag."

Lola stood up from the chair, causing a squeal on the linoleum. The sound woke Sammy. He jumped down—ready to go with his new family.

Lola took a step and then stopped.

"Why did you ask about my real name?"

"Because if you lied about it I would have left you on your own to sink or swim."

She gave me a questioning glance and then walked off toward her bedroom; her crossroad chosen—and mine too.

24

There was a hotel called the Pink Palace on the Venice boardwalk back then. It was run by Esther Maron, a woman who had once been married to a friend of mine who died. The Palace was a more or less safe haven for anyone wanting to drop out of sight.

"Will this do?" I asked the mother whose grief had finally come to an end. We were standing in the parlor of a fairly large two-room suite. From the third-floor window you could see the rippling Pacific in fading summer light.

"It's beautiful here," she said sadly.

"You know the drill, right?"

"Don't talk to anyone I know. Definitely don't tell anyone where I am. Just look at the water and wait for you to call or come."

"Me or Fearless Jones."

I put a hand on her shoulder. This caused her to turn away from the eternal sway of blue.

"I could have saved Craig if he told me the truth," I said.

"I'm not lying to you, Easy. I'm not no fool."

"I want you to stay here until I say otherwise," I told my dead client's mother.

"I might decide to go out to the desert," she said. "Palm Springs. A place called the Summer Sands. If I'm gone from here that's where I'll be."

"Anybody else know to look for you there?"

"Only Craig."

* * *

Feather was asleep on the downstairs divan near the koi pond. She was using an old army blanket that I'd brought home from the European campaign. I sidled up next to the settee wondering if I should let her sleep out the night where she was. But then Sammy jumped up on the blanket and began licking her face mercilessly.

Feather woke up laughing, pulling the puppy from side to side by his jowls and ears. They were best friends for life just that fast.

"What's his name?" Feather asked.

"Sammy."

Suddenly a high-pitched bark shouted out. Sammy stopped romping and jumped down to the floor, where Frenchie sat erect, staring at the interloper. The puppy crouched down in obeisance and another relationship was formed. The pup was already nearly twice the size of the little yellow dog, but Frenchie was the boss.

"Sorry I'm late," I said while Sammy sniffed and Frenchie nipped.

"That's okay, Daddy. I was waiting for you but I guess I fell asleep. Whose dog is that?"

"Yours."

She stood up to hug me, then leaned back to appraise my appearance.

"What you lookin' at?" I asked.

"Juice always told me to look you over when you come in late. He said that that was the way to tell if you were in trouble."

Jesus, called Juice by his friends, was Feather's adoptive brother. He'd been taking care of me ever since I took him in back in the early fifties.

"So what's bothering you, daughter mine?"

"Who said anything was?"

"That blanket did."

"The blanket talks to you?"

"You only wrap up in that old rag when you're feeling sad or upset."

Youth is beautiful. Feather's eyes were clear and unafraid of the monster standing next to her.

"I'm scared to meet my uncle but I really want to too."

"What are you afraid of?"

"Most of my friends get so mad at their parents. They can hardly wait to grow up and move away. They don't have fathers like you or brothers like Juice."

"What does that have to do with your uncle Milo?"

"I don't know. I'm worried that if I go see him then somebody might take me away."

"If they tried I'd send you to Monaco," I said with complete conviction.

Sammy had started licking Feather's fingers under Frenchie's scrutiny.

"To Bonnie?"

Bonnie had been my girlfriend most of Feather's life. We broke up because I didn't know how to let her help me. So instead she ran to Ghana with an infirm tribal prince—a man who needed her more.

"Yes," I said, "to Bonnie."

"I thought you hated each other."

"No, baby. We hurt each other but the love's still there. I talk to her once a month or so. That's how I knew that she and Joguye ran to Europe."

"She said she'd take me?"

"Without hesitation."

Feather yawned. I lifted her into my arms. By the time I'd carried her to the bed she was sound asleep.

I took the dogs downstairs and fed them a ritual meal. Ten

minutes later they were curled up together, asleep in Frenchie's bed.

Feather was still asleep when I looked in on her at 5:00 a.m.

I brewed French roast coffee in the electric percolator and drank the bitter brew with butter and strawberry jam on pumpernickel rye.

After breakfast I went upstairs to the roses and my daily cigarette. I then called my answering service.

"I got any messages?" I asked Renata Forman when she answered.

"Only one, Mr. Rawlins," she replied. "A Mr. Oldstein called and said that he needed to talk to you about a woman named D-Donata Delp, uh, Delphine. He said that he'd come to your office at around eight this morning. I told him that this was Saturday but he said that you'd want this information."

"Did he leave a number?"

"No, sir, he did not."

I parked in front of the WRENS-L offices a few minutes past 6:00, figuring to be there early so I could reconnoiter this Mr. Oldstein before he got to see me. I locked and bolted the first-floor private entrance and then set up a stool at the upper window so I could watch the street without being seen.

Waiting was, and is, the detective's stock-in-trade. It felt good sitting in shadow while the sun bore down on the place my quarry would reveal himself. I spent thirty-six minutes watching for what the morning would bring.

It wasn't yet 7:00 when a late-model emerald-green Caddy pulled up behind John's Pontiac. There was no one on the street that early on a Saturday morning.

Three men got out of the luxury car. They were all big men, white men; not businessmen, but bruisers who meant business. Two wore pale-colored, short-sleeved, loose-fitting, button-up shirts. The last member of the squad was Eddie Brock. His suit looked to be sharkskin. Fitting attire.

The men walked as a unit to the front door. I couldn't see them when they got that close to the building, but I heard the doorknob refusing to turn and then the muscular jostling of the lower door. I checked the .45 revolver in my hand and silently praised Whisper Natly for insisting that the access door on the bottom floor be solid, steel reinforced, and anchored in an unmovable frame.

Downstairs the men banged and pounded; then it sounded like they were trying to pick the lock. When everything failed they moved back to the curb and looked up at my spy window.

I leaned into the darkest corner, still watching. Brock peered into the shadows that cloaked me. After another failed foray at the entrance the men went back to the car and waited for an hour and forty-seven minutes.

Sitting there watching from darkness, I wondered what had changed. Why did Eddie Brock mean me harm? And how much harm? No one worked on a Saturday. He and his men could have killed me easily.

I waited a full hour after they'd gone before going back downstairs to my car.

I'd made it up to Sunset and was tooling down the Strip when, on impulse, I stopped at a phone booth and called Terry Aldrich's hippie house.

I was leaning up against John's Pontiac and drinking a paper cup of coffee when Milo came down to meet me.

"What's up, Mr. Rawlins?" he asked me.

"You wanna meet your niece?"

"You guys live here?" Milo asked as we strolled down the blue-brick path of Brighthope Canyon. "I mean, this is like a rich man's neighborhood."

"You can't have one rich man without a hundred poor standing right behind him," I said, quoting the long-ago philosopher Sorry.

For some reason the quote silenced the young uncle.

The door to Roundhouse was locked. This I took as a good sign, giving me hope for no sensible reason whatever.

I used my key and we walked in.

"Feather!"

"Yeah!" she hollered from upstairs.

I realized that Milo had yet to cross the threshold.

The two dogs, yellow and black, came out barking, already a perfectly calibrated guard team.

Beyond the yelps and woofs I could hear Feather's fast feet on the third floor.

"Come on in, Milo," I said to the suddenly shy hippie.

He sidled left and right before putting a foot forward. As he came into the raised foyer Feather hit the top step of the first-floor stairway. He'd made it two paces into Roundhouse and Feather was halfway down when they beheld each other.

From this first encounter I knew that I'd made the right decision. They bore the same expression: eyes wide with mouths slightly agape. They'd stopped moving and started feeling.

"Milo," I said, "meet Feather. Feather, this here's your uncle."

The dogs went silent and retreated toward the koi pond.

Feather descended and Milo stepped up. When they came into proximity Milo put out a hand that Feather grabbed by the wrist. She pulled him into a filial embrace, holding on tight.

When they finally let go Milo just looked at her, amazement across his face.

"What?" Feather asked.

"You," he said. "You look just like Robin did, like your mother did when I was a kid."

"Should I go upstairs and make breakfast?" I offered.

"Come on, let's sit near the pond while we wait," Feather told her uncle.

That day, after the troubled early morning, was an oasis, far away from the Kilian job. Feather taught her uncle Milo how to swim. He showed her a family photograph album with pictures that included her mother and went all the way back to her great-great-grandparents who'd migrated to the U.S. from northern England before the Great War.

Breakfast and lunch were huge meals created by me and devoured by youngsters who had been starving for each other's company for what felt like forever to them.

"Why does my grandmother hate me?" Feather asked Milo in the middle afternoon.

We were all, humans and dogs, sitting around the koi pond. I hadn't thought about Eddie Brock or dead Craig Kilian in hours.

"She doesn't hate you," Milo said. There was a maturity in his voice I hadn't noticed before. "She's afraid of you."

"Afraid of me? I'm just a kid. What could I do?"

"It's not what you would do," Milo said. "It's who you are. You see, our parents brought me and Robin up to be good Americans, to believe in others. We learned their lessons, but when we started living lives where we knew all kinds of different people who had different ideas, they became afraid of what might happen. Robin lived with a black man and then I grew up and grew my hair long."

"But my mom was a good person," Feather argued against absent grandparents.

Milo heard her and managed not to cry.

At around 4:00 I suggested that Agosto Longo give Milo a ride back down to the Strip.

"I think we've had enough for the day, don't you, Uncle Milo?" I said.

He and Feather hugged goodbye.

I called Agosto on Brighthope's closed-circuit phone and sent Milo down on the funicular. He left the photo album for Feather and she hugged it tight, not letting go even in her sleep.

25

I was looking out from the veranda at the sliver of the ocean. There was a half moon just out of sight that made that little strip of the Pacific glitter. I had been graced with one of the most important moments in my daughter's life. She was no longer alone and rudderless; she had a history.

When nighttime deepened I was still staring. The Brighthope phone rang and, reluctantly, I headed for it.

"Hello?"

"It's the French girl," Cosmo said.

Not a trio of killers at any rate.

"Send her up."

I met Asiette at the dais where the funicular docked. She ran into my arms and kissed me like we had been apart for years. I didn't complain.

"I am so sorry, Easy," she said when the kisses subsided. She wore a pale and thin silk violet dress that fluttered slightly.

"For what?" I asked, putting my arm around her and guiding her back toward Roundhouse.

"I broke up with Stefano at dinner tonight," she said as if that were an answer.

"Why?"

I'd like to say that it meant nothing to me that a beautiful

Frenchwoman dropped her rich Italian boyfriend and then ran to my bed. I'd like to say it didn't matter but in fact I felt it in what prim romance writers called *the nether regions.*

"He was angry that we are lovers," Asiette explained.

"I thought everything was open season until somebody came up with a ring?"

"Not open for tall handsome black men who aren't impressed by Stefano's wealth and fancy clothes."

I stopped on the blue-brick road and kissed her. I had to.

She smiled and, when we started moving again, she said, "He wasn't the right man for me. And . . . and after tonight I will have to stop seeing you too."

I think she wanted me to say something or ask something, but I stayed silent because I agreed with both of her decisions.

"Because," she continued, "as long as I see you I will want you."

We made love as quietly as a couple can when they know this might be the last time. Afterward we sat intertwined on the veranda beneath a quilt of silver and gold cloth.

The telephone rang.

"You 'ave replaced me already?" Asiette teased.

"I told her not to call until after you fell asleep."

"Easy?"

"It's kinda late, isn't it, Lola?"

"I can't sleep and I don't know what to do. As long as I knew I'd be talking to Craig in a day or so I felt calm, peaceful. But now he's dead and . . ."

"I understand," I said. "I have a son about Craig's age."

"You do?"

"He's adopted but I love him so much that I couldn't imagine the world without him in it."

We were both silent for a time there.

"Did you just want to talk to with somebody?" I asked after a while.

"Donata Delphine used to work for the Stephanopoulos Talent Agency."

"Oh." I scribbled down the name on a little pad I kept next to the first-floor extension.

"I had forgotten it before. She just mentioned it that time Craig brought her over. It's up on Sunset, the talent agency is. She told me that she got fired because of dating one of the clients."

"I thought she was a burlesque dancer."

"She does a lot of things, but through all of it that girl has ambition. She won't stop until she's on top of the mountain or underneath it."

"Anything else about her?"

"Like what?"

"Who else she worked for, if maybe there was somebody angry when she got dismissed. Maybe the name of the client she was dating."

"I don't, I don't remember. She turned up her nose at the little bit of money the modeling agency paid. Like all young, beautiful women she thought she was worth her weight in gold."

I felt a hand on my bare back and actually gasped.

"What's wrong?" Lola asked.

"Nothing," I said, turning my eyes to Asiette. "I just thought I saw a mouse."

The French girl had donned her violet dress and also an old orange, button-up sweater that I let her wear sometimes when she got cold.

"Oh my God," Lola moaned. "You got to fumigate. If you see one there's a thousand."

Asiette kissed me and then moved on along the inside stream. The touch, kiss, and the fact she did all this while I was on a call meant that she was emphasizing the break between us. We might never see each other as lovers again.

"One time me and Craig had to move out of my house for a week because of rodents," Lola was saying.

I let her talk because it seemed to make her feel better.

As Lola jabbered Asiette made her way to the door and let herself out.

"It was just a shadow," I said. "Nothing real."

I didn't sleep that night. Asiette's overly dramatic breakup made me feel alone. And because I had serious problems before me, I found that I was able to concentrate on how to pursue a case where the client was dead. I still hadn't accomplished the tasks Craig and his mother had set before me. The man Craig had stabbed and the woman that man had savaged were yet to be accurately identified. And there was a third man, that's what Christmas Black said.

"How old is Uncle Milo?" Feather asked at the breakfast table later that morning.

"Twenty-five or six," I said. "Why did you want him to swim with you?"

"He needed a bath," she said, crinkling her nose. "Can I call him sometime?"

I wanted to say no. I wanted to protect her from anything that might bring her pain.

"There's a number in my phone book for a guy named Terry Aldrich. Call there and ask for Milo."

She grinned and nodded.

"But, Feather," I said in a stern tone.

She looked up at me, sans smile.

"I don't want him up here unless I'm with you."

"Okay."

After that we ate our shirred eggs and bacon, strawberry jam on pumpernickel, and figs cooked in their own juices.

When the house phone rang I was wondering about the Stephanopoulos Talent Agency.

"Hello?"

"I need to see you," Melvin Suggs rumbled.

"It's Sunday," I complained.

"And you think murder's gonna take the day off and go to church to confess?"

"Talk about what?"

"Face-to-face," he said. "The usual place."

When Melvin was gruff like that he most often hung up without another word. But the phone made some airy noises and a woman's voice came over the line.

"Hey, Easy," Mary Donovan said. "How are you?"

"Okay. How about you, Mary?"

"Still in the same skin and liking it just fine, thank you very much."

Our chatter seemed to be about nothing on the surface of things, but Mary and I communicated on subterranean levels. Just the fact she got on the line told me that this meeting with Mel was going to be something serious.

Mary liked me because she loved Mel and believed that I was his best friend in the business of being a cop.

She might have been right.

26

Roger's twenty-four-hour diner was on Exeter in the heart of downtown—as much as LA had a downtown back in those days. The restaurant had a plate-glass window-wall that looked out on the street. In the old days Melvin would order three eggs over easy with sides of pork sausage and maplewood bacon along with a slab of baked ham.

But that morning he supped on a cup of oatmeal with no raisins, brown sugar, or cream.

He was sitting in a booth next to the window frowning at his repast when I slid into the seat across from him.

He looked up, a beast with beautiful eyes, and squinted.

"It's a couple of things," he said.

I was wearing a blue sports coat, cotton brown trousers, and a yellow shirt open at the throat. If Mary's implied warning was as bad as it sounded I might get arrested and forced to take a mug shot; if that was the case I wanted to look good.

"Yesterday evening," Suggs recited, "a report came in from a San Bernardino heist that went down two and a half months ago."

"I remember that one," I said. "They stole the whole armored car."

"Along with three guards—presumed dead. They got away with something like eighty-six thousand dollars."

"How many in the crew?" I asked.

Mel didn't like his flow interrupted but he said, "A witness happened to be driving by just as three Negroes wearing construction clothes were winching what he later realized was an armored car into the back of a big rig."

"Would'a had to been a semi," I said, adding, "hardly worth the weight on a serious crime like that for less than thirty thousand dollars apiece."

"Is there any dollar amount that would make it okay for someone to murder a man?"

"Aw, c'mon, Mel. You know what I mean. You think I could do something to help you and San Bernardino find these guys?"

"And so we come to Craig Kilian," Suggs replied.

I felt a chill at the back of my neck and wished, absurdly, I had killed that long-ago German soldier.

"What about him?"

"He was shot dead at close quarters and nobody heard a thing," the head cop opined. "We found a stack of hundred-dollar bills from the armored car job in an envelope in his closet. The wrapper was from the bank the car was delivering for."

I loved being a PI. The work suited me. It didn't matter much that Suggs was wrapping a chain around the box he thought I was in. The case was starting to come clear and I liked that.

"I have no idea about any money from a robbery," I said. "The kid wanted me to find a girl named Dee Dee. I couldn't and went to his place to tell him so."

"You happen on the name of Alonzo Griggs," Melvin said, holding up his left thumb. "He's been suspected of midlevel bank robberies and heists throughout Southern California." That brought out the point finger of the same hand. "Now your *client* shows up dead and you're the one that found him." The fuck-you finger accompanied that little sarcasm. "You wanna tell me right now where this Dee Dee is buried?"

Melvin Suggs was the best cop I had ever met. He was dogged, courageous, and as honest as a man steeped in crime can afford to be. He worked for the most racist police department I had ever encountered (and that's saying something for a southern boy) but still managed to do what was right more than fifty percent of the time. Any lie I told him was likely to come out sooner or later.

"Look, Mel. Craig Kilian came to me almost a week ago with a story about having gone camping out at Blood Grove."

"Where's that?"

I told him everything up to, but not including, Eddie Brock's visitations and Lola's real name. Melvin let me go on as his oatmeal congealed.

"But the Alonzo that the kid told you about was shot," Suggs said. "There wasn't a knife wound on him."

"I know."

"Why didn't you come to me?"

"Blood Grove ain't your jurisdiction."

"There had been a murder."

"I didn't know that. The kid said that when he woke up in the morning there was no body, not even any blood. All I had was the questionable testimony of a shell-shocked vet. What the fuck would you do with that?"

"If there was a murder I would have acted."

"And the first body I found I called your man."

"You didn't tell Anatole you were looking for that man already."

"Like you said, the man I found was shot. As far as I knew this was a completely other Alonzo and a heck of a coincidence." The ice under my feet was getting a little thin.

Suggs sat back and stared at me. I was absolutely sure that he was thinking about ordering a slab of ham.

"Talk to me about the heist," he said at last.

"The first I've heard of it is here at this table."

"How do you expect me to convince anyone of that?"

"You know me, Mel. I'm good at what I do. If I thought that

there was one shred of evidence, much less a stack of hundred-dollar bills lyin' around, do you think I would have left it for the LAPD to find? And then call them to come find it?"

That was the first smile I got out of him.

"So what have you come up with?" he asked.

"I told you."

"You told me the facts as they happened—maybe. What I'm askin' is what do you think they mean?"

I liked Melvin, couldn't help it. If they fired him from the force I'd bring him into the agency. I liked him but I didn't trust anyone except maybe my children.

"Kilian obviously lied about something," I said. "I don't know about any heist, but the fact that that money made it into his apartment says that there was more involved."

"Uh-huh," he said, expecting more.

It was one of those crossroads Sorry and Robert Johnson had warned me about. Me putting the cops on Brock, a man I was sure had his fingers in a lot of pies, would be like shaving my head and then drawing a big white bull's-eye on the back of my skull.

"I found a picture at Alonzo's that might have been the girl Kilian was looking for."

"You held back evidence?"

"Look, man, either we talkin' or I'm walkin', all right?"

Melvin looked around to make sure no one was watching and then nodded.

I took the picture I got from Alonzo Griggs's wallet and handed it over.

"So this is the girl the dead vet was lookin' for?"

"I suspect so but I don't know for sure. I showed it to the kid and he acted like he didn't recognize her. But I had the feeling he was hiding something."

"What else?"

"I should be askin' you that."

"What does that mean?"

"Come on, Mel. We talkin' here, right?"

Policemen hate giving civilians information. It's like a river flowing upstream, birds migrating north for the winter.

"The SBPD have a couple'a their guys here in LA lookin' for the black crew that took down the armored car. One name they floated was Alonzo Griggs."

"Why didn't they come question me?" I asked. "Is that why you're here now?"

"They haven't heard your name."

"Wouldn't Anatole tell them?"

"I told him to keep it to himself. The three SBPD detectives got a room at city hall. Some deal they got with the mayor. Chief Brown doesn't like that they're given special treatment and has asked me, personally, to find the perpetrators and make the arrests before they do."

"So now you got me in the crosshairs."

"I'm just sayin' that you got a problem that dovetails with mine."

We were both pretty quiet there for a moment. Now I had two police departments, two dead bodies, maybe three more dead bodies, a gang of desperate heist men, a gangster, and a grieving mother pressing up against me.

All that might have gotten me nervous if it weren't for my participation at the Battle of the Bulge.

My expression must have communicated that thought because Suggs smiled and handed me a card. It was his regular business card but on the back he had scrawled, *If Ezekiel Rawlins presents this card to you call the number below . . .*

"I see you expected me to take you up on this," I said.

"You get six percent of all monies recovered and I forget about your little misdemeanors."

* * *

I went home to get Feather and then drove us both up to a motel I knew in Isla Vista. There we swam in the ocean; I for forty-five minutes and she for two and a half hours.

Exhausted, we went to Benny's Seafood Shack and ate shellfish until the sun went down.

Our room had two single beds and we were both dead tired.

"Daddy?" Feather called out from the darkness.

"Yes, Genevieve?"

"I'm not gonna use that name."

"Okay. What were you going to ask?"

"I think my life is just about perfect."

"Me too," I said, and then I was asleep.

The Stephanopoulos Talent Agency was on the south side of Sunset Boulevard a few blocks east of La Cienega. The Gruen chronometer said it was 11:07 in the morning when I parked John's green Pontiac across the street from there. It was a cheaply constructed building, three floors high with the front walls made from glass. The visual effect was something like the plastic ant farms that children used to watch emmets aimlessly tunneling, their hearts thundering for a queen that does not exist.

There might have been eighteen employees and of them there were only women visible. No elevators, so you could see them climbing and descending the stairways, sitting at desks, and walking from here to there. The women were of all races. That was the late sixties and rock 'n' roll had taught us that difference sold. These women were office workers but they were hired for their age and looks as well as their secretarial skills. This made sense to me because the business concerned itself with beauty. That's what they bought and sold.

Fourteen minutes passed before I got out of the car. The lag was because I had learned to reconnoiter a place before going in. That way you knew what to expect, or at least had a good idea how things worked. Most detectives learned that skill on the job, but I had been practicing my entire life. Poor blacks from the Deep South had to keep on the lookout for trouble; either that or fall into its trap.

* * *

I walked in the front door and up to the high podium-like reception desk. A young woman with impossibly long eyelashes looked up from a paperback book she was reading, giving me an insincere smile. She had Asian blood and also some Caucasian flowing in her veins. There was something darker there too but I couldn't quite tell what.

"Can I help you?" She dog-eared the book and laid it facedown.

"What you readin'?" I asked.

The question threw her off her game a little. It wasn't the kind of question that should be on my mind. At least not the first thing I'd ask.

"*Myra Breckinridge*," she said with a twist to her lips that added, *Something you wouldn't know a thing about.*

"Oh, that book by Gore Vidal. Came out last year, right?"

"Um. Did you read it?"

"Only skimmed," I said. "There was too much sex for an old man like me."

The young woman's practiced smile turned into an honest grin.

I looked up at the high wall behind the reception desk. There were dozens of photographs tacked there upon a huge corkboard. Mostly women in various glamorous, and sometimes naked, poses. But there were also a few young men models—and one older one.

"I'm Sata," the literate receptionist offered.

"Easy Rawlins."

"That's a good name. How can I help you, Easy Rawlins?" Sata looked me up and down. I assumed that was habit for a modeling agency: most people who went in there were either in the market—or on it.

The picture with the older gentleman wasn't him alone. Five young miniskirted women stood around him smiling and touching.

Somewhere in his early forties, he wore sunglasses and a tight-brimmed Stetson. But that didn't fool me.

"Who's that?" I asked Sata, "one of your brawny man models?"

"That's Brock Oldstein. He's the owner."

"I'd like you to tell Mr. Oldstein that Easy Rawlins came to see him about Donata Delphine."

"Oh," the child of many continents said. "Um, Miss Delphine doesn't work here anymore."

"Then it'll be a short conversation."

Sata had become wary of me, showing that Miss Delphine was persona non grata and that I now fell under that shadow.

"May I have your contact information please?" The receptionist's language turned proper and her shoulder—cold.

"Mr. Oldstein already has my number . . . and now I have his."

Sitting in the driver's seat of the borrowed Pontiac, I was slowly coming to consciousness about the case I should have turned down. It's like I had been knocked out and in the middle of a dream while coming to—there was reality and then there was the dream.

In the year 1929 at the age of nine I arrived in the Fifth Ward. I was already a man and on my own. I'd jumped a boxcar outside of New Iberia and spent one day and two nights in there with dark, desperate men. I never talk about that ride . . .

After that I spent more than a week wandering the streets of the Fifth Ward asking people if they knew my grandfather, Winston Marquette, a man I had never met.

Eleven days I wandered. My mother's father most probably lived in that district somewhere, but even if he had moved, someone might remember where to. Finally, on my twelfth morning without breakfast, I came upon a woman they called Mad Mary.

"Winston Marquette!" she ejaculated. "That niggah can drank some wine. He used to come up to see me when I had a nice place.

We'd drink and then he'd have me callin' out to Jesus, thankin' the Lord he give me a body could feel so good."

Mary was weathered like a seaward wall that had taken every gust and squall the Gulf of Mexico had to offer. Her hair was coarse and half gray, her eyes still looking for that bottle of wine and a chance to praise Jesus. I remember taking her hand and squeezing it.

"I'm looking for Mr. Marquette," I said. "He's my grandfather."

"You poor child."

Along with pity Mary gave me a possible destination.

"There's a gang'a big palm trees on t'other side'a the north-bound railroad tracks, that's where Crackers Street is at. If you take Crackers across the tracks it comes Algo and if you take Algo up past three cross streets you'll see a brash blue house on your left. That there is Juanita Ferris's house. Behind that is a dirty yella shack. That's where the bastid Marquette used to live at. Maybe he still do."

Everything she said was true. The cluster of palm trees, the cross streets, the ugly blue house, and then the dingy yellow one. She was right about my grandfather too—he was a bastard. He told me that I could sleep on the front porch but that he didn't have any money to feed me or to put clothes on my back.

My grandfather and I did not get along that well, but his friend Sorry dropped by now and then to drink corn whiskey and play chess. Sorry always took the time to ask me how I was doing. After I had regaled him with my adventures and experiences he'd give me little tidbits of advice.

Sitting there across the street from the Stephanopoulos Talent Agency I remembered one day when I was tending an onion patch I kept out next to my grandfather's place.

"What kinda onion you sow, Li'l Easy?"

"Spanish onions, Uncle Sorry," I said. I must've been eleven at the time.

"You learn anything lately?" Instead of a cane the bent old man had an eight-foot driftwood staff. He leaned on it while looking down upon me.

"Me an' Billy Ray and Raymond Alexander was runnin' down this gulch like. First Billy did it runnin' through these thick bushes down there. Then Mouse, we call Raymond Mouse, he ran down the same way. I was the last to go and I made it through but I guess there was a bumblebee nest down there and that big black bumblebee barnstormed me an' hit me in the fo'head so hard that I was knocked out for fi'e minutes."

Usually when I told a story Uncle Sorry would smile. But that day he was dead serious.

"And what did you learn from that, Ezekiel?"

"I will never be last again."

Old Sorry's nostrils flared and he said, "Come here, boy. Come here."

I was a little bit afraid but that old man was one of the few people I trusted so I walked right up to him. He was fishing around his pockets for something and finally came out with a five-dollar gold piece. That was a fortune for a full-grown black man back in those days.

"I want you to keep this money with you for all the rest'a the days of your life," he said. "Keep it so that you nevah forget the lesson that bee taught you."

"Why cain't I spend it?" I asked.

"Because the lesson is more important an' it's hard for us poor mortals to remember everything. It's just not possible."

I still have that coin in my wallet. Just knowing it's there reminds me of the lesson that bee and Sorry taught—that some things we must never forget. I was thinking about Sorry; tall and thin with a high forehead and skin as black and shiny as tar. That old man who parented me was in my mind's eye when Mr. "Eddie" Brock Oldstein walked into the front door of the Stephanopoulos Talent Agency.

I could see him through the window talking to little Sata. When she told him her news he turned to look out the window. I don't believe he saw me but he knew I was there.

At that moment I understood I could not take the next step of this job on my own.

I eased out into the boulevard headed west. A few blocks away I went into Manning's Drug Store and used the pay phone to call my home phone. No one answered so I dialed another number that was answered by Matteo Longo, assigned driver for the residents of the Bowl of Brighthope.

"Did you take Feather anywhere today, Matt?"

"Down to the house where I took the hippie."

Terry answered on the first ring.

"Yeah, she's here, Easy. She's getting high with her brother out back."

I had no right to be angry with Terry. He was a hippie and hippies had a different set of rules than *straights* did. Hippies believed in free love and getting high, world peace and sharing what you have with those who don't. If I didn't want Feather to be exposed to all that, I shouldn't have put Milo there and then given her the phone number.

A very young woman wearing only a red-and-yellow tie-dyed T-shirt opened the front door of the mansion/commune; a white girl with thick, tousled black hair. She was about to ask me what I wanted but instead yawned, then stretched. The hem of the shirt rose to the top of her thighs. If she knew what she was revealing she didn't care.

"Yeah? Can I help you?"

In my sports coat and slacks she identified me as someone who was either lost or a threat. But Terry told his guests that they had to be polite to everyone.

"I'm Easy Rawlins. Terry's expecting me." I wanted to push that child aside and rush to my daughter but I had been raised on southern manners, so I stood still waiting for her to process what I'd said.

"Oh," she said. "I know about you. You're that detective guy." She said this and then stared.

"Can I come in?"

"Um. Sure. I guess."

When she stood aside I hurried across the foyer into the living room. I was headed for the kitchen but that took some fancy footwork. There were at least a dozen sleeping and partially conscious hippies spread out across the floor in sleeping bags, under blankets, and propped up on piles of clothing and knapsacks.

"Excuse me, excuse me," I said, using my hips as well as my knees to take steps forward and to the side, between arms and legs, hands and feet.

"Ow!" one big man shouted, though I was pretty sure I hadn't stepped on him.

Bounding to his feet, the long-haired, bearded man confronted me. He was in his middle twenties, big-bellied, and wild-eyed. His black T-shirt read CRAZY HOGG in bone-white letters.

"What the fuck?!" Crazy said.

I held my hands out to the side—palms up; an invitation anywhere on Earth.

Mr. Hogg looked at me and his first name shifted to *Sensible*.

"Excuse me if I stepped on you," I said. "That was not my intention."

The kitchen was empty so I went straight through the side door leading to the backyard.

There I came upon active hippies. Two lean-muscled, long-haired young men were stripped to the waist playing badminton for an audience of three naked reclining girls sunning their skins. My daughter and her uncle Milo were sitting in half lotus with another young woman under a huge avocado tree, heavy with fruit. The young woman was wearing an iridescent gold halter and bright red pants. She was in the middle of taking an epic hit off of a fat joint. This she handed to my little girl.

I held my breath.

Feather took the hand-rolled cigarette and passed it to Milo without pause.

I hadn't realized that there was murder in my heart until it evaporated. Just then Feather looked up and saw me.

"Daddy!"

I took a moment to breathe and then smiled.

Walking past the naked and semi-naked hippies, I was so relieved that nothing about the case I was chasing bothered me.

Love is a powerful balm.

The woman sitting with my daughter and her uncle rolled up onto her feet with such ease that you had to appreciate her strength. She was blond-haired with a big toothy smile, almost as tall as I, with eyes like gray diamonds. She wasn't so much beautiful as handsome in the extreme.

Feather hugged me and said, "This is Dagmar, Daddy. She's from Boulder, Colorado. She says that the college there is one of the best."

I held out a hand and the Coloradan shook it.

"Hi," she said, looking directly into my eyes. It felt as if she saw all the way to the soul. "You have a really great energy."

"You some kinda athlete?"

"Rock climber."

"Glad to meet you," I said. And that was the truth.

I greeted my daughter's uncle and suggested that the three of us go to lunch down at the Hamburger Hamlet.

". . . I was surprised myself that she came to Terry's," Milo was saying.

He'd ordered a burger with avocados, Muenster cheese, raw onions, and thick slices of beefsteak tomato. Feather got a salad and I had water.

"You know," Milo went on, "when she called and said she was coming down I thought that you'd be with her. It's some heavy shit comes down at Terry's. Not a place you'd want a kid alone."

"If you don't mind, watch your language around my daughter," I said.

That got a look from Milo. Hippies were rarely asked to watch what they said, and me claiming Feather as mine might have bothered him too.

"I'm almost grown, Daddy."

"*Almost* being the operant word."

Feather harrumphed but she couldn't repress her smile. She was happy to be with Milo and me. It felt to her like family.

After lunch I thanked Milo for taking care of my daughter. He had assured me that he'd never let her *do dope* until she was out of the house. He went back to Terry's and I drove Feather home to Brighthope.

"So what were you thinking when Dagmar handed you that marijuana cigarette?" I asked as we cruised down Sunset.

"What happened to your Rolls-Royce, Daddy?"

"I lent it to John."

"John Malcolm?"

"John the bartender. Are you gonna answer my question?"

"I don't know. I know you don't want me to smoke. But I really wanted to talk to Uncle Milo. And Dagmar had been playing badminton and came over to talk. She had the joint and shared it with him."

"I don't want you going down to that house anymore. It's too much for a young girl like you."

"Okay."

Okay. I wanted her to tell me that she'd never do drugs, drink alcohol, have sex, never leave home, and that she would stay my child forever. But all I could hope for was *okay*.

Within the first week of moving into Roundhouse I installed a telephone in a waterproof tin box on the roof. That way I could commune with my roses and talk business in a place that was private.

There I made a call.

The phone rang twelve times before I hung up. I waited a minute or two, then dialed the number again. Still no answer.

There was a new number folded on a slip of paper in my wallet. I hadn't thought that I'd ever use it, but now that Feather was safe my mind was back on the case. I felt a sense of urgency because looking for Donata Delphine felt like sitting at the bottom of a deep hole that was threatening to cave in.

"Hello," she said in her sexy, throaty, *act right or I might kill you* voice.

"Hey, Lihn."

"Easy. Where'd you get . . . Oh, sure." She shouted, "Raymond!" Then in a normal tone, "He'll be here in a minute, Easy."

It was an odd interchange. Lihn felt like an old friend from down home, someone who, with just a few words, you understood and who understood you.

"Hey, Easy," Mouse said before that feeling about Lihn could adapt into understanding. "What's happenin'?"

"I called your house first, but nobody was home."

"Etta gone to take care'a her cousin Jillian. You know Jill up north in Richmond workin' for the post office. But she got the pneumonia and is laid up."

"So you moved in with Lihn?"

"We went to a magic show last night, man. Brothah, that shit was crazy."

Raymond Alexander only gave simple answers out of the muzzle of a gun or off the edge of a knife.

"I think I might need a little help, Ray."

"That's a happy coincidence," he said. "I might need a little sumpin' from you too."

"Hold tight and I'll call back soon." I cradled the receiver and for maybe eleven seconds I wondered about the term *happy coincidence*. Then I dragged my daughter down to my borrowed car and drove.

"Where we goin', Daddy?"

"Jackson's house."

"Why can't I stay at home?"

"I might not get home on time and then all I'd do is worry."

Little Anzio wasn't very crowded at that time of day. Only the bartender and three men sitting at a far table inhabited the down-at-heel saloon. The men were speaking loudly but their words were incoherent, suffering from alcohol, three lifetimes of cigarette smoke, and the fact that each one was trying to outtalk the other.

The skinny lad named Meanie was still bartending, but due to a lack of active customers he was sitting on a barstool reading the *LA Times*.

"How you doin'?" I greeted him.

He stared at me quizzically for a moment and then said, "Oh yeah, you're that guy from the other day. The one Bernard tried to brain with that Coke bottle."

"Yeah."

"What can I get ya?"

"You keep any schnapps back there?"

Meanie grinned and said, "European theater?"

"Yeah."

"All you boys that marched into Germany got a taste for their liquor and their women." He folded the paper and stood up straight. "I got this raspberry stuff in the fridge out back. Won't take a minute."

He left through a side door and I turned my back to the bar. The men in the corner were happily shouting. I was engulfed by one of those beatific moments, certain that everything would be all right for the next few minutes. It was that peaceful lull soldiers experience in wartime. Nobody was shooting at you right then and orders from behind the lines were to hold your position. Maybe there was a letter from home in your pocket or some cards or dominoes coming out of a buddy's backpack.

Those oases of calm between battles were moments of grace rarely paralleled in peacetime.

"Here you go, Mr. Rawlins," Meanie said.

He'd returned to his post behind the bar having served up three fingers of the clear liquor in a squat whiskey glass.

I took a sip. It was sweet and chilly on the tongue but savory and warm going down.

"Pretty damn good."

Meanie smiled.

"You remember my name," I said.

"That's a bartender's job. Remembering drinks, names, and tabs."

I looked at the young man. Slender, he'd probably been in shape at one time, but now his only exercise came from those duties the bar demanded. When he moved there seemed to be a hitch involved. Like if he swiveled to pick up a bottle with his left hand, the right shoulder resisted a moment before falling into the flow.

"Vietnam?" I asked.

"Yeah." He blinked and nodded.

"What you do over there?"

"Same thing. The men in my family been tending bar since they were called taverns and decent women weren't allowed. I was the daytime bartender in the American officers' club in Saigon."

"That where you got wounded?"

Meanie took in a deep breath and nodded.

"In Saigon. Not the club, though," he said. "We was out whorin' at this hotel they called Big Fish. They served real bourbon and had the finest bar girls in the city. They only played American and English rock 'n' roll on the jukebox and after a few drinks the war seemed like it was about ten thousand miles away. The girl I was with was called, um, uh, Duyen. Yeah, Duyen.

"By the time we were through it was way after curfew. On top of that a midnight convoy was crossing the street and stopped us up for at least five minutes. Marcus was riding shotgun. I was in the back behind the driver, a Mexican guy called Ernesto. This kid come up next to the car. He couldn'ta been no more than ten, eleven. He asked Marcus for a buck. That's what he said, 'Gives us a buck, Mistah Yankee. Gives us a buck . . .' "

Meanie stopped talking for a few seconds, his eyes piercing the veil of time. History unfolded before that gaze. It wasn't good or bad, right or wrong—just a series of events that were as certain as if they had been carved in bone.

"When Marcus reached into his vest pocket, Lance, the guy to my right, said, 'Don't give that little gook shit, Marky. He probably . . .' That's when the kid slung this canvas bag he had through the air. It smacked down between Ernesto and Marcus. We all hollered. The kid was makin' tracks. I saw a white light but didn't hear the explosion, didn't hear it, but all my friends were dead."

That was the sole purpose of Little Anzio. Vets could tell their stories plainly without pity or disdain. They didn't even have to hate anymore; just feel the ride and honor the sacrifice.

"How you like that schnapps, Mr. Rawlins?" Meanie asked.

"Tastes like springtime in Bavaria."

Meanie grinned but that wasn't the end of it. A story like he told

was a gift and it was expected among our tribe to tell your tale—
like throwing another log on an eternal flame.

"We were among the first soldiers to march into Auschwitz-
Birkenau," I said as if responding to a question. "My buddy was a
black boy from Charleston, South Carolina, named Oliver Sams.
That was at the end of the war and the army had been integrated
by attrition. So many whites and blacks had been killed or wounded
that we had to come together to make up our companies and
squads. We filed past hundreds of living skeletons with the dead
piled around them and lying at their feet. The smell of rotting
human flesh was strong.

"After the victims we marched by the officers. The commandant
was in a wheelchair. He was out of it. But his number two was in
full SS dress uniform standing at attention. He was sneering at us
dirty GIs. But what did we care? We'd already won the war.

"The problem was that we were the first two black soldiers to
pass the number two. When he saw me and Oliver he said, 'Nigger,'
almost like he was a redneck from Mississippi. Oliver stopped and
said, 'What did you say?' and the number two repeated the word.
I watched while my buddy's hand went to his pistol. He asked
what maybe half a dozen times until that gun was in his hand and
pointed at the SS man. The German repeated the word and Oliver
shot him in the chest somewhere. The Nazi went down on one knee
and Oliver took a step toward him. He asked the German *what*
one more time. With gaspin' breath he said, 'Nigger,' and Oliver
emptied the clip into him."

Meanie had poured me another few fingers of schnapps. I took a
sip and again it tasted like spring.

"When I think about that day I remember the roar that came from
the skeletons, the men and women that had seen that man murder
thousands of them. They cheered his death. But what got to me was
that not one American, black or white, tried to stop Oliver. And

Oliver couldn't've stopped himself for love nor money. That whole camp—from the Jewish survivors to that SS man who just couldn't keep his mouth shut—none of us could do any different."

After a few minutes of Meanie cleaning, me sipping, and the men in the corner laughing at one thing or another, Meanie asked, "They said that you were askin' about Craig Kilian the other day."

"Craig's dead."

"Really?"

"Yeah. He was shot in his own apartment. Anyway he hired me to find a guy named Alonzo and a woman, probably going by the name Donata Delphine."

"You still lookin'?"

"I took his money."

"But there's nobody to report to."

"I like to do the jobs I'm asked to do. That way I feel a sense of accomplishment even if it was all for nothing."

The barkeep considered my words in deep self-reflection.

"Well," he said. "I don't know those names, but Kirkland Larker and Craig been thick as thieves for the past two months. If anybody knows, Kirk does."

I was thinking about the phrase *thick as thieves* when I asked, "What's Larker's thing?"

"He got drummed outta the army four years back. Two and a half of them he spent in Leavenworth."

"For what?"

"Thievery. They gave him a dishonorable discharge so the regular VA didn't like him but he had some friends in the bar. Seems like he was a pretty good soldier when he was out in the field."

I showed Meanie the picture Brock gave me, the shot of Donata Delphine.

"You ever seen her?"

Meanie shook his head. "No. But Larker had a girl. Real pretty black girl. She dressed fine and filled out those clothes like nobody's business. Kirk used to say that she was his golden ticket. Said she could get him through any door."

"You remember her name?"

"Yeah. It was an odd one. Mona Strael. I remember because I asked where the name Strael came from and she said, 'Outta thin air.' "

30

I sat around Little Anzio until closing time, which was 2:00 a.m. I was hoping for Kirkland Larker to show but he never did. Still, I sipped schnapps slowly and talked to anyone who drifted my way. Because I was buying the drinks most everyone took up temporary residence on a stool next to mine. In that way I learned a little bit.

A guy named Mike told me that Larker offered to help get him a job somewhere.

"You remember where?" I asked.

"Not really. It sounded kinda chinky. You know I used to scuba dive near Seoul. But one day I was down there and I saw about ten thousand shrimp swarming a corpse. They'd been at that guy for so long that he was no more than a raggedy skeleton . . ."

A man calling himself Captain Fell told me, "Kilian and Larker are malingerers," and that he expected both men to end up in front of a firing squad.

I didn't enlighten him as to Craig's end. I guess I didn't want to give him the satisfaction.

It was almost 3:00 in the morning when I pulled up to the Dragon's Eye. Through the alley on the right side of the establishment was the parking lot. I really had no plan in mind. Feather was at Jackson Blue's and the two bars were the only places I knew that my quarries might have been.

There were about half a dozen cars spaced out around the lot. Sounds of something akin to love came from a couple of them. I walked the perimeter, stopped in a dark corner to brood for a quarter hour or so, then headed back for my car. I was just about to put the key in the ignition when I saw Montana coming from around the side of the building followed by a blowsy businessman. She was pulling him by one finger as he staggered behind.

"Montana," I called.

"Oh. Hi, baby."

"Who the fuck are you?" the businessman demanded. He wore a blue suit that sizzled in the electric light. He was burnished tan and carried about thirty-five pounds more than a doctor would advise. Maybe at his office that extra weight was seen as strength. But in a back alley it didn't mean a damn thing.

Before I could answer the question Montana put her lips to the john's ear and whispered something.

"Wha'?" he said. "I didn't know that. How you expect me to know that?"

He looked at me with worried eyes while teetering backward and to his left, moving toward a late-model Cadillac. In the few seconds it took Montana to sashay up to me, the businessman was in his car.

"What did you say to him?" I asked the bar girl.

The Cadillac engine roared to life.

"That you were my boyfriend." She took my left hand and swung it from side to side like a country girl might after a barn dance. "You here to collect on that forty dollars?"

The Caddy and its businessman were gone. The lot seemed preternaturally quiet, the last spasms of love spent.

"Donata Delphine," I said.

"You give her forty dollars?"

"I haven't met her yet."

"Yet?"

"There's a few questions of mine that she might could answer."

"What kinda questions?" She was still holding my hand gently. I liked that.

"Montana," I said as a request.

"You remember my name at least."

"I need to know about Delphine. I'll gladly give you four more twenties if you can point me in the right direction."

"Is that what you thinka me? Like I'm just some whore that wants to get paid?"

Two of the cars in the lot started almost simultaneously. As the automobiles pulled away two young women walked past us. They didn't speak because they could see that we were still in the negotiation phase of our relationship.

Montana was staring into my eyes, searching for the answer to her question.

"What do you want from me?" I asked.

She considered a moment and then said, "I want you to give me somethin'. Something special."

I frowned, trying to decipher this request.

"And not money and not no kiss or nuthin'," she said. "Somethin' that's gonna mean somethin' to both me and you."

From my shirt pocket I took a WRENS-L business card and a cartridge pen. I wrote a number on the back of the card, then waved the stiff paper around until the blue-black ink dried. I gave this handwritten promise to her.

"What's this?"

"Two things," I said. "First, it's my business. You call the number on the front and you can get to me almost any day. That's during business hours. If I'm not there someone'll take the message and I'll get back to you quickly."

Montana was about to say something snide but she stopped when I held up a daunting forefinger.

"On the back of the card is another number. That's my private answering service. You can reach me at that number twenty-four hours a day. If it's an emergency just say so and they will call me direct. Leave a message as long as your arm. They will write down every word."

I think it was the message length that got to Montana. She wanted a connection that she could rely on and that was it.

"What if I called you right now?"

"Florence Pratt will write down the message and either wait for me to call or, if it's trouble, she'll call me."

Another car fired up and drove off. No young woman walked past us that time. Maybe it was real love for those passengers.

"She calls herself Donata Delphine but her real name is Roxanna Coors from San Diego," Montana said. "She the kinda whore don't mind how mean a man like Alonzo could get."

"He beat her?" I asked.

"Like a three-egg omelet."

"She have any other boyfriends?"

"Girls like us aren't there for friendship. No man wanna girl that look like we do to be their buddy. A friend'll tell you the truth now and then; we just say what you wanna hear. I mean, would you ask a friend to get down on her knees and spread her ass?"

That image conjured a door through which one could imagine the pain a life on your own offered. I understood what she meant too well to dally on her question.

"Donata have any regular customers that wanted her to compliment them?"

"Not that I could tell. A lotta men pass through here. Some become regulars but not the way you're talkin' about—not really."

"When was the last time you saw her?"

After pondering a few moments she said, "Must be at least four weeks."

"Anything special happen around then?"

"Not that I know. You got a cigarette?"

I handed over a Lucky and lit it for her. She took a deep draw and exhaled the smoke against my chest.

When the mist evaporated I asked, "You know where I might find her?"

"You sure this number will work?" she asked, indicating my business card.

"I am. Don't you believe me?"

"I don't know. A man like you could lie in his sleep."

"And a girl like you would be lying right there next to me."

A real laugh escaped her lips.

"She talks about Chateau Marmont sometimes," Montana admitted. "Says that she likes the bar up there because sometimes famous actors pick her up. She told me they know her at the front desk and they only take ten percent."

That was all I could ask for, but neither one of us wanted to leave right then.

"You ever hear the names Craig Kilian, Kirkland Larker, or Mona Strael?"

"Uh-uh. No. They got some answers too?"

"Time'll tell."

"You can give me that kiss now, Easy Rawlins."

31

Mouse and Agosto were sitting outside the sentry's hut playing dominoes under the weak light emanating from the doorway. It was three minutes shy of 5:00 a.m.

"Who's winning?" I asked.

"No scores. Just tiles," the son of Sicily replied. "We play through the box twice. Your friend said he wanted to wait."

"I thought I was gonna call you, Ray."

"You sounded bothered, brother," he said, standing from the little crate they used as a card table. "Thought I'd drop by and make sure you were okay."

Mouse and I hadn't seen much of each other over the past few months. I was busy working and my partners didn't like having him around. We hadn't been together much but our kind of friendship was a life sentence. Only one thing could sever that.

"Come on up," I said. "I need to get a little sleep before we talk business."

Mouse nodded.

"Thanks, Aggie," he said to the Longo brother. "Next time we can play chess."

Both men shook hands and for some reason I felt pride in them.

Raymond wore dark clothes and had a canvas sack slung across his left shoulder. He lit a cigarette as the funicular rose over LA. Under a dawn mist the city lights glittered like some phosphorescent tides I'd seen.

"You got more luck than any man I ever known, Easy."

"I wouldn't call my life a lucky one, Ray."

"I'idn't say lucky. I said luck. Good or bad it clutters around you like chickens squabblin' over a busted sack'a grain. You got this house on top of a mountain and chirren been hurt by life so bad that it would have killed a grown man. It's somethin' else . . . your kinda luck."

"What you got in the bag?" I asked.

"Maybe everything," he said.

We had a guest room on the second floor of Roundhouse. I put Ray in there and then went to undress for bed. I managed to get my shoes off but then I lay back. I do believe that I was asleep before head hit mattress.

It wasn't what you'd call good rest. I was in a small room filled with people who were hogging up the air. They had faces but for some reason I couldn't make them out. They were talking but the words didn't make any sense. On top of that I didn't know why I was there. I looked around for a door but couldn't find one.

"Easy," somebody said. The other inmates of the dream were busy hiding their faces and mumbling. It was hot in there and the air was thin. I was looking around for an exit again when I felt a sharp, sharp pain in my chest.

I looked down and saw that there was a dagger buried up to the hilt in my heart. Blood was leaking out, slowly. In an instant I understood that the knife was blocking the flow of blood and, if it was pulled out, I'd bleed to death in a room full of strangers.

There was a hand on the hilt, a woman's hand. She was black

and beautiful: someone I had searched for my entire life. Her eyes were full of questions and, I knew, her mouth would be full of the answers I needed if only I could get her to talk.

"I'm sorry," she murmured.

"About what?" I gasped.

"This," she said, looking down at the dagger and the blood across her brown knuckles.

"Is this love?" I asked, feeling foolish even using the word.

That's when she pulled the blade from the wound. Blood gushed from my chest and I was more afraid than I'd ever been. Lurching forward, I reached for her as she backed away. I tried to yell for help but my breath was gone.

I sat up in the bed in violent genuflection. I was still gasping and my chest actually hurt. I hadn't moved in my sleep. For long moments I sat at the edge of the bed trying to glean meaning from the dream.

After failing at that I showered and shaved, put on my own dark clothes, and took a pistol from a locked drawer.

Ray's bed was empty and made.

I found him downstairs sitting next to the koi pond—reading a book!

"Ray?"

When Mouse looked up, the second surprise was that he was wearing glasses. He took off the rimless spectacles and smiled in a way that I'd never seen. It was the glasses that shocked me most; the fact that he bought them, that he wore them in spite of his fierce vanity.

"Bettah close your mouth or the flies'll get in," he said. It was this old familiar phrase that calmed me a bit.

"What are you reading?"

"*The Souls of Black Folk*," he said.

"W. E. B. DuBois?"

"Is it so amazin' that I'd be readin' a book?"

"Yes. It is. I've known you more'n forty years and I have never seen you read anything but a racing form. I didn't even know you *could* read. You never went to school. And why would you be reading DuBois? That's a book most people got to build up to."

"Not just that," he said. He gestured at the rucksack sitting next to him. "I got *Up from Slavery* in there too. Booker T. Washington wrote that one. He a southern boy down to his nuts and Boisy from New England. You know them two mothahfuckahs like oil an' water."

"I don't get it, Ray. What's come over you?"

"Well," he said. "I told you how I started runnin' jobs, right?"

"Yeah?"

"That means I have to stake out people an' places in order to make the plans. Used to be I could sit in a chair on the porch hours on end an' not do nuthin'. But since I got older I get, you know, impatient. I told Jackson Blue about it and he gave me these two books here. He said readin'd calm my mind. And damn if it don't. I had to buy me some glasses but then things started to make sense."

"Like what?"

"I really had no idea that anybody was thinkin' like this except for me in my secret mind."

His secret mind.

"Your mouth hangin' open again, Easy."

"Ray."

"Yeah?"

"I wanna talk to you about this but first there's business to take care of."

Mouse still had his thumb holding his place in *The Souls of Black Folk*.

"Shoot," he offered.

"Do you know anything about a man named Oldstein, Brock?"

Mouse put his book down on the ledge of the pond.

"Big B," he said. "He's just about the ripest pile'a bad attitude you're ever likely to step in."

"I think he came over to kill me the other day."

"I doubt that."

"Why?"

"Because if Brock want you dead. You dead."

"It was a special circumstance."

"Must'a been."

"He a heist man?" I asked.

"Naw."

"So he's not connected to Alonzo?"

"Not that I know. Tell me about it."

I explained about Kilian and the girl he was after, how Alonzo fit in and then Donata Delphine. I gave him every pertinent detail.

"So," I ended. "What do you think I should do?"

"You should stop thinkin' an' start killin'."

I never thought I'd be happy to hear Raymond suggesting murder. But at least some part of my friend was still in there somewhere with the uncharacteristic reading glasses, classic Afro-American literature, and new love.

"That might be the only option," I said. "But I want to try something else first."

That afternoon found me sitting alone in the coffee shop across from the Stephanopoulos Talent Agency. I had a cup of black coffee and chose that time to have my one cigarette of the day. I lit the Lucky, not because I craved it, but the way things were going it might have been my last.

Somewhere around 3:30 I saw Oldstein/Brock walking toward the door across the street.

I ran outside and yelled, "Big B!"

The man-boulder turned his head and beheld me. He considered a minute, then nodded. He waded out into Sunset traffic as if he were the only thing on the boulevard. Cars stopped for him and not one horn sounded.

That gangster might have been many things, but all of them came from not being a coward.

32

The café was called Sheila's Snack Bar and it served liquor. Eddie Brock Oldstein preferred scotch. I ordered a Coca-Cola for the first time since returning from the war. I was angry at the soda company for allowing their German CEO to produce Fanta beverages to get around the spirit of the embargoes America had set up against the Nazis. But my protest took a back seat to the fact that I needed something unnaturally sweet to cut the fear that a natural force like Brock instilled.

I sipped on my soda and Brock downed his whiskey in one gulp.

After he'd gestured for a refill I asked, "What's your problem with me, man?"

"Who said I had a problem?"

"You come up to my office in the early morning with two thugs. That's a problem."

"I thought you were up there," he said.

"So? What you got against me? I'ont even know you."

"My money in your pocket."

"You haven't paid me a dime."

"Not what I owe but what was stolen from me."

"Why would you think I had anything belonged to you?"

"Because you were working for that worthless piece'a shit Kilian." *Were.*

"Look, man," I said. "Craig came to me with some crazy story about a man and a woman fightin' in the woods. He said that he thought he killed the man and wanted to find out if that was the case and if the woman was okay. I looked into it and couldn't even prove that anything had happened. That's it. Period. No money. No even mention of you or anybody like you."

The waitress, probably not Sheila, brought Brock his second drink.

He held the glass up to his chin and stared at me like a hunter might spy quarry mostly hidden by a thick scrim of woods. No clear shot yet, his finger was still on the trigger.

"If you didn't know what Kilian was up to, then how'd you find me?" He posed the question with misplaced arrogance, like a checkers champion at a chess match. My heartbeat shifted to a slightly higher setting. So far everything I'd said was true. Maybe I'd left out a detail or two, but that was merely omission. Now I had to lie. Luckily I had an answer prepared.

"You're built like a brick shithouse, Mr. Oldstein," I said.

It helped me to see his massive shoulders tense up. While I was paying attention to the threat, the lie passed more easily through my lips.

"Don't get all bothered, brother. I just mean I asked a few shady characters I knew if they'd heard the name Eddie Brock. And when I described what you look like I was given a few choices. One of them ran the Stephanopoulos Talent Agency."

"Who told you about me?"

"You all big and bad, Brock, but even a little motherfuckah could stab me in the back. No names."

"All right. But I do need to know the name of the girl Kilian was after."

"I have no idea. Up until right now I thought the whole thing was likely a figment in a shell-shocked vet's mind."

"Why'd he come to you?"

"How should I know? The man he thought he killed was black, maybe."

"Maybe?"

"Yeah. It was late at night in the woods. Maybe he wasn't. But if you askin' where Kilian got my name, I got no answer."

Brock studied me a little further. His stare alone, I believed, had broken many a man. But I was better than that. I was just scared shitless.

"I gotta different story to tell," he said when I refused to crumble. "I had a girl worked for me was smarter than a store-bought pair'a tits. She could juggle three sets of books would make any accountant scratch his head. After the first year she was workin' on all my businesses and with some of my partners' money too. She got knee-deep in our shit, ripped us off, and ran. We tagged a nigger named Alonzo to get to her, but she must'a paid him off or somethin'. Now he's on our list too."

"Too?" I said. "You plan to kill her?"

"Not before she gives us our mothahfuckin' money."

"Okay," I said, holding up my hands, trying to look innocent. "She took your money and bought off your boy. But I don't see where you could imagine that I have anything to do with it. Craig neither. From what he told me he didn't even know the girl."

Brock downed his shot and then held up two post-like fingers to indicate to the waitress that he now needed a double.

"Craig was Delphine's boyfriend," Brock said while nodding something to the waitress. Then he looked at me. "On her last day at work he picked her up and drove her away."

The waitress came and set down a nearly full glass. Most other men might have gotten a little tipsy drinking like that. But for somebody like Brock whiskey was fuel.

"All right," I admitted. "That looks bad for Craig and Delphine. But where it gets hazy is when I get the blame."

"Craig hired you," Brock said just before guzzling half his liquor.

"How would you even know that?" I asked.

"Craig told me with his own bloody mouth." I didn't need to

hear any more on that subject. "And if you're working for them, then you're workin' against me."

"I can see how it might look like that on the surface. But I told you: He said he didn't even know the girl. He didn't give me a name or a picture or nuthin'."

"Maybe you're right, soul brother. But common sense says that if you fall into a hole, either you climb out or you die down there."

It was unsettling that I had just recently imagined being at the bottom of a pit about to cave in. It felt like the thug was in my head.

"You got a ladder I could use?" I asked him.

"Three hundred twenty-six thousand dollars."

Melvin Suggs said that the San Bernardino heist was only eighty-six thousand dollars.

"That's how much this girl stole from you and your friends?"

Brock stared at me so hard I had hope he might bust a blood vessel.

"You can stare until bullets come out your eyes, brother. But I have no idea how you think I know anything about your money."

The bent *businessman* hadn't finished staring yet. I might have been even more afraid if I didn't know that Mouse was across the street, at the top of the building next to the Stephanopoulos Talent Agency. He had a high-powered rifle and assured me he could hit anything within a fly's width.

A housefly, Mouse had said. *Not no fat old horsefly.*

I was craving another cigarette.

"Craig told me that he got into a knife fight with a . . . a big black man out in those woods," I said. "That man belong to you?"

"What did he look like?" Brock asked.

"I told you. Craig thought he was black but it was night with no light except for the moon through the trees."

"A knife you said?" Brock asked.

I nodded.

"Our man Alonzo was shot in his own bed."

"Look, man. I don't need you to incriminate yourself and then turn around and worry about me tellin' your secrets."

"I didn't shoot him." Brock actually grinned. "I didn't have anything to do with it."

"So the girl you asked me to look for, that Donata Delphine, she's the one you think stole your money?"

"I don't think. I know." He punctuated that claim by downing the last of the whiskey.

"And why is it again that you came to me?" I said. Turnabout is fair play.

"We knew that you were working for Craig and he was a friend of DD's."

"So because of that you think they gave me your money?"

"You might know something and not even know that you do."

"Like what?"

"What did Kilian tell you?"

"Come on, man. I told you what he said. He might'a killed a black man in the woods and that man was beatin' on a white girl."

"He didn't tell you her name?"

"He said he'd never even seen her before he came up on them fighting."

Brock's stare had softened—from caveman's club to a clenched fist.

"You went to the place where he killed the man?"

I told him about an orange grove, a cabin, and not one shred of evidence.

"I believe you, Easy," he lied. "But my partners won't be so understanding as me. If you worked for Craig they will want you to answer for it."

"So the only way I can get out of it is by finding the woman you call Delphine."

"That's about the size of it."

"How long you givin' me?"

Holding out a hand as if offering to pull me out of that hole he said, "Forty-eight hours. Forty-eight hours or the same thing happened to Craig happens to you."

"Something happened to him?"

"He tripped on a pistol and shot himself in the eye."

Once again there was murder in my heart.

33

A few blocks south of Sunset, Mouse and I stopped at a block-wide supermarket. He was buying groceries for Lihn.

Groceries for Lihn. In my experience Mouse wouldn't so much as boil water for coffee, but here he was in full domestic mode looking for skim milk and *natural* cornflakes.

While we cruised the fruit and vegetable section I said, "Tell me sumpin', Ray."

"What's that, Ease?"

"Did your boy Alonzo have anything to do with a big black man with straight hair who was good with a knife?"

"You see any coconuts around here?"

"They probably up there with the citrus fruit."

"You mean the lemons and oranges?"

"Uh-huh."

Mouse drove that shopping cart like he was in the Daytona 500.

I caught up to him at a small bin of about a dozen coconuts. He was holding one in his hand looking at it with great concentration.

"How you tell if this bitch is ripe?" he asked. "Usually if sumpin' hard it ain't ready."

"Hand it here," I said.

He gave me the coconut. I tapped it with a finger and got that hollow sound.

Passing it back to my friend I said, "This one'll do."

"Ketch," he said but I thought he said, *Catch.*

"You gonna throw it?"

He looked at the palm fruit and smiled.

"Naw, man," he said, dropping the thing into the shopping basket. "Reynolds Ketch. Ketch with a *K.* He live over on Hoover."

"Where?"

"You know the Hoover Car Wash down near Eighty-Third?"

"No. But I could find it."

"He live across the street in a group of bungalows. They painted not blue and not green."

"Thanks, Ray."

"What you think is a bettah meat, Easy? Pig or sheep?"

"In my line'a business I prefer to sup on snake."

So far I had been to two domiciles that contained dead men, their mortal clay waiting at that one last station on the way to hell. I didn't want to go to one more makeshift mausoleum, but there was a breaking point coming and the best arsenal to have backing me up was information.

I drove east on Santa Monica Boulevard for a while and then went south, hooking up with Sixth Street, which I followed downtown. From there I took Hoover Street all the way into the hood.

The LA riots were almost four years gone but the devastation was still apparent. Burned-out businesses and more pedestrians than populated the streets of the rest of the city. Men and women who were the heirs of slavery trod down the avenue looking as if they were still bearing up under the heavy loads of another man's wealth.

Reynolds Ketch's apartment complex was right where Mouse had said it would be. The single-story courtyard of eighteen or so small apartments was painted turquoise and maze-like in its construction. A bank of mailboxes in front of the warren told me that the Ketch residence was number nine.

The doorway was flanked by a bushy bougainvillea with its red flowers burning brightly on the left, and on the other side stood a skinny loquat tree crowded with not-quite-ripe fruit.

I knocked on the door but nobody answered. I was wondering how I could break in when a voice called out, "Who you lookin' for?"

Directly across the concrete path was unit fourteen. Standing in the doorway was a very old, quite emaciated black man wearing jet-black sunglasses. He was leaning against the doorjamb, and his attention was aimed in my direction, if not directly at me. The plants on either side of his front door were big, healthy bird of paradise. There must have been sixty or more orange, blue, and red blossoms, each one of them seeming just about ready to take flight.

"Reynolds Ketch," I said, amplifying my voice in case his age had made him hard of hearing.

"You'ont have to yell. I'm blind, not deaf."

"Sorry, sir. I guess your hearing is so good that you heard me knock." While speaking I crossed the concrete pathway to the old man's front apartment.

Gauging the magnification of my words, he closed the screen door before I got there.

"What you want with Reynolds?" the old man asked.

"I'm Easy Rawlins. What's your name?"

"I'm Shep. Shep Williams. Used to be Shep and Zula but she died seven, no, no, eight years back."

"Sorry to hear that, sir. Were you married a long time?"

"Seem like forever. We had forever and now it's gone."

His tone of voice was oddly objective, like some celestial being commenting on the inevitability of mortality.

"I'm looking for Reynolds because a friend of mine wanted me to give him something."

"What's that?"

"A crate of blood oranges from his tree."

"I like blood oranges. They more tart than most'a the store-bought ones. I cain't see orange but I could taste it."

"Have you, um, heard Reynolds lately?"

"Not for a few days, Mr. Rawlins."

I regretted using my real name. In my business you wanted to leave as little a footprint as possible.

"Any idea where I might find him?" I asked.

"Sometimes he goes out of town for a few days, but then again he might be with his mama. She's old and he helps her out now and then. He might not be a good man but he is a good son."

"Something wrong with Reynolds?"

"Sometimes God ask the question and we give the wrong answer," he said.

I pondered this reply for a moment or two. It made a great deal of sense though I couldn't have explained why.

"Where does Mrs. Ketch live?" I asked.

"At the Poinsettia Court over on Hooper. Her name is Miss Lily Dasher."

Poinsettia Court was another single-story courtyard of maybe twenty small apartments. Another maze with a different layout. Lily Evangeline Dasher was number eleven.

Half a dozen throwaway newspapers were piled at the threshold. And there was so much junk mail jammed into the slot of the door that some envelopes had fallen among and on top of the papers.

I was sure that no one was home but still I knocked out of deference and was surprised when a sixty-something black woman yanked the door open.

She was short and skeletal but there was life burning in those eyes, glistening off that black skin.

"Yes?" It was more an accusation than a question.

"Is he still breathing?"

"You'ont look like no cop." That was back in the day when the word *cop* was a slur.

"No, ma'am."

We measured each other. I was more than half convinced that she was armed with something. After an intensity that I don't believe Big B Oldstein could have matched, the woman stepped aside and said, "Come on in, then."

The living room was the size of the smallest cabin on a second-rate ocean liner. With all the shades and curtains pulled, it was dark enough to be below the waterline.

Miss Lily Dasher stood next to a recliner chair that was upholstered in cracked brown pleather. I had my back to the front door wondering if she was going to offer me a seat or whip out a gun and shoot me.

I wasn't nervous, not exactly, but I had learned over time that because most women are physically weaker than most men, they, members of the *fairer sex*, were braver, forced to be more courageous and therefore more dangerous. A poor black woman knew that going up against a man was a life-and-death situation, so she had to be ready to risk it all. And there was something about Lily, her dark house, and the mention of the police. For her this was something serious and I didn't know if she saw me as a possible friend or a definite threat. Because of all that I kept a close eye on my hostess's hands.

For two or three minutes we maintained the silent standoff, and then, as if at the end of some test of strength, Lily collapsed onto the recliner. She was breathing hard. There was perspiration across her forehead.

"Renny called me in the middle'a the night outta nowhere," she

said, her gaze cast down upon the pitted parquet floor. "I drove out
to some roadside gas station that was closed and found him in his
car with a knife in his chest." She looked up at me. It seemed like
she'd aged a decade since letting me in.

"I brought him home," she said, putting great weight on the
words. "Brought him home to die."

The third death. The charm. I thought of Mouse telling me that
I had more luck, both good and bad, than anyone he knew.

"Where is he?" I asked.

Lily turned her head away from me. At first I thought that she
was embarrassed or maybe feeling guilty about her and her son. But
then I realized that she was looking toward a closed gray door.

"In there?"

She nodded.

I've seen a lot of death in my time. From the Louisiana backwoods
to Houston. From the European theater to the streets of LA. The
fact of death never bothered me, but the anticipation was another
thing altogether. Knowing that there was a dead man on the other
side of a closed door made me hesitant. I had to take a breath
before putting my hand on the knob.

"Oh God," Lily said when I turned that handle.

Another breath and I pushed the door open.

The bedroom smelled of infection. Reynolds Ketch was laid up
in the bed, his shirt cut open and the knife still protruding from his
chest. His dead eyes made Lily's fever look like a light frost.

Then he took in a gurgling breath.

I am not ashamed to say that I nearly ran screaming from that
bungalow.

There was a straight-back wood chair set near the head of the
bed. I imagined that Lily sat there whispering prayers rather than
calling a doctor or, at least, a friend.

I sat there next to that impossible specimen of life.

"Ketch?"

He turned those hot, confused eyes on me.

"Help," he whispered.

"What you need?"

"Call the, call the hospital. Mama won't do it."

"Okay," I said. "I will if you tell me what happened to you."

Death peered at me through Ketch's eyes and decided that I could be trusted.

"It was that mothahfuckin' Alonzo. He ripped me off. Took all'a the money from where we hid it. But I knew. I knew where he went with that girl'a his. He'idn't know that she had me up there too. He got her pregnant and I took her to that free clinic they got on Fairfax. She were mad at him and so when I took her out to Blood Grove she had me stay. I knew they were up there and I went to kill him and then make her pay me my money. But Alonzo wasn't there and when I was talkin' to her this white boy jumped in. We fell and I stabbed myself. When I came to the white boy was on the ground and Donata was gone. I made it to my car and then to a phone booth to call Mama. But she wouldn't take me to no doctor. She said if she did we'd both get in trouble."

I had about a dozen questions. I wanted to know how Lily got all the way out to Orange County and why she would let her own son die. But Ketch didn't have the time and I didn't need answers.

He said other things that I didn't understand. After a while he drifted off into a feverish sleep.

"We got to call the cops," I said to the heist man's mother.

"His fate lies with the Lord," she replied, refusing to look me in the eye.

"That's true," I agreed. "But God's watchin' whether the cops come or not. No one can escape the judgment of God."

I didn't believe any of that but I knew those words would sway her.

Shaking her head Lily Dasher said, "That boy never did do right."

In some way I knew these words meant I could do what I felt was necessary.

"McCourt," he said, answering the first ring.

"I got another body for you, Anatole. This one's still breathing."

34

I left Lily Dasher's house before the police came. That was okay because, even if my name got mentioned, McCourt would call Suggs and the chief detective would tell his minion to lay off me—for the time being.

I got back up to Sunset around dusk. The hill upon which that part of the Strip stood looked down on the rest of the city like a lazy predator idly wondering how to approach a herd of unsuspecting bovines.

The Chateau Marmont was a lovely, old-style, rambling kind of hotel. It turned its nose up at Los Angeles below and catered to wealthy and beautiful residents who did illegal things alone and with others in the upstairs rooms and the cottages out back. It was the kind of place where a man of my hue could be turned away at the front door for little to no reason. At places like the Chateau I'd have to come up with a trick just to get the doorman to answer a simple question. I could pretend to be a janitor looking for a job or maybe a chauffeur picking up a client. I would have needed to come up with some kind of subterfuge if I didn't already have a backdoor man.

A few years earlier Bo Tierce, of Riverside via Mississippi, had already languished nineteen months at Folsom State Prison. Bo had been convicted of a trio of crimes: B and E, assault and battery, and rape. This because he had a record for burglary and he'd been working as a gardener for the mansion next door a few months before the crime.

The police arrested him at his home, when his wife was out waitressing at some diner. His bad record combined with no alibi convicted him. He pled guilty for a nine-year sentence bargained down from a probable thirty. I was hired by a Beverly Hills banker named Holloway who had lost a very valuable piece of art in the B and E part of Bo's conviction. Holloway's seventeen-year-old night maid, Sorrell Hart, had a shattered cheekbone and soiled virtue, but all Holloway was interested in was his possession: a small iron sculpture of an angry crow attributed to Picasso.

Holloway had called Saul Lynx to investigate the loss but Saul was on another case and so told him that his partner Easy Rawlins was a better fit.

Sorrell was living in Gardena with her spinster aunt trying to forget about that night. She wasn't happy to see me but I had convinced Mr. Holloway to write her a severance check for twenty-five hundred dollars, and she needed, as well as deserved, the money.

Among other things I found out her attacker, unlike Bo, had a military tattoo and a small mustache. One might wonder why the police hadn't gathered this data when they first questioned the most innocent victim of the crime. The answer was simple—Sorrell was in the hospital when the investigation started and the detectives in charge had already found out that Bo had a bad temper, one or two violent charges against him, and one conviction for burglary. The police questioned Miss Hart only once, and that was while she was still in the hospital.

I identified the perpetrator, Martin Verdun, using my detective skills and police connections. Verdun was detained in San Diego. The man who bought the sculpture, Titus Crenshaw, was also a banker. After being granted absolution for accepting stolen property, Titus agreed to return Holloway's crow, which looked more frightened than angry to me. I went to Commander Suggs and reported the details of the crime just in case somebody wanted to do something about Tierce. Suggs actually shrugged when he told me that Bo would be moldering in a cell built for one and occupied by three for the foreseeable future.

"Can't you just tell them that he's innocent and to let him go?" I asked, feeling very country and simpleminded too.

"I will," Melvin told me. "And maybe they'll get around to it in a year or so. It costs you either money or time to commute a sentence that's based on a confession."

That assessment didn't sit well with me. I imagined my adopted son, Jesus, being put in jail for something he didn't do and then left to rot because nobody cared.

So I went to see Bo in prison. Melvin at least greased those wheels for me. I told the convict that another man had been arrested for the crimes he was blamed for but that the wheels of justice moved slowly for the poor. I suggested maybe that he could get a second mortgage on his house to afford a decent lawyer. He told me that his wife had divorced him three weeks after his sentence and hooked up with one of his friends.

Luckily for Bo he had a mother who owned her house outright. She sold her one piece of property and turned the money over to a lawyer named Ganns. Ganns did what looked like an afternoon of work and Bo was granted his freedom.

Bo had been raised hating black people; so had his father and grandfather and the rest of his sod-busting, sharecropping, shit-kicking relatives from eastern Mississippi. The word *nigger* to him was an endearment. But about ninety-seven seconds after we met, all that racist history fell away. I was from Louisiana, which bordered on Mississippi, and from that day on he called me Cousin Easy.

I met him at the front gate of Folsom on the day he was released. He was definitely planning to kill his ex-wife and his friend. I offered instead to drive him down to LA. One of Jewelle's employees in the maid service helped to get him a job at the Marmont.

So when I got to the front door and was approached by two young white men, at the height of their strength and misplaced arrogance, I was not perturbed.

"Can I help you?" a tallish, short-haired lad asked.

"Bo Tierce," I said.

"What about him?"

"He asked me to drop by."

"For what?"

"I don't know. Why don't you ask him?"

"I need a reason to call," he said.

His partner, just as white and tall but a little more thoughtful, came up close to us.

"Listen, man," I said. "Call Bo on the phone and say that Mr. Rawlins is here like he asked."

"I don't have to do anything you say," he replied petulantly.

He was acting as if I was oppressing him by asking him to do his job. On top of that he was asserting his God-given entitlement as a white man to banish my rights. These responses called up a feeling in me that I can only describe as revolutionary. I don't know what might have happened if the other doorman hadn't put a hand on his friend's shoulder and whispered something. The angry doorman moved aside, allowing his partner to step up.

"What's your name again, sir?" the new inquisitor asked.

"Ezekiel Porterhouse Rawlins."

I sat at the far end of the bar that was removed by the waiters' space from the nearest next barstool. Bo had served me a club soda and a small bowl of soy-glazed rice crackers. I watched him talking to and serving the six other customers he had. In between conversations he prepared drinks for the waitstaff to serve.

Tierce was an inch or so under six feet and reminiscent of a bleached lion. With dirty blond hair that washed against his forehead and ears, he looked dangerous and a little wild. He was perfect for that hotel and time. Anything a guest might want, from a marijuana cigarette to company for the night, he would do his best to procure. After all, he had sworn to buy his mother a new house.

After a round of drinks and good cheer Bo made his way to me.

"You got Mr. Charlie downstairs real hot, Cousin Easy."

"You mean the doorman?"

"Oh yeah. He said that you were rude and threatening."

"Threatening? There were two of them."

"That's what I told him," Bo said, exhibiting a hungry grin. "I said if they couldn't take care'a one man that maybe they'd like to transfer to maid services."

"How's it going, Bo?"

"This here's the best job I ever had, Cousin. Last week a young woman brought me up to her room just so she could sit on my lap."

I smiled and nodded.

"What can I do for you, Cuz?"

"Donata Delphine."

Bo's murky brown eyes had the look of the swamps where men like him and me came from.

"You in need of a little company?" he asked.

"I don't think I could afford the likes of Donata."

"Then what?"

"I'm on a job."

The bartender rubbed his nose, then glanced over at some guy in an overly green suit who was trying to get his attention.

"She's a good kid," he said. "I wouldn't want to cause her no trouble."

There were many things I could have said. But instead I just stared. Bo had the innocence of wild country in his heart. Once he owed you a debt, he would not, could not ever forget it.

"She worked the bar with three or four other girls for a few months," he said. "But ain't none of them been around lately."

"You know how to get in touch with any'a them?"

"Not really."

I downed my seltzer and stood up.

I was about to leave, but then I had an idea.

"You ever meet another bar girl name of Mona Strael?"

The ex-con bartender looked at me and smiled.

35

The bar had only seven stools but a doorway in the opposite wall led to a little cul-de-sac of a room done all in shades of red. There were seven tables and a velvet padded banquette that ran along the curved sides. Maybe twenty people, not including waitstaff, were in residence drinking and talking. Almost all of them were white. Those who looked up seemed a little surprised that their favorite redneck bartender was ushering a black man in. That wasn't the norm but, then again, maybe I was an actor or some kind of soul singer. I could have played baseball for an out-of-town team.

Bo led me to a small round table at the farthest reach of the red velvet banquette. There sat the only other Negro in the room. She was young, not quite as dark-skinned as I, with a great mane of frizzy hair that had been partially tamed by being tied at the back.

When we approached she moved her shoulders by way of greeting.

"Hey, Bo," she said, but she was looking at me.

"Mona Strael, meet Cousin Easy."

The young woman's smile broadened and her eyes expressed knowledge, if not understanding.

"The man that dragged you out of prison and brought you here to us?" she said.

"He wants to ask you some questions," Bo said. "I'd appreciate it if you gave him a few minutes."

Ms. Strael was a master of body language. She sat back and glanced at the empty chair across from her. Bo slapped my shoulder and I sat down.

"See you later, Bo," she said over my shoulder.

I was looking at this woman, trying to place her alongside other women I'd known and never really understood, women I'd loved and lost and cared for but mostly in the wrong ways. Her one-piece dress was short hemmed and middle blue. Her lashes were naturally long, fingernails lacquered but not colored, and the watch she wore had a cartoon duck on it.

I must have made a face of some sort because she asked, "What?"

"Cartoon watches the new style?"

"My little goddaughter Azalea gave me this. She said that Danny Duck would protect me."

"Azalea thinks you need protection?"

"Her mother does."

"How old is she?"

"Azalea or Athena?"

I was having a fine time. That's never a good thing on the job.

"I'm surprised that Bo told you anything about me," I said, trying to get back on track.

"Azalea's seven," Mona replied. "Her mother's twenty-three."

I was feeling a bit light-headed. Dean Martin, I realized, was singing on the sound system and the different hues of red that decorated the room seemed to swirl, like confetti caught up in a dust devil. There was something synthetic about me and Mona sitting there in a room of scarlet fabrics and white faces.

"A white man came in one night with his date," Mona said. It felt like she was throwing a rope down into that hole I was in. "The room was fully occupied. So he came up to me and asked if I was sitting here. I didn't answer because he had eyes.

"He asked me again and I didn't answer. So then he put a hand on my shoulder. I'm a woman alone and so you know I can protect myself if I have to. But this is a nice place and I didn't want to strain my welcome with some random white man's blood." She stopped there and smiled.

"So what happened?"

"His date was his undoing," Mona Strael said. "She had gone to the bartender to see if there was someplace else they could sit. The white man had just whispered to me, 'Answer me, bitch,' and Bo put a hand on *his* shoulder and leaned in just as close. I don't know what he said but the white man and his date left.

"Later on that night Mr. Felton, the bar and restaurant manager, came up to me and apologized. A few days after that Bo told me that he used to look down on black people but then one saved him when he didn't have to, when everybody but his mother had abandoned him."

My dizziness was gone. Mona shifted on the banquette and looked into my eyes.

"It costs a hundred dollars to sit here with me," she said. "Five hundred if you need me to get up."

"Did Kirkland Larker have that kind of cash?"

The sinewy suppleness went still in an instant. She sat up a little straighter and her eyes tightened a millimeter or two. The smile faded, but not for long.

"He'd raise it now and then," she said, impressing me with her resilience.

"You seen him lately?"

Her deepening smile was the rebuttal of the transparent duplicity of my question.

"No," she said at last.

"What about Donata Delphine?"

"Who?"

"Roxanna Coors."

There was a certain amount of satisfaction I felt cutting through the smug confidence that was Mona Strael. Her smile disappeared behind a look that was both speculative and deadly, causing my mood to shift from momentary pleasure to familiar caution. I felt like a child staring through bamboo bars at a Siberian tiger. I was safe, scared, and sacred inasmuch as I was destined to be sacrificed.

Strael smiled again, relaxed again.

"Would you like to come with me, Cousin Easy?"

"Where to?"

"The management has a small building behind this property. We can use it from time to time if we don't abuse the courtesy."

"I don't have the five hundred."

"You can owe it to me."

"All I need is a couple'a answers," I said.

"This is a public place and it sounds like you have private concerns."

Concerns.

"Nothing private," I assured her. "I just need to get to Roxanna."

"And why would you think I'd deign to help you?"

First *undoing*, then *concerns*, and now *deign*—I had to switch up.

"What school you go to, Mona?"

For the first time the bar girl showed actual surprise.

"You're good, Cousin Easy. I'm right down the street at UCLA. Prelaw. Now you tell me what this is about."

"There's a lot I could say. Robbery, attempted murder, actual murder, kidnapping, and big-time embezzlement. But the only thing you need to hear is that a man named Eddie Brock, also known as Brock Oldstein, has been breathing down my neck to find Donata. I want to get together with her and tell her what I know."

"Brock." The name lodged in her throat like a chicken bone. "And you want to warn Roxie?"

"I want to talk to her."

"And then tell Brock where she's at?"

"Not necessarily. But even if I did, that's better than me tellin' him that you might know where to find her."

I wouldn't have told Brock her name, but she didn't need to know that.

36

She was staying on Ogden Drive between San Vicente and Olympic Boulevards. A huge oak tree dominated the front of the property. The house itself was small and disheveled like an old dollhouse lost and then forgotten in a dark wood.

When I knocked on Donata/Roxanna's door I wondered what to do if she didn't answer. I could go around back and climb in a window or call Anatole McCourt or have someone else call the cops. If Donata was dead Brock *might* decide to leave me alone. But I knew that nothing short of homicide would ensure safety from the gangster.

I'd killed men before . . .

The door opened while I was having that internal dialogue. She didn't ask, "Who is it?" Nor did she attach the chain as proof against some big black man she didn't know. No. The lovely young woman threw the door open wide and said, "Yes?"

No more than five two, she wore a blue-and-gold satin and silk kimono. Her lustrous hair was light red like some Germans' and she had blue eyes that were both startled and startling. When she got a good look at me, the slightest of smiles brushed her generous, pinkish lips.

"Oh," she said upon taking me in. "Hi."

"Miss Coors?"

A slight tightening of her eyes and tilt of her head seemed to decipher the meaning of me using her real name.

"How is everybody down at the Dragon's Eye?" she asked.

"Montana misses you."

"She doesn't have this address."

"The mailbox says Andrews," I said in partial agreement.

"My name is nowhere on anything having to do with this house."

"I'm a very resourceful man when I have to be."

"Good to know, Mister . . . ?"

"Rawlins."

"Would you like to come in, Mr. Rawlins?"

Ah. The courage of women.

On the inside the place was very neat and modern. There was a window in the ceiling of the sitting room. This transformed what might have been a dark cove into a bright destination. The chairs and sofa were constructed of whitewashed bamboo frames fitted with thick cushions festooned in floral design. The floor was white pine and the paintings on the walls were real oils depicting nostalgic scenes of the English countryside.

"Have a seat, Mr. Rawlins."

"Easy is what everyone calls me."

"Easy," she said with a smile.

I took a chair and she chose the sofa.

"Do you need something to drink?" she asked, pulling her feet up under her butt.

"Do you?" I replied.

"That depends on what you have to say."

She had a big smile. It would be hard to imagine anything evil coming from her. Luckily for me I had a great imagination.

"So," she said to fill in my silence, "how did you find me? And why?"

"A young vet named Kilian hired me to locate a man, maybe named Alonzo, who he might have killed, and a woman the man had attacked. As far as I can tell—you are that woman but possibly the situation he related was made up."

"Craig doesn't know this address," she said.

I was glad that she didn't try to tell me she knew nothing about Craig or Alonzo or . . .

"Reynolds Ketch," I said.

Donata Delphine's features darkened.

I continued, "Ketch figured that you and Alonzo thought he died from the knife wound. So he gave me enough that I found Mona Strael."

"What do you want from me, Easy?"

"Eddie Brock Oldstein believes that you have somewhere north of three hundred thousand dollars belonging to him. After Craig hired me to find you, Brock tried to outbid him."

"And did he?" The blue of Donata's eyes contained the cold heart of glaciers.

"I don't respond well to threats and he doesn't know any other way to talk."

The woman of many names glanced at the front door. I believe she was beginning to regret letting me in.

"I haven't told Brock any of this," I said.

I could see myself—shot, stabbed, and hanging from a rafter—in her deadly frozen stare.

The feeling was so intense that I said, "Hold up, sister. I'm not here to hurt you. If I wanted that I would have traded my life for this address."

That earned me a brief reprieve.

"So you're here for Craig," she said.

"Craig's dead."

I don't know what I expected. Maybe I thought Donata/Roxanna would break down under the grief of this loss. But she didn't have any response other than a few-seconds-long spate of silence. That's all she took and it was back to business.

"Then who are you here for?" she asked. "Yourself?"

"In order to answer that question I need you to put a story

together that makes sense to me. Craig's the one that hired me and so I still see him as the client. After I hear you out I'll have to decide on what he would want me to do and then how far I'd go to accomplish that end."

She gave Craig a few seconds. My request qualified for a whole half a minute.

"I met Craig at this veterans' bar down on Western—" she said.

"Excuse me, but I have to interrupt you there, Donata. You met Craig at the Dragon's Eye when his mother got too drunk to drive and he came to pick her up. Something like that. If you want to have me on your side you have to tell the truth." I didn't know if I was right but I suspected that Lola had been less than truthful about DD.

Donata put on a big grin. Here I just called her a liar and she loved it—as if I had passed some kind of test.

"Okay," she said. "You've done your homework. I met Lola first. She told me about Craig. She thought he needed a woman like her to make him walk the line."

"But you saw something else in him," I suggested.

"He was sweet," she said. "But I'm nothing like Lola."

"His mother said that you were having trouble . . . with a man."

"Trouble with my boyfriend Alonzo, Alonzo Griggs."

"He's dead too," I said.

That didn't earn even one second.

"Craig had been going up to this cabin in an orange orchard since he was a boy. He took me there a couple of times." She paused and looked at me, gauging how much she should reveal. "I told him to meet me there in the evening but I went up earlier with Alonzo. I didn't know exactly what would happen, but . . . but Alonzo and me could get kinda kinky with sex and he went at it much harder if he was angry. He had babies with six other women and he knew I was pregnant. So when I asked him to tie me up to this tree, he did. Then I told him I got an abortion.

"I thought he would beat on me and then Craig would come and they'd fight. I expected Craig would win 'cause he'd come back from the war in the last year or two and he'd done a lotta hand to hand. I figured he'd see Alonzo hittin' me and just lose it."

"Excuse me," I said when she stopped to take a breath.

"Yes?"

"Were you afraid of Alonzo?"

"Not really."

"Even though he beat on you?"

"It wasn't that bad and he always got pretty sweet afterward. I kinda liked how manly he was, how he could go all the way out there. No, I wasn't afraid of him at all."

"So then what did you need Craig for?"

That was the sixty-four-thousand-dollar question. The lady took the time to consider her response. When she'd finished thinking she looked into my eyes and pondered a little longer.

"How much did Craig pay you?"

"My regular fee."

"Is that a lot?"

"More than you'd make working at a taco stand."

"What if I offered you fifty thousand dollars?"

One of the great things about being a black PI in the late sixties and before was that most people saw you as being poor. That way they could offer you what sounded like a great deal of money, confident that you'd sell your soul for it.

"Who I got to kill?" I said, going along with her convictions about me and mine.

"I did embezzle from Brock. Got three hundred twenty-six thousand out of him and his Mafia friends. The problem was that Alonzo, Ketch, and one other guy had done a heist in San Bernardino. Alonzo promised to hide my money until we could get away. He did hide it, but when I wanted to get at it he wouldn't give it back."

"That sounds like a mistake on your part," I offered.

Donata smiled and nodded.

"I thought he was crazy about me," she said, "that he'd do anything for a woman that gave him what he wanted. But that much cash had a sobering effect and he knew that sooner or later the San Bernardino job would take him down; something about a witness. My money became part of his escape plan."

"So," I said, "you posed for some photos of you two making love and then you shot him."

"You're a sweet man, aren't you, Easy?"

"What makes you say that?"

" 'Making love.' You're the kinda guy I'll end up marrying and raising kids with after my wild oats have flowered and gone to seed."

That was a conversation stopper. I could hear the truth in those words. Well, not exactly the truth, but a conviction she held that would probably never be achieved.

"So," I said, "we left off where you were tied to a tree and Alonzo was about to let you have it."

"I didn't realize how upset he'd get. He punched me a lot and then ran off saying that he was going to get enough wood to burn me up."

"You say he beat you?"

"Uh-huh."

"The attack wasn't that long ago and I don't see any bruises."

She stood up and opened the kimono. The only things she wore underneath were black and blues with hints of red and yellow around the edges.

"So," I said. "Reynolds Ketch shows up while Alonzo is collecting kindling and Craig gets there just in time to see another black man kicking your ass."

"Alonzo had taken Ketch's money too. Reynolds got stabbed with his own knife. Alonzo came up behind Craig and knocked him out with a big branch he'd found. After all that he cut me loose and we cleaned up as best we could. We both thought Ketch was dead and maybe Craig too."

"What about Sammy?" I asked, just to keep my finger in the conversation.

Mention of the little black puppy landed closer to her heart than any of the three murders. With rueful eyes and a sad smile she remembered her dog.

"I had just bought that little rascal. I tried to get him to come with me but he wanted to stay by Craig. Whenever I'd go after him he'd run off. Finally Alonzo made me come with him. Is Sammy okay?"

"Fine," I said. "So you and Alonzo left together?"

"Yeah. Yeah, we did, but I knew I had to get rid of him because sooner or later he'd remember that he wanted to burn me alive."

"And you're just gonna tell me all this? Admit to murder?"

"I want you to understand how serious I am here. There's money to be had."

"Where is the money?" I asked.

"Where it is isn't the only problem. How to get at it is where things get sticky. How to get at it is why we might work together."

"Seems like the men that work with you don't live long."

"I'm sorry about Craig, but Alonzo and Ketch deserved what they got."

"What about the three guards in the armored car job?"

Donata stared at me, the wide-eyed question plain on her face. That was her most telling moment.

"The three guards that Alonzo hijacked," I reminded her. "They've been missing for over two months."

"I had nothing to do with that," she said simply.

"Alonzo or Ketch never said anything about what happened?"

"No," she answered carelessly. "Why would they?"

"Don't you care?" I just had to ask.

She turned serious then, honest.

"I have never been the kind of person who feels another man's pain," she said. "If you're with me you have to accept that. I was too busy living my own day-to-day to be worried about what Alonzo or anybody else was doing."

"If you didn't care about him, how did he get hold of your money?"

I expected some kind of anger or remorse, but the innocent-looking beauty did not feel that brand of emotion. She smiled and nodded, leaned forward, placing an elbow on either knee. The kimono was still open, but she didn't care.

"The money is in small denominations—bulky, you know? And Brock was after me. I know this banker will transfer funds out of the country—slowly. Five thousand at a time. He'll do it for a flat fee."

"How do you know he won't steal it?"

"Because he wants to go to London with me. You know—leave the wife and kids and start over. I have that effect on some men."

"So you thought Alonzo was that kinda man and let him put your money with his—for safekeeping. Your bank connection was here, and carrying the money around with you was dangerous."

"Yeah. But when I asked Al for twenty-five thousand of my own money he told me I had to wait. So I waited. After three weeks of being put off I decided I had to do something. That's why I brought Craig in on it."

"But didn't you just say that Craig was supposed to find you and get mad because some man was attacking you? That doesn't sound like he was in on anything."

"I told him that a boyfriend that I broke up with had stolen my money. Then I went up to the cabin and got Al mad. Craig knew enough to help me get what I needed to."

"But Alonzo went out looking for kindling and then Ketch showed up, so the plans changed."

Donata sat up straight and shrugged.

"And did Alonzo ever tell you where the money was?" I asked.

"I went back with Al to his photo studio after we left Ketch and Craig. I told him I lied about being pregnant. Then I got him naked and took out a gun. I told him that either I was gonna get my money or I was gonna shoot him."

"And?" I asked. "Did he tell you?"

"Yeah." The nod and twist of her lips told me that this knowledge just presented another barrier. "He told me, but I realized that I couldn't get at it—not directly."

"So you needed him alive to get to the money?"

She nodded again.

"But you killed him anyway."

"Yes."

"Why would anybody kill someone when they needed him?" It's a bad sign when you start discussing murder as if it were a chore done out of sequence.

"I could see in his eyes that he thought he still had me tied to that tree." Her face was not quite so beautiful when she talked murder. "At the very least he planned to take my money and run. At most he'd leave me burned alive. He thought that I needed him too much to kill him. But as my mother used to say, there's more than one way to skin a cat."

"Ah," I crooned. "That's where I come in."

Donata smiled.

"But you're not gonna tell me where the money's at until you know that I can't do what Alonzo planned," I concluded.

"I need somebody who's smart enough to negotiate," she said. "Somebody who doesn't think in absolute terms."

Those blue eyes bore into mine like twin skies over a day-old battlefield. The land was devastated and the soldiers all dead or dying.

"Girl, you scare the shit outta me."

Donata grinned, stood up, and retied the sash of her robe.

"Fifty thousand dollars," she said. "That's all you have to worry about."

"If your money is stacked up with what Alonzo and his crew stole, then you got over four hundred thousand," I argued. "Fifty don't seem like enough."

"I'll go as high as one hundred thousand. That's the limit."

"And what about Brock?"

"We leave LA. He'll never find us."

"Brock's a killer," I said.

"Yes, he is. That's why we have to do something, Easy. Either take the money and run or just run."

"I could give you to Brock."

"He'd kill you anyway."

She was probably right about that.

"What do you say, Easy? Is it a deal?"

It was my turn to think. I should have been figuring out the right move to make but instead I wondered how I could get into so much trouble. Most people live their entire lives without experiencing what I had just sitting here, talking to Donata Delphine.

There was a trick that she meant to play on me at the last minute. I was sure of that. Roxanna Coors had the information that would save me from my own case. But she was also probably the greatest danger I faced.

"Okay," I said. "But how can I help if I don't know what to do?"

"You're going to have to trust me, Easy."

"Just looking for you I've come across two dead men. That's the kind of path you wreak. What's there to trust in that?"

"I just want my money," she declared. "And I need a man I can trust to accomplish that goal."

"And why aren't you out there trying to do that?" We were talking but the words meant nothing.

"I never leave this house except to go to the Safeway to buy food and wine. Brock would snap my neck in a minute. And you better believe he's out there looking too."

"What about my neck?" I wondered out loud.

"You got to risk something, baby."

I truly admired this woman. It felt like she was the child of evolution, a being who had mastered survival skills that most other human beings couldn't even imagine. That appreciation must have shown on my face because she made a little bow using her head and left shoulder.

"Give me your phone number and I'll call you within the next three days," she said.

"I take it you'll be in a different place."

"Don't worry, Easy. You aren't like Alonzo or Ketch, because I know I can trust you. And you're not like Craig, because you know how to survive."

I found myself hoping that the lies she told me were truth.

37

"Hi, honey." I'd called Feather down at Jackson's house.

"Hi, Daddy. Are you home?"

"Right now I am." Sammy was licking my fingers and Frenchie was watching, mumbling something in Dog.

"Can I come up?"

"I'm still pretty busy on this case. And lots of the work is at night."

"Can't I just stay there by myself? I'm old enough."

"Why don't you want to stay at the Blues'? Is anything wrong?"

"No, Daddy, I just wanna be in my own room and in my own house so my friends can call me."

"I don't know, little girl. I'd be so worried about you up here all by yourself."

"I'm not a little girl and I worry about you every night you're out working. But I can't tell you to stop."

I grunted a couple of times and sighed.

"What does that mean?" my daughter asked.

"I'll be down to get you in about an hour."

Feather fell asleep in the passenger seat. I drove and she snored. That's a song I'd never tire of.

The next morning I made pecan waffles and codfish cakes. Feather and I sat together at the ledge around the stove eating and enjoying each other's company.

"I talked to Erculi last night after calling you," I said.

"How is Uncle Hercules?"

"He told me to tell you that if you had any problem just to hit the alarm button and him and his sons will be here in under three minutes."

The elder Longo had little red buttons installed in every house just in case there was some kind of emergency. We had one on each floor.

"Uh-huh," my daughter said. She wasn't worried and I suppose that was a good thing.

"You been talking to your uncle Milo?"

"He told me that my mother used to play violin when she was a girl. He said that she was one of the best in her age-group in LA."

"So what do you think about him?"

"He's my blood," she said with unexpected conviction. "When I talk to him about our family it feels like he knows things about me that I don't, but, but it's like I feel like I always did. You know what I mean?"

"Yeah," I said. "I guess it's important to have real family."

"No, Daddy." Feather put her hand on mine. "You're my real family. Uncle Milo and his people are where I came from. But you're my father forever."

I got to work at about 9:00. I wasn't bothered to be alone because I figured Oldstein, or whatever his name was, would honor the forty-eight hours he gave. I was pretty sure that he wouldn't have found Donata on his own and that money was the primary issue on his mind.

I went to the window of my office and looked down on the hippie yard. The youngsters were going back and forth from the greenhouse bringing various chemicals and tools to bear.

I noticed, not for the first time, a dark sedan parked across the street and down a few houses from the hippie house. The sun was beating down hard and there was no respite of a breeze.

I trundled back to Niska's desk, making myself comfortable there. I find that at times if I change small patterns, like sitting at Niska's desk, for instance, I gain a different perspective and maybe even a slightly altered way of thinking.

Sitting at the innocent student's desk, I considered Mouse's suggestion of killing Eddie Brock. He was a bad man even Melvin Suggs couldn't protect me from. But killing was such a final thing.

I tabled the notion, and then there was a knock on the front door.

It could have been the grim reaper tapping on my chamber door. Maybe I should have run, but this was my office. You only die once, but giving in to fear was endless defeat.

A small, balding white man stood there at the threshold dressed in a cheap gray cotton suit. His only outstanding feature was a bright yellow and deep red pansy in the buttonhole of his lapel. Behind the small man was a slightly taller guy who was slender. He was dressed in rust-colored trousers and a similarly hued square-cut shirt. The blouse had the vague pattern of leaves across it, like a fleeting memory of autumn.

They were both white men. Neither one smiled.

"Mr. Rawlins?" the front man asked.

"That's me."

"My name is Mr. Jericho and this is my associate, Orrin Cause."

"What can I do for you, Mr. Jericho?"

"May we come in?"

I considered the request. Orrin Cause gave me pause, no apologies for the rhyme. He had dead eyes and posture reminiscent of a dancer—a dancer of the dead.

"Sure," I said. "Come on in."

I got behind Niska's desk and gestured for my guests to take the chairs that were there.

Jericho looked around the room while his associate stared at the wall behind my head.

Still taking in the room Jericho said, "It has been brought to my attention that a man I know has come to you with a problem concerning missing funds."

Jericho's eyes settled on mine as he achieved the last word.

"If you're talking about a client of mine I can't tell you what I'm doing for them or why."

Cause's left shoulder moved forward an inch or two.

"That is an honorable position, Mr. Rawlins," Jericho said, "and I applaud you for it. But I'm afraid I have to press the question."

"Maybe you could get this man you know to give me the okay," I suggested.

Jericho smiled. I was not sure this was a good thing.

Seeing this duo together made me think of some two-headed mythological monster or demigod come to Earth to pass judgment or to quench a thirst for revenge.

"I believe you know a gentleman named Rufus Tyler," Jericho suggested.

My tongue actually went dry. Rufus Tyler was more widely known as Charcoal Joe because of his skin color and his superior sketching abilities. Joe was the most feared and respected man in the black community, and beyond.

"Uh-huh," was all I could utter.

"Why don't you give him a call?"

"I don't have Joe's number."

Orrin Cause stood and placed a slip of paper on Niska's desk.

"You have to understand, Mr. Rawlins," Jericho said. "I'm not a man who appreciates being rushed and I have no desire to hurry you. But in this case time is of the essence."

There was something about the smaller man's tone. It was the voice of someone who held the reins of authority. I took in a deep breath, picked up the slip of paper, exhaled, and then dialed.

There was one ring before the receiver was picked up.

"Yeah," a man said.

"Let me talk to Joe," I said.

"An' who the fuck is this?"

"Easy Rawlins."

A soundless moment passed and then: "Easy?"

"Hey, Joe. How you doin'?"

"Gettin' ready to go down to the California Club. One of the governor's men wants to talk."

"I'm sitting here with a man named Jericho. He seems to think that you have something to tell me."

"Jericho? That's easy. He will never threaten you, so you have to make sure not to cross him because you will not make it to the other side of that street."

"Huh. How's your wife and son?"

"They okay. He's off at school bein' a genius and she's more beautiful every day. How 'bout your li'l family?"

"They're okay."

"Remember, Easy. Walk softly, now."

I hung up and practiced breathing again. Then I went into my speech.

I told Jericho about Craig Kilian and his untimely death; about Eddie Brock and his missing money. About a girl named Donata that I was still looking for and a man named Alonzo who was already dead.

"And what do you plan to do about all this?" Jericho asked.

"I plan to stay alive."

That got the crime boss to smile again. He made a hand gesture that was familiar to Orrin Cause. The rust-clad gangster got to his feet, reached into a pocket, and came out with a fat envelope. This he deposited on my desk.

"That envelope contains two thousand six hundred and sixty-four dollars," Jericho said. "That's my lucky number. That's what

I'm giving you to keep me informed about what's happening with your case."

I didn't reach for the money. I didn't tell him that Donata/Roxanna had offered approximately thirty-eight times that much.

"You seem like you might have come from the country, Mr. Jericho. Is that true?"

He smiled again and nodded.

"Me too. I was born on a farm and lived around people who possessed what wealth the land had to offer but very little money. Those people traded in favors. You know what I mean?"

"I do."

"So at the end of this thing with Brock and the money, if you are satisfied I might want to ask a small favor."

Jericho gave me a curt nod, stood, and turned. He followed Orrin Cause through the front door.

38

Back in my office I decided on a .22 revolver for the rest of the Kilian affair. That caliber didn't have much of a kick and I felt I might need to be accurate with each shot. There was too much threat for me to rely on manhood alone.

I made a call. After about a dozen rings I hung up. A few minutes later I repeated that process with the same results.

The next call was answered on the fourth ring.

"Pink Palace," a mature woman's voice warbled.

"Hey, Esther, she's not answering her phone."

"She's gone, Easy. Said that you knew where to."

"That I do. How much I owe you?"

"Nothing this time, darling. Lola took me out drinking every night. She showed me more about this area than I could guess and I've lived here fourteen years."

"Thanks for making room."

"I hope she's okay."

"Me too."

With that thought in mind I dialed yet another number and asked a question. After that I cleaned and oiled my .22, washed my face and hands, then decided to take a walk around the block.

The front lawn of the urban farmers' house wasn't cut, but they kept it watered. In among the long blades of grass were tiny yellow flowers teeming with the insects that loved them. The big front window used American flags for curtains. A few houses down the dark sedan had not moved.

I went to a Winchell's doughnut shop and got a bear claw and a large cup of coffee, black.

He was standing out in front of our outside office door by the time I returned.

"Easy," he said.

My friend wore a tan-and-brown tweed jacket and dark brown trousers. His checkered white, lime, and dark green shirt was open at the collar. Thinner than I and an inch or two taller, Fearless Jones had a friendly smile, a slight limp, and a right hook that Sonny Liston would be cautious of.

We shook hands and slapped shoulders.

"What you into, brother?" he asked me.

"You must be gettin' old, Fearless."

"Why you say that?"

"Because the man I knew down Texas never looked before he leaped."

"You'ont have to tell me," he said on a grin.

"Let me put it like this," I said. "It's so bad that I needed to call on you."

"All right, then. You ret to go?"

"What you drivin'?"

"That Ford Edsel you gimme. I had it painted purple, though. That's my favorite color."

Back in those days the ride through the desert was both bleak and beautiful. We had to pass through Claremont and Redlands first, but once we were past those cityscapes there was just buff-colored ground and a Joshua tree here and there.

* * *

"So you sayin' the man hired you is dead?" Fearless asked from behind the wheel of his purple Ford.

"Yeah. That's right."

"Then why don't you just walk away?"

"Mainly because of the gangster, that Brock. But even if it wasn't for him I'd want to see this thing through."

"Is that smart, Brother Easy?"

"Is it smart to stand up against four men because they insulted a woman in your presence?"

Fearless laughed and said, "But I knew I could beat them."

It was midafternoon by the time we reached the Summer Sands, a gated apartment complex at the northern end of Palm Springs. The compound had high adobe walls and a big iron gate with an armed guard lounging under the shade of a huge metal umbrella that was painted orange.

"Can I help you?" the big-bellied, fifty-something white man asked Fearless.

Mr. Jones turned to me and asked, "Who is it you said?"

"Lola Thigman-Kilian," I called out.

"Does she expect you?"

"Yep."

"What are you doing here?"

"Coming to see Lola Thigman-Kilian."

"But what's your business with her?"

Staring the sweating white man in the eye I said, "I'm her florist."

He didn't like me, I didn't like him, and Fearless just didn't care.

"Can we come in?" my friend asked.

The guardian sighed and said, "Unit twenty-two."

He went to a cubbyhole in the wall and reached in. A moment later the iron gate slid to the left.

* * *

"Who ya lookin' fah?" a woman called out in a shrill voice. Her accent was from New York like my friend Izzy Abromovitz. I fought next to Izzy from Italy, through France, and into Germany—where Izzy died.

Fearless had parked out in front of unit twenty-two, a dark red door in a long pink building. No one answered our knock.

"Lola," I said, answering the nosy New Yorker.

"Oh." The woman seemed a little disappointed, or maybe jealous. "She's down by the pool. That's where she is every day in her swimsuit. Never swims. Just lolls around drinkin' martinis."

"Which way is that?" I asked.

"That way." She waved her hand like batting at a fly but I got the idea.

There was a broad swath of impossibly white tile between the main building and the blue pool. Two or three dozen sunbathers sat and reclined on the chaise lounges sipping on drinks and chatting, sleeping, or pretending to sleep. There was even one man reading a newspaper.

Lola was installed next to the water, laid back and completely relaxed. No one was swimming and the water looked somehow synthetic.

Lola's bathing suit was navy and her skin an ivory hue. You could see in her curves, and how she moved them, how some men get lost on their way home.

"Mr. Rawlins," she exclaimed when my friend and I walked up.

"Lola."

"And who is this?" she asked, getting an eyeful of Fearless.

"Fearless Jones," I said. "An associate of mine."

"Come, join me." Sitting up to make space on the lounger, she offered Fearless the spot next to her. I grabbed a nearby aluminum-and-green nylon chair.

"Do you have news for me?" she asked when we were all settled.

If you had just met her and didn't look too close, everything about Lola seemed happy, satisfied. But a second glance would hint at the weight around her eyes that whispered sorrow and maybe even a touch of remorse.

"I don't have any report yet," I said. "I came out here because I want to put it all together."

"What do you mean?"

"It's like this," I said. "Craig hired me because he said he got into a fight with a man he didn't know over a woman he never met."

"Okay, but, so what?"

"He said he didn't know her but you said that Craig introduced you to her some time ago and that she was having trouble with a boyfriend. If that was the case he could have been going out there planning to kill her man."

"But then why would Craig hire you?"

"Maybe guilt," I offered. "But more likely, after her boyfriend was dead Donata ran out on your son. When he hired me he wanted to find out where she might be."

"She was naked and that man was slapping her. Craig did what any good man would do."

"That's the general story, but you can see how maybe it doesn't hold together . . . not completely."

"What other reason could he possibly have?" Lola asked. She was good at pretending to be honest.

"Money," I said.

For a brief second Lola froze. She was gazing at something over my shoulder.

"Excuse me," a man said.

He was tall and lean like Fearless. One might have called him a white man if he wasn't wearing a suit truly that color.

"Yes, Mr. Graham?" Lola purred.

"Is anything wrong?" the man called Graham asked Clementine.

"Why, no. Why do you ask?"

"Um, these men are friends of yours?"

"This is Mr. Rawlins and Mr. Jones. They're from LA."

Before Graham could say any more I stood and held out a hand. After a moment's hesitation he grasped it and gave me an abortive shake.

"Pleased to meet you, Mr. Graham. Lola and I are friends. She asked me to drop by if I got the chance and so here I am."

"Are you planning to stay with us, Mr. Rawlins?"

"Plans haven't gelled yet."

He didn't like the answer but I had a pretty good grip. He nodded and moved on as if his questions were merely out of courtesy.

"Motherfucker," Lola said after Graham was past earshot. "They treat us like trash and then say thank you very much."

Us.

"So, you were saying, Easy?"

"Donata worked at the Stephanopoulos Talent Agency, a place that's owned and run by gangsters. She was also well-known at a sex club called the Dragon's Eye. Because Craig lied, I have to wonder why any of what happened did happen. I've been thinking about it for days and the only thing that makes sense is you."

"Me?"

"You were a stripper, right?"

"So?"

"Come on, Lola. We're not virgins here. I've known a lot of people, women in the life. Once you're in, you're likely to keep a toe in the water."

She wanted to lie but could see that I wasn't having it.

"Okay," she said. "Yes, I went to the Eye sometimes. It was the kind of a place where a man might buy you a drink and nobody looked down their nose at you. One night my car wouldn't start and I didn't have cab fare. I had to call Craig. He came and had a drink with me and Donata. After that he gave my car a jump."

"Yeah, but, it's not just her," I said. "You knew Alonzo too, didn't you?"

"He was a photographer," she said, somewhat reluctantly. "He took a few pictures of me."

"He also heisted an armored car."

"I don't know anything about that."

I took out the hundred-dollar bills she had given me, placing them next to her martini glass.

"What's that?" she asked.

"The money you gave me to pay for Craig's investigation." I was watching her closely.

"I don't understand," she said.

I sat there silently watching. But her confusion did not turn into fear.

"What?" she asked at last.

"The cops found a stack of hundreds like this in Craig's apartment."

She leaned away.

"When they ran the serial numbers they found them on a Treasury Department warrant," I said. "From that armored car job in San Bernardino."

The aggrieved mother looked down at the money and then up at me. It slowly dawned on her how she was implicated in her son's death.

"If you don't tell me about it, there's no way that I can protect you," I said.

"I don't know anything about a robbery. All I know is that Donata got this windfall and then her boyfriend, that Alonzo, took her money and put it with his. That's what Craig told me."

"Put it where?"

"I don't know. She said that he said he put it somewhere safe. But when she wanted to get at it he kept putting her off."

"Was Craig involved with this, um, windfall?"

"He gave me the hundred-dollar bills, but that was a while before he got in the fight with that man."

"Did he know Alonzo?"

Lola looked away and said, "Definitely not. I knew him like you said, but I didn't want Craig to know how I made my extra money. My son thought Alonzo was the straight-haired man."

Staring bullets at her I asked, "What do you think, Mr. Jones?"

"I believe her," my friend testified.

That was good enough for me.

39

We had drinks at a small place called the Malmar until the sun went down. There Fearless told stories about the old days and the war. I was at the front more than once in that conflagration, but Fearless spent most of his time behind German lines—causing all kinds of havoc. He didn't regale us with tales of bloodshed, however. He talked about the countryside and the wildlife, about people he'd met and the solitude that only a terrorist could appreciate.

At nightfall Lola invited us to a club she knew called Venus Cove, an intimate nightspot that had only nine tables.

No one questioned a white woman accompanied by two black men being guided up to the front. We had steaks and bourbon with baked potatoes and broccoli cooked so long that you could have mashed its green stalks with a fork.

After dinner and four rounds of top-shelf whiskey, Lola's defenses started to lag behind her words.

"Women don't have it easy in this world, Mr. Jones," she said.

They don't have it easy and most of them loved Fearless.

"Ain't that the truth," my friend agreed, patting her forearm. "From birthin' babies to buryin' their men."

Lola took the hand and squeezed it.

"You think anybody cares about a woman or a girl gets dragged by her hair and fucked or beat up just so a man could pretend he's a man?"

Fearless was too well-mannered to answer that question.

I sipped on my whiskey and waited.

"You wouldn't let that happen, now, would you, Mr. Jones?"

Fearless clasped her hands in his. She looked up at him with moist eyes and I knew that at least her feelings were for real.

"You know we're trying to do right by you, Miss Kilian," he said softly.

Lola pressed her forehead against Fearless's steel-band fingers.

That's why I had brought my friend. He worked for the detective agency from time to time. Fearless was the best bodyguard money could buy. But it was his power and the honesty in the eyes of most women that I hoped would solve the riddle of Craig and his mother. Lola could sense that Fearless would protect her no matter the odds. And in the face of those odds he was most likely to come out victorious.

"I know you are, Mr. Jones. I know you are," she said. "I don't deserve it. I did introduce my baby boy to that woman. She was just like me. I'd look at her and see myself."

Fearless lifted her chin with a finger and asked, "What did she do?"

"Women like us don't do things," she confessed. "Not really. We motivate the men that mistreat us, make them do things."

"Like what?" Fearless asked.

"Rob and steal and, and kill."

"She made somebody do all that?"

"That Alonzo stole an armored car along with all'a Donata's money and hid it in a garage somewhere."

I knew Fearless would open Lola up. I could never tell if he understood that he was part of the interrogation. But that hardly mattered.

The lights went down and as they did Lola leaned forward to give Fearless a gentle kiss on the lips. I felt a pang of jealousy. It wasn't that I wanted to kiss Lola but that Fearless was the kind of man who women wanted to taste the moment they saw him.

"Got my tweed pressed," a man's amplified voice crooned. I turned as he sang, "Got my best vest."

I didn't even know there was going to be a show. Four men were on the small stage: a horn player, drummer, pianist, and Frank Sinatra. The musicians were all black men.

"All I need is the girl," Sinatra sang, and I was put completely off my game.

He performed six or seven songs, ending with "My Way." After that he introduced the band, on loan from Duke Ellington, and thanked the club manager, whose name I've forgotten.

When the lights came up he walked over to our table and leaned down to kiss Lola.

"Hey, babe," he said. "Who're your friends?"

Then he pulled up a chair and joined us!

For ten minutes Frankie and Lola chatted like old pals. They had indeed known each other a long time. Thinking about it, it shouldn't have been a surprise. They both worked different ends of the same circuit.

When Sinatra got up to go he gave Fearless a quizzical glance.

"Do I know you?" he asked.

"You came to LA one time in fifty-nine," Fearless said. "Your manager talked to my man Milo Sweet, said you needed some black bodyguards."

"Yeah, you knocked out that big drunk who was jealous that his girl was giving me the eye."

Fearless shrugged and Frankie shook his hand.

Lola offered to let us sleep at her place after the show. But when I told Fearless that I could sleep in the car he got the message.

Fearless and I pulled off onto a dirt road ten miles outside of town. There I took the front seat and Fearless the back. There were at least a million stars out that night. Every minute or so you could see the trail of another fallen one. Thinking back on it now,

I am reminded of the time when the night skies were ruled by distant suns.

I woke up with the sun in my eyes and a crick in my neck. If Fearless felt cramped it didn't show on his face.

We stopped at a little stand in 29 Palms and had date shakes for breakfast.

Sitting at a redwood table on the outside patio, Fearless said, "Easy, look over there."

Standing maybe a dozen feet from us was a bird that looked like a large rooster if that rooster had grown to twice its normal size. It had very long, featherless legs and turned its head slowly to regard us. It took one long languorous step, then another. The third step came more quickly and by the fifth footfall it was moving at least ten miles an hour. That speed doubled by the eighth span and then the bird was gone.

"Roadrunner," Fearless said. "Outrun ninety-nine percent of men."

"We should get going," I said.

"Tell me sumpin', Easy."

"What?"

"What you plan to do about Lola?"

"Why? Don't you trust me?"

"Better'n that. I respect you. An' you know that's somethin' rare."

"You mean most people don't think I'm all that?"

"It ain't no insult, Ease. It's just that most people is afraid'a you 'cause you know folks like Mouse an' Charcoal Joe and that crazy Redbird. But I ain't afraid'a pain or death so I don't go there. Other people amazed at how smart you are but my friend Paris is the smartest man I ever met, even smarter than Jackson Blue."

"And so why *do* you respect me?" I asked.

"Your honesty," he said with a straight face.

"Honesty? I lie all the time."

"Only 'cause you're into the shit. Every pig farmer knows that there ain't no way to clean out a hogpen without gettin' messed. But you cleanin' it up and in the end you do the best you can. In the end the truth come out.

"That's why I'm askin' 'bout Lola. She lost her son. That's enough grief for any mother."

When I can afford it I let my heart listen to Fearless. He knew people better than most, and though he couldn't beat an eight-year-old at checkers, he was rarely wrong about things that mattered.

"I hear ya, Fearless. I like her too. But she pulled me into this thing with her son and if my count is right there's at least five men dead behind it."

Fearless stared at me like an avenging angel weighing sin. Then he sniffed and stood up.

"Let's go, man," he said.

Back at the office I showered and shaved, made oatmeal with raisins and cream, then sat at my desk trying to figure out what to do next. I'd learned a few things from Lola and Donata, Reynolds and Mona Strael, but I was no closer to getting my hands on the money that might save my life.

There was a call I should have made, but a rare bout of procrastination stayed me.

The hippies were working hard in the yard and greenhouse. I noted a man walking from the black sedan down toward Pico. Taking a pair of binoculars from the window ledge, I studied the man. At least that felt like I was doing something.

He was maybe five ten with short brown hair, wearing a yellow short-sleeved shirt that had little designs on it but I couldn't make them out. He had on khaki shorts and incongruous black leather shoes.

"Hm!" I grunted and then turned to my phone.

"McCourt," he answered.

"You got to Ketch?"

Anatole paused and then said, "We did."

"He still alive?"

"Don't ask me how."

"So where's he at?" I asked then.

"I don't work for you, Rawlins."

"I know. But Suggs wants me to find out some things. Ketch is a big part'a that."

"When I sent his name up the line I got a call from the Organized Crime Taskforce."

"What they want?"

"They say that Ketch and two of his friends are on their radar."

"For what?"

"They wouldn't tell me. Why were you on him?"

As a rule I don't share information with most cops. But rules are sometimes meant to be broken.

"As far as I've heard they're heist men."

"LAPD doesn't have a thing on them."

"I can't be sure about this but I believe they don't shit where they sleep."

It was a fair lead. He could do things with it. He might even end up helping me.

"Well?" I said after a moment or two.

"At Mercy," he said and then he hung up.

I made it downtown to Mercy General Hospital's emergency care wing in under an hour.

Ketch had been given his own room to die in. He had oxygen tubes attached to his nose and two IV stands feeding medicine and sustenance into his veins, drop by drop. There was a big electrical console set up next to him, taking readings through wires that were somehow attached to two fingers of his left hand.

Four other people were crowded in there with him, each one ministering in their own way. One nurse was standing off to the side writing something on a pink sheet of paper attached to a dark brown clipboard. Another white-suited sister of mercy studied his attachments and readings. In the farthest corner Lily Evangeline Dasher sat rubbing garnet prayer beads in her left hand and muttering prayers or curses under her breath.

Standing over Lily was a sturdy black man in work clothes designed for heavy labor.

When I came in, the man looked up and approached me.

"This is just the family," he explained, holding up a big hand swollen with muscle developed over many years of physical labor.

"I'm Rawlins, the one that called the police to come save him."

The man's eyes got wide. I couldn't tell if the workman was grateful or enraged. He opened his mouth but at first no sound came out. Even his vocal cords were torn over my deed.

"Tremolo," he said. "Tremolo Dasher, Reynolds's half brother. Um . . . how did you know to go to my mother's house?"

"I'm a private detective," I said, taking a business card from my breast pocket. "My client's a man who said that he witnessed a stabbing. After looking into it for a while I came up with your brother."

"Where is this man?" The tone of his words expressed his mood clearly. He was furious at everything, looking for anywhere to vent that rage.

"Dead."

Frustration was so strong in Tremolo that he shuddered, crushing my card in an involuntary fist.

"If the man hired you is dead, then why you here?"

"You know the kind of business your brother's in."

"I never had anything to do with that." He might as well have added, *I was the good son.*

"I'm not sayin' you did. But lookin' into findin' him I came across some, uh, some unsavory sorts. I need to find answers or I might end up bein' the next one need a hospital."

"I wanted him to go straight," Tremolo said through gritted teeth. "I asked him to come work with me."

"Doin' what?"

"Construction support. I worked for this guy Pitman runs a whole fleet of heavy-duty equipment. I even got Renny to work at one of our sites for a while. After he met that girl I thought he was on the way to goin' straight."

"What girl?"

"Mona. Mona Steel, sumpin' like that."

"But something pulled him back into the game, huh?" I was treading water, waiting for the wildebeest to come a little closer.

"One day he didn't show for work and the next thing I know I get fired, and then, then he's like this."

"How long ago was he working with you?"

"Why?"

"Tryin' to develop a timeline to figure out who might'a done this." He didn't seem to like the explanation so I added, "You wanna find out, don't you? You want justice for Reynolds, right?"

"He quit over three months ago," Tremolo admitted. "Him and his buddy."

"Who's that?"

"A guy named Plennery, Dennis Plennery."

Reynolds Ketch chose that moment to die. The machine he was attached to emitted a high-pitched sound like an electric scream. The nurses hurried Tremolo and me out of the room. Attendants and doctors were rushing down the hall and then past us to get to Ketch.

"Mama. Mama!" Tremolo called through the door.

I felt bad for mother and son, but I had other business to attend to.

In a phone booth on the first floor of Mercy General I consulted the detective's greatest tool of the day—the phone book.

41

It was a plain-looking bungalow-style house on Forty-Sixth Street a few blocks west of McKinley Avenue. The siding was composed of dingy, overlapping, lime-colored aluminum slats. The roof was flat and the front door open behind a closed screen. The lawn was mostly bare earth sporting a few swaths of dying St. Augustine grass. No tree or even a bush afforded any shade from the relentless summer sun.

I was half the way to the screen when a small boy appeared from nowhere and shot me four times with a silver-painted plastic cap pistol.

"Bang, bang!" the boy yelled.

I heard a giggle and then saw, off to the left, a girl-child, maybe four, two years younger than her brother.

"Is your father home?" I asked the grinning girl.

She had six pigtails with five yellow ribbons and one blue one tying them off at the ends. She was barefoot in a stained but still bright red dress. She shrugged her little shoulders in an exaggerated fashion saying either that her father wasn't home, or she didn't know if he was home, or maybe she didn't understand what I was saying.

"Daddy's in jail," the boy shouted.

Before I could turn and ask the little assassin if his father was named Dennis Plennery a gruff woman's voice asked, "Who you talkin' to out here, Theodore?"

The screen door slammed open and a young light-skinned woman came out. Looking at her I imagined that Dennis must have been fairly dark because the boy and girl were the dusky color of pecans.

"Alan Fredericks," I said to the sensibly protective mother.

"Penny," she snapped at the girl. "Get in the house and put on your tennis shoes."

The little girl laughed, skipping behind her mother and into the house.

The boy, Theodore, was moving around the edges of the yard, shooting his cap gun at phantoms.

"Am I supposed to know you?" the mother dared me.

"I was Ketch's friend," I said. "His mother called me to the hospital."

"Hospital why?"

"He was stabbed. He's dead."

She wanted to ask more, but the reality of death stopped her.

"Fredericks, you said?"

"Alan," I agreed.

"My name's Corrine." She took a step forward to offer a hand. "Why don't you come in, Alan."

"No, Mama," the little cowboy protested. "He dead. He have to stay out here an' play with me."

The house was larger and more substantial than I expected. The wide living room had buff-colored shag carpeting and ornate sea-green furniture. The coffee table sported a dozen or so small standup frames containing photographs of Corrine and her family. That was the first time I saw Dennis Plennery. Tall and gawky, he held himself like Clark Gable with Corrine playing the role of some starlet on his arm. He was dark-skinned, as I had imagined, topped off with a bushy mustache.

The flat fan situated in the side window brought a much-needed breeze through the hot house.

Corrine left the room and returned with two glasses of ice water. She put these on an end table that separated two short sofas placed at a perpendicular angle to each other.

"You look a little parched," she said. "Sit down."

The way she arranged the glasses meant that we had to sit on separate sofas.

What impressed me was that she hadn't lost her composure over the fact that a friend of her husband had been murdered.

"Where's Dennis?" I asked.

"He in jail waitin' charges on four counts," she said. "All the money he had and all he got is a fuckin' cheap-assed public defender."

"What they got him on?"

"Niggah got a wife an' two kids at home, but he in a bar on Slauson gettin' in a fight over a bitch cryin' 'cause her man slapped her one time."

"That only sounds like maybe one count," I said, biding my time again—waiting for what I needed to come to me.

She raised one finger and said, "First there's assault because he broke the boyfriend's nose."

Theodore and Penny came into the room laughing and running, hiding and shooting off caps.

"Boy, what I tell you about shootin' your gun in the house?"

Theodore stopped and looked down at the shag floor.

"Not to do it," he said.

Corrine held up a second finger and said, "Then he had a gun in his pocket and, third, a switchblade too. Penny, what did I say about your shoes?"

"Bu' I not ou'side, Mama. Shoes is for ou'side."

"Go—put—on—your—shoes." The force of the young mother's voice ran Penny from the room.

"What's number four?" I asked, mostly to derail the mother's fury.

"What?"

"The fourth count they got on him."

"Oh. Yeah. Then, when the police came, instead'a just sayin' that he was protectin' a woman got attacked, he tell the cops to fuck off, an' when one put a hand on his shoulder, Dennis pushed him. An' you know Dennis got a strong arm, so that cop stumbled and fell down."

"Resisting arrest," I said.

"Niggah just don't know how to ack."

Corrine's words were harsh, but it was obvious how hurt she was. I figured that's why she was so willing to invite me in; she needed an adult to complain to.

"Damn," I said. Though the story was common enough it felt daunting to know how much trouble you could get into while trying to do what you felt was right.

Corrine heard the meaning behind my one-word exhortation.

"It's all like TV at first," she said to an unspecified audience. "There you are still in high school an' just about everything he do drive you crazy. From the money in his pocket to him kissin' you with his teeth, from all night long to knowin' you ain't never had real love in your life before. An' if anybody come up on you he got his gun and his switchblade, his troops too. Make you feel like a goddamned queen.

"Then you marry him an' find out that he been doin' that stuff with about a dozen other girls; that he got three kids and he's still married to some woman down in Mississippi. One day you wake up and you want to change the channel."

"Why not leave him?" I asked, even though I knew the answer.

"Why? We know all the same people. Where I'm'a go nobody know me and Dennis too?"

"You afraid of him?"

"Not like you might think. Whenever I see him I'm that fifteen-year-old girl. I remember them kisses like they was yesterday. I need to take my babies and go somewhere where he cain't talk to me no more."

It was a little too much truth for the young mother. She put her chin down and turned her head away, trying to hold back despair.

"What you say about Ketch?" she asked a far wall.

"Somebody stabbed him in the chest and he died. And here this happens about the same time Alonzo got killed."

"Alonzo?" That turned her attention back to me. "He's dead too?"

"Shot in his own cot."

"An' so why you here?"

"I'm Lily Dasher's cousin. She told me to come here to warn Dennis."

"An' how do you know Dennis?"

"Just from around. When I went to the hospital, Tremolo, that's Ketch's brother, Tremolo told me that Ketch told him that Alonzo was shot and killed. Lily said to tell Dennis because she knew the three of them ran together. She also told me that he had a wife and children and they should know if there was danger out here."

"An' what the fuck I'm supposed to do about it?" she challenged.

That was my entrée; time for me to shine—darkly.

"I had heard around that Dennis and them had a big score not that long ago," I said. "They say that the money got hid. That sounds like a payday for somebody willin' to take some risks."

"And that somebody is you?"

"I could tussle when I need to."

Corrine looked at me with new eyes; eyes she might have used on Dennis when she was in high school.

"What you askin' me, Mr. Fredericks?"

"I wanted to talk to Dennis," I said. "First to warn him if he didn't already know about his friends, and then . . . well, maybe to see if he needed any help he was willin' to pay for."

"I already told you he cain't even pay a lawyer."

"Oh yeah. And I heard you too."

"So that's all?"

"I don't know. I mean, maybe if you could give me some information about your husband and, and his friends, then I could give you money to get far enough away so that Dennis won't find you to talk to."

"You think I'm'a turn on Dennis fo' the little change you got in your pocket?"

"More'n twenty-fi'e hunnert dollars."

"You lyin'," she said speculatively.

"Swear to God."

"Niggahs been sayin' shit like that to me ever since I was thirteen."

I took the envelope that Mr. Jericho's man Orrin Cause had given me and put it down between us on the end table.

"Two thousand six hundred and sixty-some dollars," I said.

Faster than either of us could move, Theodore ran up and grabbed the envelope. But before he could make good his escape Corrine yanked him by the arm, hard.

The boy hollered in pain. His sister ran up and wrapped her arms around her mother's offending wrist.

"Don't you ever come up and take my property!" Corrine yelled, shaking the little cowboy and his wailing sister. "You keep your goddamn hands to yourself!"

With that Corrine dropped Theodore on his butt and plucked the fallen envelope from the floor.

Holding each other, the children ran crying from the room.

Their mother looked at me and asked, "Can I count it?"

"Be my guest."

Two times she shuffled through the twenties, tens, and ones. When she was satisfied I held out my hand. She hesitated but then passed the bills over. I put them back in the letter casing.

"What you wanna know?" she asked.

"Did your husband and Alonzo work together at some kinda job?"

"Yeah. Construction. I think the company was called Pitbull an' it was out in the Valley somewhere."

"How long ago did they quit that?"

"'Bout three months past. Dennis said that he hurt his shoulder liftin' sumpin' too heavy but there was blood on the bandages. When he took 'em off it looked like somebody had grazed him with a bullet."

"You know anything else about the place he worked?"

"Him and Alonzo had been hangin' out with this white boy worked there. They came by here a time or two. He had this black girlfriend one time and then a white one."

"What was his name?"

"Um, uh, oh yeah, it was Kurt. No, no. Kirk, Kirkla, somethin' like that."

"What kinda stuff they talk about?" I asked.

"Nuthin'. Just man talk. Sports and how much they hated their jobs. That was the first time I evah heard a white boy complain about work. I guess we ain't all that different."

The young mother looked up at me—minds thinking things that might as well have been in foreign tongues.

While Corrine and I stared, the children slinked through the living room to the screen door and out.

"Is that enough for some'a this money?" she asked.

Maybe it was. It didn't really matter because I was just as superstitious as Jericho. His money felt like a curse smoldering in my pocket.

I stood up and Corrine quickly followed suit.

I handed the envelope to her. She snatched it and then took out the money to make sure I hadn't pulled a switch.

* * *

Outside the children were playing with a tomato bug. Penny was brave enough to let the little red-horned caterpillar crawl on her skinny arm.

I came over and squatted down between them. From my wallet I took a two-dollar bill and handed it to the boy.

"Sometimes adults lose their temper," I said. "But they still love you anyway."

Then I took two one-dollar bills and handed them to his sister.

"Whatever he gets, you get," I said. "Remember that."

42

Another gas station. Another phone booth.

Melvin Suggs had a secretary named Myra P. Lawless. She was elderly by 1960s standards. Fifty-six years old. Melvin paid Myra top dollar because she knew how to find out anything in one-tenth the time anyone else could. She worked long hours and never complained about men being men. Not that she let anyone walk on her. It was said that one time she slammed a pinching burglar with a folded metal chair.

Myra tolerated my company because she liked Fearless. Sometimes, when Fearless went with me to see Mel, he would sit in the outer office beside Myra's desk talking about anything from flower gardens to World War II.

"Commander Suggs's line," she answered.

"Hey, Myra."

"Hello, Mr. Rawlins, how are you?"

"Fine. How's Puggs?" Puggs was her dog. Her pet in lieu of a husband.

"I had to put him on a diet. Doctor said that he needs to lose three pounds."

"For a dog his size that translates to about forty-five pounds in man-weight."

"That's exactly what I tried to tell my sister when she said it wasn't that much."

"People don't even understand their own place in the world," I said.

"How can I help you, Mr. Rawlins?"

I explained about a construction company owned by a man named Pit-something, maybe Pitman, somewhere in the Valley.

"Let me look into it," she said. "Are you at a phone where I can reach you?"

"I'm kinda on the move today."

"Well, call back in half an hour and I should have something."

The next call was to my home phone.

"Hello." Feather was out of breath, the sound of laughter echoing in her voice.

"Hey, baby."

"Daddy!"

"You sound happy."

"Uncle Milo and Dagmar came up to visit. I thought it was okay because you said I couldn't go down there anymore but you didn't say we had to stop seeing each other. We've been having swimming races and I beat them every time."

"They aren't smoking marijuana there, are they?"

"Um, uh, no . . . I mean, only up on the roof."

I took about ten seconds of silence to show my disapproval and then we started talking again. She went on about her school friends and what they were doing and where they were going for their summer vacations. She said that she'd like to go see Boston and New York and London too. We'd gotten a letter from her adoptive brother, Jesus. He and his little family were doing fine down in La Jolla.

I closed my eyes for a while there listening to her chatter. I never really understood the word *blessing* before she and her brother came into my life.

"Are you coming home tonight, Daddy?"

"I'm gonna try my best. It's kind of a complex job."

"Uncle Milo and Dagmar are goin' to a concert in Griffith Park tonight, so could you try to get here before I go to bed?"

"I'll try."

Myra gave me the address of the Pitman Construction Company on Lankershim Boulevard in the San Fernando Valley.

"Rinaldo Pitman is listed as the manager but a Leon Starr is the owner through his company Sherman Construction. Pitman has been arrested twice on assault charges but they were both dropped."

"Thank you so much, Myra. That was a great help."

"You're very welcome. Say hello to Mr. Jones for me."

One more call, to Jewelle Blue, and I was on my way. When it came to commercial construction she knew just about every player in the business. And they were aware of her connections and the amount of money that was there to be made.

On the drive through Laurel Canyon over to the Valley I was thinking that I was glad not to have seen Dennis Plennery. I'd talked to, dealt with, and encountered enough bad men to last me a month, maybe two. I was looking forward to a simple business where men worked hard and then went home to their families, TV programs, and pets.

Pitman Construction took up an area of about two and a half city blocks. It housed at least forty trucks, from van-size to sixty-foot tractor trailers that could move many tons of cargo. They also had cranes, bulldozers, cement-mixing trucks, and a dozen or more highly specialized vehicles that a city like LA needed to grow as fast as seaweed under the South Pacific sun.

The front gates were open so I cruised down the unpaved dirt path that led to the only office building on the lot. This was a two-story structure that looked like a pair of mismatched train cars stacked one upon the other.

There were men all over the place, driving and banging, toting and smoking cigarettes.

A white man with a mostly bald head and broad shoulders emerged from the front doorway of the train-car building. He was on the short side but built like a fireplug. Even the way he walked seemed to seethe with anger.

He strutted over to where I'd gotten out of my car.

"Can I help you?" he shouted.

"Hi," I said, extending a hand. The angry man waited a moment before deciding to shake. When he did it was with a show of great strength.

I extricated my hand from the viselike grip, saying, "My name's Rawlins. I'm a private detective investigating a robbery."

"Nobody stole anything around here."

"I just have a couple of questions."

"Time is money, Rawlings. And you don't do a thing for me."

"Ten minutes at most," I assured him.

"I don't know you," he said. "And I haven't had an extra ten minutes since my wife and I made our fourth child."

"You had an Alonzo Griggs and Dennis Plennery working for you, right?"

"I don't know you," Pitman said again. "And because of that I'm gonna have to ask you to leave."

"Do you know a Leon Starr?" I asked.

It took Pitman a simmering moment before he said, "Get the hell offa my property!"

I looked him in the eye, letting him know that he didn't scare me but maybe he should be scared. Then I went to my car, retraced the route I had taken, finally coming to a 76 gas station across the street. In yet another phone booth I called a number that Jewelle had given me. Then I parked on the street and went to stand out in front of the construction company fence.

The gate had been shut and locked behind me.

A guy in jeans and a dark green, uniform-like jacket strolled over to keep me company. He was tall and lean, white with a scowl on his face that spoke, I supposed, to the lack of a mother's love.

"You should move on, son," the white man advised, a hint of the South putting a spin on his words.

"Did you study history in shit-kicker high school?" I asked him.

"What the fuck you say to me?"

"Come on out past the gate and I'll whisper it in your ear, Huck, honey."

"Faggot nigger!" he exclaimed.

"More than enough to kick your ass, peckerwood."

It was at that moment I realized that I was ready to kill Eddie Brock Oldstein. I was almost mad enough to pull out my pistol and make the half guard come out and face me.

Maybe I would have done it but there came behind me the honk of a car.

Driving up to the gate was a Cadillac limousine painted in shiny metallic gold.

While the security guard ran to open up the gate, the back door of the Caddy opened and a small white man leaned out.

"Are you Easy Rawlins?" he asked.

"I am."

"Get in."

The back of the limo was opulent. It had seating for eight or nine men. There was a bar replete with five kinds of whiskey, ice, crystal (not glass) for drinking, and even a telephone.

"This phone works?" I asked.

"Yes, it does," Leon Starr said. "Jewelle Blue called me on it just a little while ago. We do a lotta work together in downtown LA.

That's why I agreed to this. She told me that you were a private investigator. I hope you don't intend to cause me trouble."

"I can honestly say that anything I do will be better for you than if I did nothing."

Starr was a little thicker than Mr. Jericho but they seemed to be cut from the same original cloth. He stared at me, still wondering if he was making a mistake bringing me into his business. But Jewelle was a dynamo of construction in Southern California at that time. She could open doors for him that no mayor or governor had access to.

I rode with Leon Starr to the double-train-car offices of Pitman Construction. We walked into the building unmolested and through the entrance to Rinaldo's small office.

When Pitman saw me again, I was sure that he planned to throw a paperweight or something, but . . .

"Hey, Rinaldo," Starr said. "This man Rawlins needs some questions answered. I'd appreciate it if you gave him a few minutes."

"I'm pretty busy right now, Lee," the angry man said in a forced tone that approximated reasonableness.

"You'll have to put everything on hold until Mr. Rawlins has asked his questions and you have answered them."

Capitalism is a feral beast but I love her when she works for me.

"Okay, I guess," Pitman said.

I turned to Leon Starr and said, "If you don't mind I'd like to discuss my business with Mr. Pitman alone."

The boss gave me a stately nod and left the little office, closing the door behind him.

Pitman was no longer angry. His expression can be best described as befuddled.

"Who are you?" he asked.

"I'm the guy who knows the man your boss needs to do business."

"What do you want?"

"Alonzo Griggs and Dennis Plennery," I said. It was then that I noticed Pitman's fists—they were flushed sledgehammers.

A shudder went through the squat man's shoulders.

"The, um, the uh, those, those men worked here. I hardly ever saw 'em. You know, just muscle on the job."

"You fired them?"

"No, no. They quit. I mean, really they just stopped coming in."

"How long were they here?"

"I don't know. Here, lemme get my secretary on the line and you could ask her." He went as far as getting behind the desk and picking up the receiver.

"What do you think would happen if I called an LAPD commander to search every property you had for something bigger than a breadbox?"

"What are you talking about?" he asked.

Maybe he really didn't know. But he was afraid of something. He was a cornered creature and I had to be careful that he didn't go mad.

"So what was it?" I asked him. "You spent too much money on the girlfriend, lost it in Vegas, or maybe both. You had to sell out to Starr so your kneecaps didn't get busted. Then Alonzo offered you a big-time payout and all you had to do was turn your back."

I knew part of the story from Jewelle. The rest I surmised.

Pitman's mien was rueful sorrow. In a bind for quick cash, he said yes when it should have been no.

I knew that moment all too well. Most black men of my generation do; men born as second-class citizens, living third-class lives. The grandsons, great-grandsons, and great-great-grandsons of slaves. Those men would be sitting around a card table late at night drinking hard liquor for temporary relief of the pain that hard lives and hard labor bring. They talk about sex first and then naturally come to discuss their children and those children's mothers. On some nights, like the one Pitman was remembering, the men who didn't have good mothering, who didn't listen in the pews to what the minister was laying between the lines, who didn't believe in law because they had never been the recipients of justice—those men crossed a line in their minds. One of them says, why not? Why not do that thing that they think we do anyway? Maybe it's stealing a bag of coal that won't be missed or allowing that beautiful white daughter to enter when she comes knocking. Maybe it's running your car over some soused-up peckerwood stumbling down a country road in the dark of night, alone.

Why not is the question and most often drunken oblivion is the answer. But sometimes, sometimes you wake up in the morning with that question still in your mind. Why not? They took every-thing else. Why not take something precious that's theirs?

That's how it starts and most often it's the beginning of the end. Pitman knew all these things in that long tunnel of silence he was in. I knew it too. The guards were kidnapped, probably killed. That's a capital crime; that's shackles, bars, brutalization, forced labor, and a sudden return to the lives of our ancestors.

Pitman was a white man but he knew these truths as clearly as any descendant of slavery. He cleared his throat mightily.

"What are you getting at?" he wheezed.

"Come on, man," I said. "Alonzo, Plennery, and a man named Ketch offered you some thousands of dollars to let them use a big truck and maybe to store it someplace. You might have convinced yourself that it was just a truck but you know that when the cops get hold of it, you will be on trial too. You'll be up in Q with the niggers and spics, more aware of bein' a white man than you have ever been in your life."

Pitman began to sweat. It was like I had become the narrator of his nightmares. His breath was labored and his rage transformed to despair.

"Look," Pitman said, trying to wrest back control. "We were workin' on a block of new row houses down in Compton. We got a steel-gated work area down there with a double-reinforced series of storage units inside meant for construction vehicles. Plennery told me that I could make um, some, some money if I filled out the paperwork for him to drive one of those vehicles with Alonzo as the nighttime guard."

"What kind of vehicle?" I asked.

"I left that blank on the request form."

"What else did they need?"

"One of the storage units for the more expensive equipment. Yeah. One'a the lockups."

"And what's in there now?"

"Nuthin'. I looked just a few days ago. There wasn't nuthin' there."

43

We all—Starr, Pitman, myself, and a company jack-of-all-trades named Bob Bester—took a ride out to Compton in the golden limousine. The chauffeur had turned on the air-conditioning, but sweat dripped off Pitman's brow anyway. He didn't want to be in that car. I couldn't blame him.

Starr had called a special connection he had at city hall to tell them what he expected to find at the Compton installation. I called Anatole and Melvin but they were out together on a triple homicide that happened in Hollywood the night before.

Nineteen sixty-nine was an interesting year. There was strong anti-war action from the colleges and universities and all kinds of black political insurgence. The sleeping giant of white guilt was awakening and there seemed to be some kind of hope for the future. If you were innocent enough, or ignorant enough, you might have believed that things were improving in such a way that all Americans could expect a fair shake.

But of my many flaws, neither innocence nor ignorance played a part. We were on our way to the scene of a movable crime; a crime committed by black men. I was already guilty simply because of the color of my skin. It was even worse because my brethren had committed the crime. My head would be considered for the chopping block no matter how guilty the liberals on the Westside, or in Washington, felt.

I was as frightened as Rinaldo, but he didn't have the great luck of being on the battlefields of World War II. The fear of being huddled in a foxhole with two-hundred-pound shells exploding all around gave the beating heart perspective that no peacetime experience could equal.

The Compton installation was even larger than its Valley counterpart. We pulled in through double gates and drove the equivalent of a block and a half to a triple-gated area where a dozen or more storage areas were used for cargo, construction paraphernalia, and, of course, earth-moving vehicles. The storage units were constructed from iron slabs that formed the walls and roofs for containment. Starr wasn't fooling around protecting the tools of his trade.

"It's twenty-six-A," Rinaldo said when we exited the car. "But like I told you, there's nothing there."

We walked down one path, turned left on another, then went quite a ways to get to 26A.

There was a huge, complex lock at the center of the garage-like door of the unit. The metal door was slatted, fifteen feet in width and twice that in height.

Bob Bester went up to the lock. He was maybe five ten, with a thatch of white hair, the gait of a male ballet dancer, and a grin that was irrepressible. He was a strongly built man, like an old-school middleweight with some pop.

He took a crazy-looking keychain from a pocket and used six or seven odd-looking devices on the door. After these machinations a small slat slid open. Bob stuck his arm in up to the elbow, did some kind of blind manipulation, then yanked his hand out. A few seconds after that the slatted wall began to rise, each iron plank folding neatly and loudly into the one above.

This revealed a big empty garage with a dirt floor.

"You see? You see, I told you. There's nothing here," Rinaldo said. "I never saw nothing either. I don't know what they did."

Pitman was right as far as any vehicle or object was concerned, but there was something there: a weak scent. An odor with which I was quite familiar.

"There any units out here that don't get opened very often?" I asked Bob Bester.

That man might have been some kind of genius. He looked at me with gray eyes that were almost white. Slowly understanding filled those glossy orbs. Then he nodded, giving me a little smirk.

"Yeah," he said. "Yeah. The hazardous materials containment unit. That's where we keep explosives, corrosives, and stockpile toxic waste."

"Why don't we go over and take a look in there?" I suggested.

This unit was smaller, protected by yet another iron barrier.

Bob Bester performed his magic and the garage door lifted. The pall that flowed out caused the two men to cough. Pitman, who was already in a heightened state of distress, actually vomited.

Bester handed me a handkerchief upon which he had drizzled a few drops of camphor. Putting this over my mouth and nose, I walked into the dim cavern.

The armored car was there. The back door was closed but the lock had been broken. The three guards were in different parts of the otherwise empty vehicular safe. They had fallen where they were shot.

A bright light suddenly illuminated the scene I was already trying to forget. You could see clearly that the dead men were decomposing where they lay. Foul-smelling puddles had formed under each one of the deflated bodies.

"Nobody move!" a voice boomed.

Eight or nine men in unfamiliar uniforms were rushing in. They toted serious-looking rifles. The invaders would have been frightening if it wasn't for the fact of the smell of death. Try as they might, the armed troops could not hold their rifles steady when their lungs filled with the miasma of the dead.

The heavily armed cops were from San Bernardino. A special military-like team of officers that our mayor had let in, in order for them to find the men who took their armored car and its guards.

They identified Leon Starr, shook his hand, and told everyone that they had to wait in an office that could be locked—everyone except me, whom they clapped in chains and dragged off to yet another room.

"What was your job in the heist?" the mustachioed young man who led the strike team asked. His name was Borland and he had no patience with trash like me.

"I'm working with the LAPD, brother," I said. "I'm the one who located the car."

He slapped me hard enough to hurt an office worker. For somebody of my persuasion it was just the promise of things to come.

"The fact that you knew where it was proves that you're one of the gang," he said.

"It proves that I have a logical mind."

He used his fist that time. I was seated on a three-legged stool and so fell to the concrete floor.

"Get up!" Borland yelled.

My hands were cuffed behind my back but I knew from the timbre of his shout that he didn't give a damn about my restraint.

I staggered to my feet and he gave me an uppercut to the gut.

"Stop that this minute!" a familiar voice commanded.

Behind Borland and his two assistants were Anatole, Melvin, and four LAPD uniforms.

Borland turned his head to regard them, then swiveled back and socked me on the jaw.

I was on the floor when Anatole McCourt took the three steps that brought him from the door to Borland. The blow the Irish cop threw was so fast and so hard that my torturer had to be unconscious before he hit the concrete.

44

I don't think there had ever been another moment in my life where I felt so much glee and so much pain at the same time. McCourt lifted me to my feet with one hand—he was that strong.

"One of you men get him out of these cuffs," he barked at Borland's officers.

The command was obeyed immediately because Anatole was not the kind of man you ignored.

Suggs was at my side holding my left arm. I guess I was a little unsteady on my pins.

"What's going on here?" Suggs asked the man working to unlock my chains.

"Nigger knew where the armored car and the dead men were," the guy behind me said.

Anatole gave the man a questioning look.

"What did you say?" the head cop asked.

"We knew that the, that the crew was nig—was Negroes and this one knew where the car was hid. He musta known we were closin' in and figured to get to the money before we did."

"But you said that there wasn't any money," Melvin challenged.

My hands came free and the cop behind me backed away.

And then a really amazing thing happened.

Borland climbed to his feet and Anatole hit him again! The jab traveled no more than six inches but the San Bernardino cop collapsed in a heap. Anatole turned his head toward the other out-of-town cops, daring them to complain.

They had nothing to say.

Rinaldo Pitman was arrested, charged with conspiracy, and held over for other, yet-to-be-filed charges.

When the three of us were alone in the unit boss's office Anatole McCourt asked, "Why weren't they questioning him?" It was unclear if he was addressing his question to his boss or me.

"He just saw three of his uniformed white brothers dead in probably the worst way he could imagine," I said. "And there I was, of the race that slaughtered them. He was just gettin' his pound'a flesh."

"But you didn't do it," Anatole said.

"Doesn't matter."

"It always matters."

"So what you got for us, Easy?" Melvin interrupted.

"This isn't even the case I signed up for," I told the cop, once again treading water, guarding myself from men who didn't see themselves as threats. "Like I told you already, Craig Kilian thought he stabbed a black man named Alonzo."

"Only the guy's name was Reynolds Ketch," Anatole interjected.

"Probably, yeah. The three of them—Ketch, Griggs, and Plennery—did the heist."

"Who's Plennery?"

"He's the third heist man."

"And where's he now?"

"In your jail system somewhere. He assaulted a citizen and then a cop. Him and Griggs worked for the construction company so they could get a truck big enough to move the armored car. They planned on taking the car here and hiding it so the police would think the guards ran off with the money themselves; at least that's the way it looks to me. Even with the witness the plan would have probably worked if I wasn't trying to find that girl for Craig."

"That Donna somethin'," Melvin said, nodding. "Where's she now?"

"Donata Delphine, also known as Roxanna Coors."

"Yeah," Melvin said. "Her."

"Only things I can tell you about Delphine is where she wasn't. She ran away from Alonzo, her job, and LA as far as I know." I hoped Mel couldn't tell I was lying. Luckily I got a little help from his subordinate.

"You have that friend," Anatole stated. "That Raymond Alexander."

"Yeah?"

"He's known nationwide as a heist man."

"Alleged heist man."

"This is a heist."

"This is a travesty," I said. "Any good thief worth his salt would never go after a payload under half a million. Too many men and moving parts."

"Let's get back to Delphine," Melvin said.

"Commander Suggs," a strong voice declared.

At first I was happy for the interruption. Melvin could smell that Roxanna/Donata was the linchpin of the crime. And even though I'd already given him what he wanted, he was still a cop and wouldn't let any detail slide.

When I turned to see who it was who spoke I was mildly surprised. He was a tall, skinny man in an olive-colored suit, tan shirt, and no tie. Eggshell white, he had a military haircut and sallow cheeks. His eyes were ten percent larger than would be expected and his face was smaller than it should have been.

For all his deformities this man projected confidence and intensity.

"Yeah?" Melvin replied.

"Joe Cox," the new player said. He walked forward, extending a hand for Mel to shake. "FBI. We're taking your prisoner." There was no ask in his deep voice.

The armored car was moving money between banks. And banks were the province of the federal government. With that thought in mind I was already beginning to miss Officer Borland and his brigade of San Bernardino bullies.

Mel told Cox that I was not a prisoner but rather a confidential informant they'd used to find the armored car and its hijackers. That just made it easier for the feds to detain me.

I was chained again and dragged off to a more or less nondescript black Ford sedan.

Special Agent Cox and his minion, Special Agent Donahue, had staked out an interrogation room at the downtown LAPD precinct, made available to them by the mayor.

"What was your job in the crew?" Cox asked.

I was continually impressed by that deep voice emanating from such a thin body.

"I was looking for a man that my client thought he might have grievously injured," I said for the fifth or sixth time. "He thought the man's name was Alonzo but really it was Reynolds Ketch. Both men are now deceased. It was only after the fact that I realized they were involved with the armored car job."

"The police reports say that your client," Donahue said, "was also involved in the robbery."

"Maybe he was. I don't know. I was informed of that theory after my client had been murdered."

Donahue was a big son of a bitch. Not Anatole's size but an intimidating presence still and all. It was a toss-up whom he disliked more—me or skinny Cox.

"Where's the money?" Cox asked.

"I don't know."

"Who ordered the murder of the guards?"

"I have no idea."

"You understand that the federal government is not afraid of exercising the death penalty."

"Half the people on the street where I was raised were of the same mind."

These questions and maybe six or seven like them occupied every moment of every hour that I was shackled to a chair in that room.

The interrogation lasted seven or eight hours. I wasn't allowed to go to the toilet nor was I given any water, which, thinking back on it, was probably a good thing. I was physically uncomfortable but what bothered me was that they wouldn't let me make a phone call. Feather would be worried.

When Cox and Donahue gave up for the day I was transferred to a holding cell in the basement of police headquarters.

"I'd like to make a call," I asked the police escort the FBI agents turned me over to.

They didn't speak; just brought me to a steel door painted lime green. The door opened, seemingly of its own accord, and the silent cops pushed me through.

There was a prisoner already in the room, sprawled out on one of two cots and reading a Santa Anita racing form.

Hope springs eternal.

He looked up from his studies and said, "This here is my bed."

I sat on the other and looked around the eight-by-ten cell while my roommate read.

Prison is many things. It's a daily challenge to survive, a self-contained community awash with potential allies and enemies, and anger, even hatred, so deep that it would have warmed the cockles of hell.

My cellmate was a tan-colored man, his face containing the elements of many races. He was once handsome but a hard life had worn down his features until they only hinted at some underlying humanity.

"What's your name?" I asked him.

Taking his time, marking his impossible next bet with a pencil stub, he looked up at me. That stare lasted maybe half a minute. Maybe he was still trying to pick the right horse.

"Pardlo," he said at last. "Fenster Pardlo."

"I'm Rawlins. Easy Rawlins."

The name earned a brief frown from my cellmate.

"What they got you in for, brother?" he asked.

"The wrong color in the wrong place at the wrong time."

Pardlo grinned. He was missing a lower front tooth and a toothbrush. Something about his faded countenance set my teeth on edge.

"That's funny, but I know what you mean. What they put on the arrest form?"

"Let's just say I knew where the bodies were buried. You got anything I could read?"

He had a day-old *LA Times* under his stained mattress.

Reading the paper reminded me of my ex-girlfriend, Bonnie Shay. She read the *LA Times* and the *New York Times* every morning. Two or three days a week she got her hands on the original *Times,* the one from London. Later on she married a black African named Joguye Cham. Cham was at first royalty and then became a rebel in western Africa, fighting against American and European imperialism.

From nowhere a man began hollering piteously from a distant place outside our cell.

"I won't do it again!" the man yelled and then he grunted from a heavy blow. "I won't—" Another blow landed.

I couldn't hear the thudding fists but I felt them in the man's howls. After the beating was over the victim whimpered for some time before someone said, "If you don't stop that snivelin' I'm'a beat you again."

And he did.

"Rawlins," Pardlo said with offhanded speculation. "Easy Rawlins. You're that guy knows Raymond Alexander, right? The one they call Mouse?"

My sympathies for the man being beaten evaporated. I cut my eyes at Pardlo but said not a word.

"I did a job with him on United California Bank three years back," my cellmate declared.

A man can't be proud of everything he do, Uncle Sorry once said to me. *All he can hope for is to learn from his mistakes and pray he don't do it again.*

I don't know what there was to learn when I leaped from the bed and grabbed Pardlo by his shirt. I slammed him into the wall, caught him, and then slammed him again.

"Help," he gulped.

I hit him in the jaw with my fist and then slammed the right side of his neck with an elbow. I kneed and kicked him and then lifted him from the floor.

"Help!" he shouted, and I threw him clear across the cell.

On the floor Fenster Pardlo was grabbing at his shoe. Too little too late. I was on him with three heavy punches and then I snatched the shiv from his hand.

"Help!" he yelled again, louder than the man we'd already heard.

I pressed the metal edge against Pardlo's throat hard enough to draw blood. My ears were hot and a rage passed through me that I hadn't experienced in many years.

The multiracial spy looked up into my eyes with fear that went all the way down to species. There weren't any words or bargains— just his death written on my face like a verse out of the Old Testament.

I was going to kill him. I had to kill him after all I'd been through. It was just Sorry's gentle admonition that held me back for a second or three. Just enough time for the police to come through our cell door and throw me off.

They took the shiv and then beat me with their truncheons. But physical damage wasn't their goal. They dragged the bleeding, banged-up, backstabbing traitor from the cell, leaving me innocent of murder through no fault of my own.

No one had come to the aid of the other man we heard being broken and brutalized. Combat was considered little more than polite conversation between inmates. But Pardlo was a spy. He was there to betray me and so fell under the protection of the law.

45

I hate the FBI. They think they're so smart that they can't be wrong. It's never a mystery to them but a foregone conclusion. They were sure that I robbed the armored car and killed those guards. The only trick was to get my confession. That's why my heart told me to kill Fenster. I didn't have to confess. All the snitch had to do was say that I admitted to being involved in the heist and both Raymond and I would end up on the gallows telling jokes until the final punch line died on our tongues.

My heart was beating so hard that it hurt, but I didn't have the luxury of concern.

I lay there thinking of what might be the key to the money I never possessed but that I owed still and all. The ticket on that debt was my life.

Kirkland Larker kept coming to mind. He brought my name into the mix. He sent Craig Kilian to me. He sat at Dennis Plennery's table drinking beer, even dated Mona Strael.

Mona Strael.

A key worked its way into the lock of my cell. I hoped my new roommate was as see-through as Pardlo had been.

The door opened and Melvin Suggs came in followed by his number two. McCourt had to bow his head to make it across the threshold.

I sat up and asked, "What brings you guys here?"

"It's a city jail," Melvin explained. "There's no real charge. I got a judge to kick you loose."

"I gotta get to a phone."

"Okay, but I already got in touch with Jackson Blue. Him and his wife and child are up on your mountaintop. Your little girl is just fine."

The Chateau Marmont was easier getting into the second time. The doorman was a dark-skinned brother on that particular day. When I told him where I was going he just waved me by.

Bo Tierce was making drinks at a furious pace and so just smiled and nodded at me. I went on through to the small lounge, where I spied Ms. Strael talking with a paunchy middle-aged white man. While they talked I walked up and waited patiently.

After a moment or two the man turned to me. He should have been wearing Brooks Brothers gray but instead he sported a lavender ensemble that would have made any man not performing on a Las Vegas stage look ridiculous.

"Can I help you?" he asked. You could tell by the timbre of his voice that he was used to being obeyed.

"It's the lady," I said.

"Don't you see us talking here?"

"I know. But it's a question I believe she wants to hear—about a man named Kirkland Larker."

Mona stood up.

"Excuse me, Mr. Beam," she said. "This will only take a minute."

Out in the carpeted hallway Strael confronted me.

"What the fuck do you mean by walkin' in on me like that?" she demanded.

"You'd rather me send Mr. Brock?"

"I know people too," she averred. "I could put somebody on you just as easy."

"If that's the way you wanna play it."

Mona actually sneered. She looked into my eyes, imagining me not existing at all.

"Mona," a man said. It was Mr. Beam in his garish Carnaby Street suit.

"Go away, Peter," she said. "Just go away."

She didn't even look at him.

After he was gone she said, "What have I done to you?"

"Brock was after money that your friend Donata stole," I said. "Now, because I worked for Craig a minute and a half, Brock has transferred that debt to me."

"But you didn't take it."

"That's right. And I truly do wish he had your powers of perception and objectivity. But let's face it—that man has only two gears—to kill or to maim."

"And what do you need from me?"

"Where Larker is and where he might think we can find the cash."

"I can't tell you that," she said.

"Your funeral." I meant it too.

I had taken maybe three steps toward the stairs when a hand grabbed my left biceps. She pulled hard enough to turn me around.

"Please," she said. "You don't know what that ape does to women."

"Then help me. This is the last guy who should get what he's after."

"I don't know where the money is. Plennery and Alonzo took it."

"Where does Kirkland fit in?"

"He worked at Pitman Construction. Alonzo introduced him to Donata and from there she pulled him into whatever crimes they planned."

"How did you get mixed up in it?" I asked. I wasn't expecting the truth but maybe just a lie transparent enough to give some kind of hint at what might have happened.

"I thought you knew."

"Knew what?"

"Donata was at UCLA too. She was in the actuarial sciences department. We had English Lit together and it didn't take long before we saw that we were a lot alike. You know what I mean. Not black but . . . you know. She'd been working at the Dragon's Eye but that was too much for her schoolwork. So I brought her here. We worked the lounge together for a few months. She did three nights a week. In the daytime she worked for Eddie's modeling agency. When things were slow we talked. One night, a few months ago, she invited me to go out with her and her boyfriend and his white friend Kirk. She said that she thought this friend would like me and if I liked him we could have some fun.

"Her boyfriend was Alonzo but you know that. He gave me some money and we had a good time. Kirkland worked construction. Alonzo got him to get him and his friend Plennery jobs on the yard. A little while after that they pulled him into some kind of robbery they planned. I didn't know what. I thought maybe they'd steal and sell some heavy equipment.

"Kirk and Alonzo were kinda kinky, you know. Switching partners and takin' pictures. They had some good cocaine and our semester was over so I really wanted to let go a little."

Mona stopped talking for a while, her face expressing the bittersweet memories of sex and drugs somehow translating into relief.

"What was your part in the thefts?" I asked then.

"Nothing really. Roxanna wanted to bring Craig out on a double date with me and her and Kirk. We went to that big restaurant at the LA airport."

"Why?"

"Roxie uses people. That's how she got Kirk to get Craig to hire you."

"But what would I have had to do with it?"

"Roxie knew that Craig would just get hurt and she really liked the kid. She moved to the house over on the Westside and told Kirk that she'd cut him in on the money if he made it so that Craig would go on a, you know, on a false trail."

"So I'm the decoy?"

"You didn't know anything. Kirk thought that you'd run Craig in circles long enough that he could get his hands on the money and run."

"Larker knew where the money was?"

"They knew that it was on one of the lots of the Pitman Construction Company. At least that's what he told Roxie."

"But it wasn't true?" A cold breeze seemed to come down that hallway. It wasn't real but I think Mona Strael felt it too.

Mona brought both hands to the sides of my jaw and peered deeply into my eyes. We held that gaze for long seconds.

"Roxie kinda liked Craig," she said at last, "but he was crazy for her. That's just the way it was. Craig was a good guy. He was immature but he was a man too. That's why someone could push hard on him but he wouldn't break. That's why he'd rather get shot than tell where Roxie was."

I had different notions about the young vet's demise. In my mind, Brock and a pet thug or two came in on him with guns out. That triggered the kid's shell shock and he shifted into battle mode. He had practiced hand to hand on some of the best in the world—the Vietcong. That meant that he could inflict serious damage in the shortest possible time.

When push came to shove Brock had to kill him. And once the shots were fired, he and his men had to go instead of searching the apartment. He had just enough time to go through the kid's pockets and come up with my card.

"So," I said. "Kirkland is smart enough not to tell Craig what's what but he does tell you?"

"And I don't wanna have nuthin' to do with it," Mona swore. "I wanna be a lawyer with an office and businessmen clients. I don't wanna run off with that white boy on stolen money. I'm not like Roxie."

"You could have just turned Kirkland away," I suggested. "You could have said no."

"Say no to a man who killed people as a profession over in Vietnam? A man who's got armored car money and a gangster's money too? Say no to a man that says he stole that money for me?"

Mona's beautiful face had tied itself into a sour knot. I felt for her.

"He said that?" I asked. "He stole it for you?"

"Yes."

Kirk used to say that she was his golden ticket. Said she could get him through any door; that's what the bomb-blasted bartender, Meanie, told me that Kirkland had said about Mona. It wasn't exactly corroboration—but it was close.

"Tell me something, Miss Strael."

"What?"

"Would you mind if Kirkland gets into trouble over this shit?"

"No," she said without hesitation. "Not in the least."

"He told you that he had the money?"

"He said that he could get it anytime he wanted but he was safe from harm because he didn't know where it was."

"He had it but he didn't know where it was," I parroted. "You got somewhere you could go outta town? A relative or somethin'?"

"Yes. Up in Oakland. My aunt Maude."

"Anybody down here know about her?"

Mona concentrated a long moment and then shook her head.

"No," she said again.

"Nobody. You sure? Not no friend or cousin or ex-boyfriend."

"Maude's my mother's sister, but Mama passed."

I waited a few moments while Mona let the severity of her truths sink in.

Then I said, "Go up there right now, tonight. Tell Bo that your sister's sick down south and you have to go to her. Tomorrow morning take a leave from school if you have to. Tell them that your grandmother died. Gimme a number to call you and I will when this is all over."

It was a sign of how scared Mona was that she didn't voice one complaint. Eleven minutes after my offer she was gone from the Chateau Marmont for good.

The hotel still had those fancy phone booths where you could sit down and shutter yourself in for privacy. I dialed a number and allowed it to ring at least thirty times.

"He'o?" she answered at last.

"Lola, go splash some water on your face and then come back and talk to me."

"Ho'on," she gasped.

Maybe three minutes passed.

"What do you want, Easy? Is it about Craig?"

It was her question that resolved the data that flitted around in my mind like confetti.

"You said that Craig used to go up to Blood Grove with that old boyfriend of yours, right?"

"That's right."

"Did he ever store stuff up there?"

I could hear her breath through the receiver; great huffs of reluctant air.

"Maybe," she said after six or seven bellows' worth. "It was, um, it was where they kept farm equipment."

"Farm equipment?"

"Yeah, yeah. Not tractors and stuff but little things like pruning shears and long sticks with tin cans on the end to pick oranges with. It was like a, like a little shed. When he was little Craig used to play that it was his fort. Why? Did he leave me something there?"

"Do you know where this shed's at?"

"I never went out exploring. The men did that."

By the time I got out of the booth Mona was gone. Bo told me that she had a sick uncle down south and had to go help him. I don't think he believed the story but he knew my business well enough to start practicing the lie.

I got cozy in the phone booth again and dialed a number I knew well.

46

"Hi, Daddy," she said. "Where are you?"

"At the end of this case," I said. "I'll be home for the rest of the summer, I promise."

"Then can we go on a vacation?"

"Sure. Where would you like to go?"

"San Francisco. Uncle Milo says that it's just amazing up there."

"We'll make plans day after tomorrow."

"Okay. Daddy, I'm tired. I think I have to go back to bed."

"You do that, honey. I'll see you later on."

Jackson got on the line after that.

"What's happenin', Brother Easy?"

"You busy?"

Somewhere around 2:00 a.m. Jackson Blue pulled his indigo-colored Jaguar up in front of P9 headquarters.

I was parked across the street when he arrived. He was wearing tan workpants and a white T-shirt that had seen more than its share of wear. I crossed over to meet him. Just as my foot hit the curb a police cruiser pulled up behind the dark, dark blue Jag.

"Keep your hands where we can see them," one of the cops said. They both had pistols out as they exited the squad car.

Palms up next to his ears, Jackson greeted them: "Evenin', officers."

"Keep quiet," one of the cops ordered.

They were on us but that was nothing new. What was different was that Jackson showed no fear.

"What are you doing here?" the first cop asked me. He was five eight in lifts and the color of butterfat-rich French vanilla ice cream. His eyes glittered.

"Doin' research," I answered honestly.

"You want me to go upside your head, boy?"

"Excuse me, officers," Jackson said. "My name is Blue and I'm senior vice president of P9 North America. I have identification right here in my hand."

My friend brought his right hand down slowly. When his arm was parallel to the ground I saw that he was holding some kind of identity card.

"Take a look," the shorter cop said to the taller one.

The partner wasn't wearing a cap. He had brown hair and a long face like Stan Laurel's, but vacant of any sympathy. He glared at the card, looked up at Jackson, then stared at the picture ID again.

"Well?" the short cop asked, his pistol pointed somewhere around my intestines.

"It says he's senior vice president, Jackson Blue."

"Shit."

"That's what it says, Sy. It's his picture too."

I glanced at Jackson. He was smiling. A man who spent an entire lifetime being afraid of his own shadow, smiling in the face of two white men with guns. It was the middle of the night but it was indeed a new day.

"Can I help you, officers?" someone asked.

Another white man, this one in a brown and tan private security uniform, had come out of the central doors of the block-wide building.

"Mr. Smollett," Sy said. "This man here says he's some kinda vice president."

"That's Mr. Blue," Smollett said with deference. "He's *the* vice president. Only man above him on this continent is the CEO."

The hatless cop handed Jackson's ID back. Sy lifted his pistol so that it was aimed at the middle of my forehead.

"What about this one?" Sy asked.

I knew from long experience that only the slightest shift in the situation could leave me dead on the pavement.

"Is he with you, sir?" Smollett asked Jackson.

"Yes, he is, Mr. Smollett. Easy here is my research partner."

"Researching what?" Officer Sy asked. He could have crushed diamonds with the weight of that question.

"That's privileged information, officer," Jackson said in a condescending tone.

I wished he wouldn't be so brave with a gun being leveled at me.

"Sy," the other cop said. "Put the gun down, man."

That was a life-on-the-line moment. Sy wanted to put me down. His whole world had been dashed by Smollett calling Jackson *sir*. He was further vexed by his partner, who was saying, *Put your gun down because I can't have your back in this.*

The Civil War had ended more than a century before but the remnants could still be felt, still killed over on any street corner in the country.

Sy gazed deeply into my eyes. I tried my best to look like just some other guy. A few seconds ticked by and then the officer of the law lowered his gun.

The twenty-seventh floor of the P9 building was a huge library. When we walked in a hundred lights sprang to life. There were literally thousands of books on the shelves. The odd thing about them was that they were all the same size, in the same dark green bindings.

"You got every property in LA County in these?" I asked Jackson.

"Every property, property owner, and tax history of every parcel in the entire United States," my friend corrected.

"How's that even possible?"

"Seven maids with seven mops," he replied.

He searched down the volume I needed. I, in turn, looked up a series of lots at the eastern end of the San Fernando Valley.

47

Lot AL3-47 occupied a lowland field about a mile and a half beyond the cabin where Craig Kilian stabbed Reynolds Ketch. As advertised, the bunker-like storage facility contained hand tools used for the cultivation of orange trees.

P9's library was good enough to guide me, but it wasn't perfect. I took the same footpath that led to the cabin and then kept going toward the shed. Arriving at the unit, I saw that there was a long dirt path leading there from the far side of the Blood Grove plantation. Parked at the end of the path was a bright red four-door Buick Electra.

My hand went automatically to the high-velocity .22 in my pocket and I crouched down into the tall grasses I'd trudged through. I could see the structure; therefore, logic had it, whoever owned that car might have seen me.

For at least ten minutes I stayed still, my palm sweating against the butt of the small-caliber gun. Nothing stirred. The unit was still and mute.

I had a decision to make. If I had gone unnoticed I might be able to get the drop on whoever it was in the little storage unit. But if they had seen me they could execute an ambush. If I tried to backtrack they might follow and bushwhack me from behind.

There were other options. I could circle around back, set the building on fire, and wait for the driver to rush out. But the stolen money could very well be in the unit. I didn't think that Mr. Jericho or Eddie Brock would appreciate me turning their wealth to ashes.

I could wait for hours and hours as I often did in war.

Or I could carefully approach the little hut, armed and ready.

My patience had worn thin, so I decided on the straightforward option.

It was a small building, a tarpaper-and-pine toolshed, surrounded on three sides by shrubbery. The path to the front door was laid in brick. Upon that brick was the body of Kirkland Larker. He'd been shot a few times in the chest. There wasn't much blood, so he'd probably died immediately.

His skin was still warm to the touch.

There was an expression of innocent surprise on the veteran's face. He looked like many dead boys I'd seen on the long road to Berlin.

Next to Kirkland's corpse was a metal footlocker. It didn't take much imagination to see that Lola had known where the storage shed was located. She'd called him or his accomplice, telling them to go there and collect the blood money.

Whoever she called got there, but the money was well hidden just in case someone from the orchard needed a pair of pruning shears. Unlucky Kirkland and his armed confederate had been searching for a while. They knew I was coming. One of them knew I was there.

A sound, from off to the left, somewhere in the shrubbery.

Ever since Craig Kilian had come so silently into my office I had been remembering the war and the things I had to be able to do. The sound might have been nothing, but I pivoted, went down on one knee and aimed. The shot was no more than a pop. Before I registered the bullet thudding into the door behind, I fired twice.

She screamed once and the shooting stopped.

* * *

The woman I first knew as Donata Delphine was leaned up against a broad bush that held her like a thick, springy pillow. She was bleeding from the chest and in pain.

I took off my T-shirt, balled it up, and pressed it against the wound. The .32 pistol was in her hand but she didn't have the strength to lift it. I took it from her anyway.

"Help," she pleaded.

"Don't talk," I said.

"We can still make a deal."

"After we stop the bleeding."

"Help me and we can split the money," she offered, a dying soul trying to make a deal with the devil.

"Like you did with Kirk?" Thick black blood seeped through my fingers.

"Please," she said, and then she died.

There I was on my knees trying to save another enemy combatant on a very different field of battle. I wondered what happened to the German soldier I didn't kill. I wondered if I would survive this operation.

That same afternoon Rufus Tyler, aka Charcoal Joe, set up a meeting between me and Mr. Jericho at an Italian bar on Angeles Street downtown. We sat at a small round table while Orrin Cause watched us intently from a stool at the bar.

"You have something for me?" were Jericho's first words.

I told him the truth: ten minutes earlier I had called Brock and told him where the treasure tomb was located.

"I gave him the long way round," I said. Then I dictated the driving directions.

"And the money?" Jericho asked.

"It's in four green metal footlockers in the storage unit."

"All of it?"

"As far as I can tell."

"How much more do you want for this?"

"Breath will do me just fine."

Jericho smiled.

I winced and said, "And there's a couple of other things."

"What?" he asked.

"First there's a guy named Oliver Shellbourne, a real estate developer downtown."

"What about him?"

"He's been trying to bully a friend of mine to give up on a property. Her name is Jewelle Blue and I'd like you or one of your associates to ask Mr. Shellbourne to stand down."

"Done. What else?"

"The woman stole your money and her fool got themselves killed up there. I didn't sign up for grave-digging duty."

Jericho peered at me. It felt as if he was looking into my soul; like some hell-spawn angel deciding whether or not I could be turned.

Finally he said, "You didn't ask for this, Mr. Rawlins. Go on home. The details will sort themselves out."

Details.

The next morning Brock Oldstein was found shot in the temple, sitting behind the steering wheel of a tan Volkswagen Bug on El Molino Avenue in Pasadena. The afternoon edition of the *LA Herald Examiner* reported that Dennis Plennery was arrested in a jail cell for the San Bernardino armored car job. He was being charged with the murder of the three guards and suspected in the deaths of his two partners—Reynolds Ketch and Alonzo Griggs, both of Los Angeles.

Craig Kilian's death had already been reported as a criminal death perpetrated by an unidentified assailant.

* * *

Forty-eight hours after the shootout at Blood Grove I got a phone call at my office.

"Hello," I said carelessly, putting down an article about the intelligence of octopuses.

"Mr. Rawlins?"

I hesitated and then said, "Miss Kilian."

"Hi, Easy, um . . . did you go up to that storage place?"

"I did."

"Did you find anything?"

"No. I think there might have been something there, though."

"Oh? Why?"

"There was a trapdoor hidden under a big wood box. But somebody had moved the crate and cut off the padlock on the trapdoor. The space underneath was empty and it looked like something heavy had been dragged across the floor. You didn't tell anybody about me asking you about the place, did you?"

"No. Of course not." She sighed. "I suppose that's it, then."

"Yes, ma'am. I guess it is," I said. "Sorry about Craig."

Lola gasped and hung up.

I was pretty sure that she'd been in contact with Donata Delphine, that together, along with Larker, they made the plot to sideline Craig while they planned to get at the stolen monies. The one thing they were unable to understand was the bond between Larker and Craig. Kirkland had broken into the hazardous materials garage, taken the money, and handed it over to his friend. They were comrades and certain not to betray each other.

The only problem was putting me on the case.

Lola bet everything and lost it all.

* * *

Neither Kirkland Larker nor Donata Delphine was ever heard from again. Every now and then I think that the closest I ever came to death was at the hands of that woman. She was a nearly perfect predator in a world that scared the shit out of me.

48

It was 6:50 a.m. the next morning when I knocked on my back-yard neighbors' front door. I waited maybe thirty seconds before Stache answered. He was shirtless, shoeless, and more than a little perturbed that a black man in a powder-blue sports coat was standing on his porch.

"Yeah?" the hippie grumbled.

"Excuse me," I said. "You don't know me but I have an office in the building on the other side of your backyard. Third floor."

"So?"

"I get there early in the morning and open my window to get some fresh air. Usually I see you coming out the back door with a watering can."

"Okay," he said, wondering.

A woman in a red robe appeared a few feet behind him.

"What is it, Rick?" she asked.

"Hold up, Linda," Rick said, looking at me.

"Well," I continued, "I can see not only your place but the whole block, and I have been noticing lately, maybe the last two weeks or so, a dark sedan parked a few houses down. The men sitting in that car wear shorts and bright shirts but they also have on black leather shoes."

Linda had come up beside Rick by then. She had red hair and a face beautiful enough to adorn a Renaissance painting.

Rick's brown eyes were working out the warning.

"Well," I said again. "I just thought I'd say that. Recently I found out that I've got a hippie in my family."

"Um, uh, thanks," Rick said.

I nodded and smiled, then turned away.

Niska made it in at nine to nine to find me once more sitting at her reception desk.

"Hi, Mr. Rawlins. Anybody else here?"

"Saul asked me and Whisper to come up north to help him out. He said we'd both be back down by Friday." I stood up then and moved aside.

"And how have you been while I was gone?" she asked once back in her chair.

"I thought spending the time alone would be restful. I was wrong. How was the retreat?"

"It was okay, I guess. Did you get the money from Mr. Zuma?" our receptionist/office manager asked.

I told her about my experiences with the collateral Rolls and how many times I had to discuss my temporary ownership with the police.

"That's awful," she said when I'd gotten through the tale. "Did you pick up another job while I was gone?"

I thought about Kilian and his mother, Brock and Jericho, the police and the FBI.

"No," I said. "Didn't you like the meditation retreat?"

"I met this guy. He's kinda cute."

That night Feather and I planned a vacation up to San Francisco. We'd bring her uncle and Dagmar too, if she was still with him by then.

ABOUT THE AUTHOR

Walter Mosley is one of America's most celebrated and beloved writers. A Grand Master of the Mystery Writers of America, he has won numerous awards, including the Anisfield-Wolf Award, a Grammy, a PEN USA Lifetime Achievement Award, several NAACP Image Awards, and a lifetime achievement award from the National Book Foundation. His books have been translated into more than twenty languages. His short fiction has appeared in a wide array of publications, including *The New Yorker*, *GQ*, *Esquire*, the *Los Angeles Times Magazine*, and *Playboy*, and his nonfiction has been published in the *New York Times Book Review*, the *New York Times Magazine*, *Newsweek*, and *The Nation*. He is the author of the Easy Rawlins series, including, most recently, *Charcoal Joe*. He lives in New York City.